specters

For Loule and Bert
with warm regards

Bu

21 00

specters

Radwa Ashour
translated by Barbara Romaine

Interlink Books

An imprint of Interlink Publishing Group, Inc.
Northampton, Massachusetts

First American edition published in 2011 by

Interlink Books
An imprint of Interlink Publishing Group, Inc.
46 Crosby Street
Northampton, MA 01060
www.interlinkbooks.com

Library of Congress Cataloging-in-Publication Data

'Ashur, Radwá.
[Atyaf. English]
Specters / by Radwa Ashour ; translated by Barbara Romaine.
—1st American ed.
    p. cm.
ISBN 978-1-56656-832-6 (pbk.)
I. Romaine, Barbara, 1959– II. Title.
PJ7814.S514A8913 2010
892.7'36—dc22
                                2010024958

Cairo street scene cover painting © Andesign101
Book design by Juliana Spear

NATIONAL
ENDOWMENT
FOR THE ARTS

This project is supported in part by an award from the
National Endowment for the Arts

One

The valley was full of ghosts. Silent ghosts that tilted with the setting sun to settle in their turn into the depths of the earth, where the shrouded river carried them on boats in its headlong course toward the east. Silence. Then a sound—faint at first and then rising, it would still be echoing in the valley years hence.

She heard only the three that particularly concerned her: her husband and her two brothers. They had gone, and would not return. The door was closed upon their voices, closed tightly and locked with a key secured within her breast. She carried on. She was twenty-five years old, she had two children and a third still in her belly. Six months later she gave birth to a girl.

"I will tend the little ones and my bit of land, and it is no one's business but my own."

Her cousins hated her independence, hated her refusal to marry any of them, and then they hated her capability in managing her own affairs day by day, as if she were not a woman. Even when their anger subsided—the open and the covert hostility—still they kept watching her, waiting out the test of time, to prove to her and to themselves that it was futile to try to break with the customs established by their fathers and grandfathers. She disappointed them. She raised the children, and their needs were met. Still the men's eyes followed her. She was beautiful, and her inaccessibility only made her more appealing. She did not miss out on participating in celebrations and lamentations: she sang at weddings, and at funerals she surpassed the professional mourners, no matter how much they improvised.

"Shagar is stubborn and arrogant!"

"Shagar is strong, above shame!"

They calmed down, and once again made a place for her among them; she accompanied the women carrying jars of water from the river or going to it with their tubs for the washing. Those men who had desired her, or loved her regardless, concealed their desire, pretending to forget it until it seemed, in fact, forgotten.

"A woman equal to ten men!"

This is what they said on the day when the news spread in the village. She neither suppressed the announcement nor revealed any details of what had happened. She said to her first-born son, "Tell your uncles that the girl is dead." They came, saw the body of the slain girl, and they asked, "Who, when, how?" She kept silent. For 40 days not a word fell from her lips, so that they thought she must have been struck dumb. But when her voice returned, she did not speak of the matter. It was as if her nine months of pregnancy and her daughter's fourteen years of life had fallen away, or had never been. She went back to tilling the earth with her two sons, who, like her, were vigorous, strong, and disciplined. Their hard work paid off, and they bought two new parcels of land, then turned around and sold one of them to pay the dowries for two brides.

Shagar danced on the wedding night, then again for the circumcisions of her ten grandchildren. By the time the youngest of them went to the *kuttaab*, the house—*maa shaa'allah*—was full of young people, who ploughed the land and sowed it with seed, tended the crops and harvested them, then ploughed once again. Thus in her old age Shagar was left to her leisure, and then the ghosts came to her.

At first the meetings were silent. The ghosts would come in to her, and sit there diffidently mute. Words did not come to her, either. She would steal glances at them, and then, perplexed, go back to staring at her hands. She did not know whether she should greet them and make them welcome as guests—since they had been away— or whether she should leave matters up to them—since the house was theirs and they could conduct themselves in it however they liked, and speak if they wished or otherwise remain silent. As the meetings grew frequent, the intimacy of conversation was gradually restored to them, and so they made up for all the years of separation. Sometimes she questioned them, and sometimes she talked, but most of the time she listened. They had a great deal to say about the forced-labor trenches at Atabat al-Jisr, about thirst, and about wages never redeemed for bitter toil. All this they had lived and endured over the course of several months. How could this be? She wondered, amazed, for she had lived as best she might, she had married, produced children, been widowed, raised children and grandchildren, and had chafed against the family when they chafed against her. What for her had seemed a full life was, compared to a story like theirs, an insignificant trifle.

She listened. She didn't take her eyes off their faces, or their hands, which clenched and relaxed along with the flow of their speech. When all the family members gathered for dinner and for the cups of tea served afterwards, she repeated for them some of what she had heard. Caught up in her narrative, she did not notice that the children were exchanging glances and holding in their laughter. And if she did hear laughter escaping from one of them, she said, "Stop playing, children. Listen to the story of your grandfathers."

Then her frailty confined her to bed. She could eat only pieces of bread dipped in tea boiled with sugar, following the noon prayer, and this would last her until the same time the following day. The light dimmed from her eyes; she could no longer see more than the shadowy figures of her sons and their children. The ghosts remained, clear as the sun, and they warmed her with their companionship. One day she was taken unawares by the thing she had never expected: they brought her daughter with them—her daughter, whom she had never seen since the day she had beaten her and then found her stretched motionless on the ground.

Shagar gave a shrill cry that terrified the household and the neighbors. They came running. She didn't see them, she didn't hear their questions. She was howling and raking her cheeks. The only thing she saw, standing before her, was her daughter, in whom time had not diminished the slightest detail, from her eyes, her braids, her dress patterned with delicate white flowers, even her breasts just as they had been— time had not filled them out, as if the girl had still not matured.

Shouting and weeping and angry accusations were followed by reproaches and sorrowful exchanges conducted in whispers. They immersed themselves deeply in their mournful talk. Unconsciously, Shagar reached out to her daughter, and they clasped hands.

The daughter did not come and go like the other ghosts. She stayed by her mother's side, keeping her company, not leaving her even when Shagar began to confuse names and her gaze wandered. And then Shagar was gone. Her sons bore her on their shoulders, wrapped in her shroud. The grandchildren followed them, along with the rest of the family and the neighbors. They left the house and proceeded to the mosque. They prayed over her. Then they brought her to the cemetery.

"Why 'Shagar'?"

It wasn't a question: it was an abrupt expression of displeasure. They took it as a question. "We named you after your great grandmother."

"Your name is Shagar? 'Tree'?"

"A tree is big and tall. And besides, it could be a mango tree!"

The second part of the statement was to forestall objections, for who but an idiot would not approve of a mango tree?

In the neighbors' garden was a mango tree, a towering one, whose rough-barked trunk, firmly rooted in the ground, diverged just like the other trees into three thick sections, which in turn sprouted limbs too difficult to count as they appeared and disappeared amid the dense foliage. The tree was more than just a pleasant thing to look at from the nursery window. She craved its fruit, which she would gather with her eyes when it was still small, green and hard. She would observe it as it ripened and plumped. As if outsmarting her, it only ripened during the days of the summer holidays: she would hear the thud of the ripe fruit hitting the ground and she would run to the window, only to see the neighbors' children competing for the biggest fruits, the ones that were the size of two fists put together. When her father would bring her mangoes, she would eat her share greedily, her appetite doubled by the fact that even as she savored the sharp sweet taste and penetrating fragrance of the fruit, she was ruled by a craving suspended in the lofty branches of a tree whose fruit was not hers for the taking.

"Like a mango tree!" she said proudly. The girls moved back and she advanced on them. "Like a mango tree: trunk standing tall, fruit sought by all!"

She won this round at school. At home, though, she could only be reconciled with her name once she knew the story behind it.

It was the locus of a disagreement between the two sides of her family; more to the point, it had supplied an arena for covert wrangling between her paternal grandfather and her maternal grandmother. Her grandfather, Abdel Ghaffar, had made the opening sally. He told Shagar about it. "I suggested that we name you Aziza, but Gulsun Hanim didn't agree, so I said, 'Let's call her Shagar—what do you think of the name Shagar?' At that she seemed even more annoyed. She said, 'If the name *must* begin with *sheen*, then let it be Shuaykar or Shukriya.' If she hadn't raised her voice and stuck her nose in the air and strutted around like a turkey… if she had said nicely, 'What would you say to a different name?' then I would have gone along with her wishes. But she pursed her lips and turned her head away as if I'd said, 'Let's call the girl "Dung Beetle."' I lost my temper. I said, 'We're going to call her Shagar, and that's the last word on it.' And your father said, 'By God's blessing, congratulations on Shagar!'"

In the light of these revelations it was easier to interpret that first photograph: Shagar, swaddled in white, nothing showing but her face, with the wide-open eyes and thick black hair just discernible. Sitt Gulsun was holding her on her lap, her arms encircling her, all but enveloping her with her generous bulk. She was frowning, not looking at the infant. She stared straight in front of her, a hint of malice in her expression. Was this because Shagar's grandfather Abdel Ghaffar was standing in front of her and she, looking at the camera, had to look at him, or was she still smarting from the wound she had taken from her defeat in the battle over the name?

Gulsun Hanim did not accept the name, but neither did she refrain from using it. She seized upon it the way an enemy pounces on his opponent's weapon and snatches it away in order to use it against him. With biting sarcasm she emphasized the letter *sheen* each time she uttered the name "Shagar," vindicated by her own contempt. When did Shagar herself enter the fray? She no longer remembers anything but her automatic alignment with her paternal grandfather's camp. She clung to her name. She barricaded herself behind it. It became the standard that waved over the army to which she belonged.

The no-man's-land between the two camps was no more or less than a long wooden table that separated two chairs: to the right as one entered the house, the chair in which her grandfather Abdel Ghaffar habitually sat, and across from it on the left, the one in which her grandmother

Sitt Gulsun sat. Shagar would say, still half-asleep, "Good morning, Grandfather. Good morning, Teta." She would go into the bathroom, brush her teeth, wash her face, put on her school uniform, and leave the house in the company of her father, who would take her to school before her parents turned to their daily tasks. As they were leaving, her grandfather would lift his head from his newspaper and say, "Goodbye!" Her grandmother would follow suit, without pausing in her needlework. At four o'clock in the afternoon everyone came home. Her mother would turn the key in the lock and the door would open upon Sitt Gulsun, still absorbed in her embroidery, while her grandfather dozed in the opposite chair. He would be roused by their appearance, open his eyes, and smile.

His powerful memory and robust frame belied his age; only the wrinkles in his face and the dark brown spots on the backs of his hands gave it away. He was a tall man; his awe-inspiring presence was accentuated by the gravity of his dark-colored *jubba*, which highlighted the shining whiteness of the robe beneath it. These were the clothes he wore when he went out. At home he wore a white *jilbab* and, over it, in winter, a brown camelhair *abaya*.

He had an inexhaustible supply of stories about sheikhs and effendis, the Wafd and the king, the English and Saad Pasha, and the wholesale market and those who worked for it. Her father didn't hear these stories; he went back to work in the evenings, and she didn't see him again until the following morning. Her mother didn't hear them, either. Did her maternal grandmother hear them? She couldn't help but hear them as she sat there in the chair opposite, working on her embroidery, but she didn't laugh along with Shagar and her grandfather, nor did she show any sign of emotion when the bullet struck the youth in the chest, killing him, and his companions took him up and carried him, shouting, "Long live Egypt!"

To begin with, Sitt Gulsun produced three pieces, which were mounted on wooden frames: pastoral scenes—men and women clad like royalty in old-fashioned European garments, herding their sheep in fields adorned with flowers. She hung the pictures, displayed in gilt frames, in the parlor. Then she became set on changing the fabric of the chairs, so that she could replace it with the new needlepoint she had done: once again, shepherd-princes. Sitt Gulsun fretted whenever the door to the parlor was opened, even for the purpose of cleaning the room. Her anxiety mounted when visitors came and sat on the chairs, sipping the drinks they were served. She kept her eyes fixed on a guest's hand clutching his glass of tea, shifting her gaze only to fasten it upon the guest's "silly" wife (as Sitt Gulsun referred to her after they had left). "My heart just about stopped every time she laughed. I said to myself, 'This night won't end well—the tea will be upset all over the needlepoint upholstery.'" And if guests came with their children, it was an actual crisis. Then would come a scowling visitor who never laughed, and who brought no children with her, and you would think she would be the ideal guest. But she would leave and Sitt Gulsun would say, "Her face was yellow as a lemon with envy. By God, I don't think we should admit any guests to the parlor—we should entertain them in the hall!" She would prepare incense, and pass the censer seven times over the needlepoint cushions and the three framed pieces. Then she would get a slip of paper, from which she would cut out the shape of a woman, pierce it several times with a pin, and then burn it, muttering prayers under her breath. Finally she would leave the room, carefully locking the door.

The locked door did not rouse Shagar's curiosity or any desire to cross the threshold. She knew what was behind the door: a set of gilded chairs crowded the room, so that only narrow passageways were left between the clunky furniture, passageways made still narrower by a table whose black marble surface Shagar could never look at without being reminded of the time she had bumped her head on its edge. The blood had poured from her head, resulting in a trip to the hospital and several stitches. After this the wound had healed, and all that remained of it was a fine scar beneath her right eyebrow, and the echo of a child's mockery—one of her schoolmates had laughed at the white bandages around her head. The three pieces in their frames and the upholstered cushions made her all the more eager to flee from the room. There was just one thing that she wished she could remove from it: a picture of her mother and father, their wedding portrait.

Her father was laughing; it seemed that he wanted—out of respect for the portrait—to restrain his joy and show himself a somber bridegroom. But laughter got the better of him, so that he appeared suspended between two states: the animation of a young man who has won the girl of his choice, and the ritual sobriety of a formal wedding and the portrait that fixes it in the eyes of the family for all of posterity. Her mother stood beside him in a long white gown whose splendor was incongruous with the childishness of her face—a face in which sweetness, innocence, and a little uneasiness could be discerned. She too was suspended, between girlhood and womanhood: the girl fearful and wondering, the woman accepting her own diffident role. Her father had been twenty-seven years old, her mother seven years his junior.

Shagar studies them now, years after their deaths. She is aware, now that she herself is past 50, that she is many years older than they. In the never-changing portrait, her parents are mere children, and she has become, with the passage of time, mother to her own parents.

x.⚎.x

What happened? Why did I leap so suddenly from Shagar the child to middle-aged Shagar? I reread what I have written, mull it over, stare at the lighted screen, and wonder whether I should continue the story of young Shagar, or return to her great grandmother, or trace the path of her descendants to arrive, once again, at the grandchild. And the ghosts—should I consign them to marginal obscurity, leaving them to hover on the periphery of the text, or admit them fully and elucidate some of their stories? And should I confine my narrative to the ghosts of the grandmother's acquaintance, or expand the subject to include succeeding generations of ghosts? And would anyone put up with such writing? Matters could come to a decision to erase what I've written, and begin instead by setting down my own story directly. And Shagar? Should I keep her and interweave our stories, or drop her and content myself with telling about Radwa? But then, why did Shagar come to me when I started out writing about myself? Who is Shagar?

I moved the cursor to the list of files and pressed, then moved it to "shut down," and the white screen was replaced by a black one. I turned off the machine and went to bed. My sleep was disturbed by dreams about which I remembered nothing but their oppressive presence. I woke up exhausted, as if at the end of a long day. As I sipped my coffee, I once again considered the problem of what to do about Shagar.

I turned on the computer and selected "Word," then opened the "Shagar" file. I wrote:

What's with you, Shagar? You conduct your life like a decrepit old mule. Would horses turn into mules? And this heavy, overflowing wagon—what did it look like at the beginning of its journey—a tub full of fragrant jasmine, or is it just that memory endows the past with what it never contained? In the morning, everything looks difficult. What are you afraid of? Has fear defeated you, or is it defeat that you're afraid of? Or are life and death stripping down shamelessly and having it off on your bed, while you watch, totally helpless, soundlessly screaming? You say these are all illusions, you'll get rid of them; you get up and go to the sink, get your toothbrush, and—Good Morning!—your coffee. The dust of battle hasn't settled yet, but you—as you drive your car across the overpass you are seduced by the details: a palm tree standing proud, a roaming cloud, the river's current; another driver rudely passes you, so you curse his father in a loud voice, only to discover that your voice doesn't reach him, because the car windows are all the way up.

(The warrior had died/ A man came and said, "Don't die, for I love you very much!"/ But the body— alas!—went on dying./

Two more came, and they said to him:/ "Don't leave us! Take courage! Return to life! / But the body—what sorrow!—went on dying./

Next came... (all of his loved ones)/ they surrounded him; the sad figure saw them, and emotion stirred him/ he rose slowly/ he embraced the first person; and he proceeded to walk.)

Shagar signed her name and the brown envelope that she had previously sealed and submitted to

Control two weeks earlier was handed to her. She took the envelope and headed to the examination room. She looked at her watch: precisely seven minutes before nine. She waited two minutes. She handed the envelope to the supervisor, who slit it open. He gave a sheaf of examination papers to the proctors, who spread out rapidly among the rooms and corridors in order to distribute the papers to the students. At exactly nine o'clock, the test began.

From the time she had become obliged to walk with a cane, she had accepted her condition with a calm that surprised her. Had she become reconciled with the problem? What *was* the problem with a 50-year-old woman's having to walk with a cane because of her afflicted leg? She'd had plenty of time for running, so what harm was there in entering her sixth decade accompanied by a cane to remind her that the child and the girl, and the glory of the woman in her thirties and forties, were all behind her now and had left her to the business of getting on with her journey toward old age? She forgot about the cane, forgot it was there. But during the examination she remembered it. She deplored the way it thumped on the ground, annoying the students, disturbing their concentration, and not allowing her to approach them quietly in order to cast a quick glance over their answer booklets and secretly ascertain whether or not they were copying from cheat-sheets they had brought in with them. The cane had become a sort of alarm bell; the students raised their heads and looked around, or kept their heads down, whether from shyness or because they had something to hide. She annoyed those who were sitting there in peace and quiet, concentrating on their answers, and she alerted the young cheaters with her early warning system.

She no longer walked around during examinations. She entered the examination room and chose a spot that allowed her to observe the students: a military guardsman supervising the prison complex from the highest watchtower—she lacked only a rifle to brandish in the faces of the prisoners... God, what sort of role was this?

The test ended. The proctors collected the answer booklets. She went back to her office. She ordered some coffee. She sipped it. She signed some papers. She talked to a student about the topic of his research. She went down to Control to pick up the answer booklets. She counted the papers, and signed for them: 556 answer booklets for a fourth-year test on modern history. One of the interns had been responsible for tying them up with a length of twine. The office boy carried them to her car. At home, she placed them in her office, and locked the door. Tomorrow the annual ritual would begin.

In bed, she closed her eyes to sleep, but then she saw the papers she had corrected in the course of thirty years. Tens of thousands of answer booklets rose up around her like pillars, closing off all open space and leaving her a small, confined area in which to sit. In her hand was a red pen. Her glasses rested on the bridge of her nose. A booklet was open before her, lines of responses overflowing its pages. She opened her eyes. Alarmed, she raised herself to a sitting position. She sat cross-legged on the bed.

No, it's not so! There is always a window, some light, a bird in flight. Don't deny it, Shagar—and it was never just one bird. They always come to you, always surprise you, these unexpected birds that emerge from among the papers and carry you with them into open space.

Who's calling at this hour of the night? She picked up the receiver. "'A successful woman?' What's that got to do with me? 'The criteria of success?' Madam, it's the middle of the night!" She hung up, and disconnected the telephone.

Two

Was the place as desolate as it felt to me? Did the emptiness roam the corridors with the nuns' footsteps? They have no footfall; their progress is soundless. I watched, following the movements of their bodies and their wimples: head-coverings of starched white cloth whose edges extended incomprehensibly outward—unyielding: that was the edge of the wimple. The rosary and the cross hung from the sash at the waist over the folds of the robe, which might be white or brown, and which concealed the body entirely, leaving it to a pair of thick socks and low-heeled leather lace-up shoes to cover the feet.

My father accompanied me to school—I remember that, along with the nuns' clothing and my own fear, and the dampness as I cowered in the back seat of the school bus. It would stop to let a student off in front of her house, then continue on its way, only to stop again and let off another girl, while I sat divided between two conflicting feelings: the desire to make it home and the wish that I could stay in the sun-drenched seat rather than get up in my wet dress and have to make my way to the door in front of the rest of the students, the monitor, and the driver.

The nun said, "You must eat!"

"I don't want to!"

She fixed me with a stern look and repeated the order. I reached out toward the food. The girls sat on two wooden benches that faced each other across a long table with bowls lined up on it, one for each girl. I lifted the spoon to my mouth. Chewed. Swallowed. Then the cycle was repeated. The third time, the food was propelled from my innards onto the table, my clothes, and the floor. When I got home I said I wouldn't go back to school.

The following academic year, my father accompanied me to another school. It wasn't a convent school. It was a French school whose name was written in Roman capitals on both sides of the bus, which picked me up at my house on gloomy winter mornings, and brought me back again when the noonday sun poured through the tightly shut glass windows. The monitor—tall and thin, with extremely short, white hair—was very strict, and she had a strange name. Mademoiselle Rée did not permit any talking, so the children deferred their noisemaking and gave themselves up to the exhaustion of their long school day, to the warmth of the winter sun, and the rhythm of the bus's motion. The bus would come to a stop, and the children would be roused from their stupor as if they had been asleep, and as they were getting off the bus they would utter two sentences, each in a different language, the first in French, addressed to the monitor: "Au revoir, Mademoiselle," followed by the Arabic, addressed to the driver: "Maᶜa al-salaama, yaa osta."

The first primary school photograph: four rows of boys and girls between the ages of five and six dressed in school uniforms. Radwa is to the far left of the last row, short-haired, pale-faced, gazing out. Not the facial features, nor the eyes' intelligence, are revealed here, but rather a scattered look and a trace of fear. This situation was apparently not prolonged; children, after all, reshape their own worlds, and they adjust to circumstances, too. At eight, at nine, at eleven, Radwa sits cross-legged on the ground in the first row, or perches on the wooden bench in the second row. She is laughing, and yet she is not. A gleam in the eye, a slight tilt of the head or torso, a barely discernible slant to the seated posture, betrays the assumed seriousness of a child who has crossed her arms on her chest and made do with a sober smile appropriate to the occasion. In class, away from the photographer, she chatters, talks loudly, quarrels with a classmate. The school punishes her with a zero that will go down in her monthly record, and the zero is confirmed with a red circle.

The most important thing at school is its vast playground. Our laughter, no matter how loud, dissipates there. We run unchecked there, for we do not collide with the teacher's desk or the blackboard or one of our classmates' schoolbags. We leave the playground to re-enter the classroom, and this makes us sad; then we leave it once more to ride the school buses home, which doesn't seem so sad, since there something awaits us, something to look forward to. We count the coins we have with us, and get ready.

We get on the bus and settle in our seats; the monitor counts the students, pointing with her index finger, and once she has ascertained that none has lagged behind, she closes the door and says firmly to the driver, "Let's go, yaa osta." The buses pull out, one after another, slowed down by their number and by the heavy traffic in the adjoining street, onto which the back door of the school gives access. Here stands the apple-seller, offering apples coated with a layer of red caramel. The seller offers his goods, crying, "Les pommes, les pommes." We reach out through the windows of the bus with our coins, and the vendor stretches out his hand with the sweet. The apples are fixed on wooden sticks, which we all hold like lollipops, licking them slowly before biting into them.

The only thing that matches the pleasure of that three-o'clock apple is the subterranean cavern situated—throughout my school years—at the farthest end of the left side of the playground. The place is a cellar, accessible through a rear door within the building, and with a window overlooking the playground. Facing this rear door the parents would line up in rows following the payment of fees at the beginning of the year. I stand beside my father, waiting our turn. At last we arrive at a wooden counter that separates us from the women who work inside. My father presents the receipt for the fee payment, and a lady comes with a bundle of new books and note-books. She gives back the receipt, with the book-store's stamp imprinted on it. My father carries the books, while I carry the schoolbag—empty until now—and as soon as we make our way up to the next floor we turn aside to fill it with books. I carry the bag on my back so that its weight doesn't prevent me from skipping. At home, I leaf through the books. I press my nose in between their pages, and inhale the smell of new paper. I run my hand along its smooth surface. I gaze at the pictures and the writing.

In subsequent years, I will stand before the window with the iron bars that overlooks the playground, waiting for the saleswoman to fill my order: a book or a notebook. With pleasure I let my eyes take in that place, where all I see is one side of the books carefully stacked on top of one another. It has never happened to me, nor have I ever heard that any of the other students at the school chanced to be allowed to pass to the other side of those iron bars on the play-ground-side window, or the wooden counter at the door whose access was on the ground floor of the building. The place was nothing but a depot for the sale of schoolbooks, and yet it was sur-rounded by a certain magic and mystery. It had the allure of dimly lit places. We reach out our hands because we can't stop ourselves, even though we know that we cannot reach our ob-ject.

In 1956 the administration changed. The school was nationalized, and in place of its French name it acquired an Arabic one, which appeared on the notebooks and diplomas, as well as on the school gate and the bus, all written in large, clear script, beneath which, printed small in parentheses, was the old French name. We no longer studied the history or geography of France. Egyptian teachers came to teach us the history and geography of Egypt—in addition to a new subject called National Instruction—in Arabic. Some of the foreign teachers left. The mathematics teacher did not leave; he stayed on to bestow upon us his contempt, at every occasion or on no particular occasion. As he scolded us, his face would blossom with the signs of his disgust, as if we were flies that had fallen into his soup, filling him with both loathing and rage at having his food thus fouled. His message reached us, whether by way of his words or his looks or his gestures, and it was always the same: It was useless, we were hopeless, our horizon was completely closed off, and the best we could hope for was to content ourselves with reading and writing, so at least we could pore over our horoscope in an obscure corner of the newspaper to pass the time while waiting for our husbands to come home from work.

Madame Michelle likewise stayed put. She taught French to us throughout the four years, during which we moved with her from level to level until it seemed to us that she was like Fate in the tragedies we studied: no refusing it, inexorable, inescapable. Yet she was more like a character from a comic play: in her fifties, with a large nose and tiny eyes and, covering the upper third of her forehead, bangs curled into a tube, which she took care to pat now and then in order to reassure herself that the curl was still intact. She would raise her hand sometimes to her hair and sometimes into empty air—the latter gesture combined with an abrupt movement of her head (always exaggerated), which we interpreted to mean that she was angry or disappointed or about to faint from the shock of an incorrect answer. The bell would ring, signaling the end of the class, and Madame Michelle would turn toward the mirror she had hung on one side of the classroom to have a quick look at her face, pat her tube-like bangs, extract a compact from her purse, and, with sharp, nervous gestures, dab the powder brush quickly over her face, especially her nose. Then she would close the compact, put it back in her purse, collect her papers from the desk, and hurry out, her shoulders swinging to the right and to the left in rapid, mechanical repetition. Following with our eyes the movement of her shoulders, we didn't laugh—we merely sighed.

Madame Michelle assigned us to write an essay in which each of us was to compose a "self-portrait," as she called it. I wrote, "On the Nile and our house and my mother, father, and brothers." I said, "I like chocolate and mangoes and the fragrance of new books and riding a bicycle and stories." I concluded my essay with a discussion of my school performance. I said that I excelled in my studies, and that I was intelligent enough, and that Dr. Papazian, the Armenian dentist who took care of my teeth said, "Radwa, you are a remarkable child, and in the future you will do well in whatever career you choose."

Madame Michelle collected the notebooks; a week later she returned them to us. I opened my notebook only to find that my grade was a two out of ten. Before I could summon the courage to ask the reason for the grade, Madame Michelle called out: "Mademoiselle Ashour." I stood up. "Read the last paragraph of your essay!" Hesitantly, I read. What had happened? What had made her so angry? Why all this sarcasm and mockery over the statement: "I believe that I am intelligent enough"? She said, "Intelligent enough, naturally, to write a terrible essay that exposes your foolish pride and your stupidity—a bad essay complete with five spelling errors. There are five spelling errors in the essay!" Would it do for me to say something? Some justification seemed called for, so I gave it a try: "I'm sorry about the spelling errors. I thought I knew how to spell those words correctly, and if I'd had any doubts I'd have gone to the dictionary—I didn't mean to be careless. And since French isn't my first language…" She cut me off. We shall read from Corneille's *Le Cid*," she announced. "Open your books."

Five students had forgotten to bring their books, and unfortunately I was one of them. First came the collective scolding: "*Inshallah! Inshallah!*

This is how you conduct your lives, and you always will! Carelessness, oafishness, and disorganization!" There was nothing new in the wording or the scornful, sarcastic tone. What was new was the dressing-down for which she singled me out in particular: "Mademoiselle Ashour, you are hopeless. I shall drop you from my records as if you didn't exist!" And with that she turned her face dramatically away.

She didn't drop me from the record, though. The following week, I asked permission of the Arabic language teacher to go to the washroom, and she let me go. I went, and came back. Madame Michelle was standing near the door waiting for the bell that would indicate the end of Arabic class and the beginning of French class. She questioned me and I told her, "I went to get a drink." She made no comment; the bell rang, and the Arabic teacher left. Madame Michelle entered the classroom and opened the lesson with a lecture on our disrespect for the Arabic teachers and the general laxity that pervaded the classroom when they were there. The generalized character of the scolding dissipated my anxiety. "It's all right," I thought, "Madame Michelle is just going to deliver her usual lecture that we all know is meaningless." She started the lesson, then suddenly looked in my direction: "Mademoiselle Ashour, go get a drink!" Startled, I got up from my chair. I went to the washroom, turned on the faucet, and drank. I went back to class. After a few minutes, she called on me again. She indicated the door with her hand, and emphasized the gesture with a motion of her head in the same direction. "Get up, go get a drink," she said. I didn't get up right away this time, for I was overcome with confusion. She repeated the order with irritation, so off I went toward the water faucet. I stood beside it, crying. Then I wiped my tears and washed my face. I went back to class. I sat hunched in my seat, hoping only that Madame Michelle would forget I was there, in class or even on earth. But her eyes came back to settle on me and issue the order for the third time that I rise and go get a drink. Did the French teacher soften and relax at last when the tears poured from my eyes, or was it merely that she was finally satisfied of having achieved her goal when she saw the irrefutable evidence of her crushing victory over me, in the terrified face of a helpless child? She continued the lesson.

Madame Michelle doesn't like me, perhaps because I don't like her, I told myself. She doesn't like Fatima or Nabila or Siham or Soha or Zaynab. Why? Madame Michelle likes Françoise, and she becomes sweet and calm when she interacts with Janine and Mireille and Jocelyne. With Ingrid Ziegel she's sometimes impatient, sometimes not. When Ingrid is absent, Madame Michelle insults the Germans and makes fun of them; when Ingrid is there she doesn't. She is more patient, less sharp-tongued, with Mireille Cohen and Renée Licha and Madeleine Aboulafia and Madeleine Mizrahi and Fortunée Saleh. The art teacher likes them more than he likes us. He chose Renée to play the part of the

Oriental princess at the Christmas party. We occupied ourselves with decorating the Christmas tree and constructing a small model of the manger. We surrounded it with straw and placed little figurines in it. We gathered in a circle around the art teacher as he prepared Renée for her role. He put pink powder on her skin, with a touch of red on each cheek, black for the eyes, and lipstick for the mouth. He arranged her hair. He stepped back two paces and studied her face critically, then smiled.

Ingrid said, "My dress isn't suitable. Can I borrow Radwa's dress?" She directed this request to the art teacher. He looked at me and said, "Your dress is beautiful—could you lend it to Ingrid for half an hour for her to perform her dance?" I didn't care for the idea, but I said, "Of course—no problem."

I exchanged my dress for Ingrid's outfit and sat watching the dramatic scene. Ingrid followed it with a dance I had become familiar with previously when there was a television show about Eastern European folk dances. She crouched low to the ground and extended her legs one at a time skillfully and rapidly: she extended one leg and then withdrew it at the same time she extended the other, and repeat the sequence several times. She stood up, then spun on one foot while crouching again. She leapt to her feet, leapt, swerved, and crouched once again to resume the original leg movements. I followed the dance with my eyes, divided between my admiration for Ingrid's skill and my intense focus on the hem of the dress, which was trimmed with white fur and dragged on the floor each time Ingrid went into a crouch and turned and executed her leg movements.

The episode with the dress didn't taint my relationship with Ingrid, which had begun and continued in a spirit of affection and in this respect differed from my relationships with Renée and her sister, with Madeleine and Irène, perhaps because of the air of superiority that I sensed in their conduct, or perhaps because of their veiled mockery and contempt, the winks and nudges when the National Education teacher or the Arabic teacher discussed the tripartite aggression or the Algerian Revolution or Abdel Nasser. Gabi was different. There was nothing provocative in her behavior—she was always gentle and sweet in her comportment. And the other girl, too, whose name I don't remember—she was pleasant. A slight and delicate-featured girl, she whispered in my ear: "Radwa, would you be willing to put your name on a statement against the execution of Jamila Bouhraid?" I read the document and gave it back to her. She asked, "Do you agree with what's in this?"

"Of course I agree with it," I told her, "but what good will this sort of letter do? The French will execute her anyway!"

She replied, "My family says that a stay of execution is possible."

I signed. I was surprised to the point of disbelief: the significance of the statement, the worth of a signature, and the behavior of this little Jewish girl, so different from that of most of the Jewish students.

One morning, three employees of the Ministry of Education approached all the students in the class, bearing red pens and scissors in their hands. (The previous day, the teacher had made sure each of us would bring her copy of Molière's *The Miser*, as well as her copy *Ancient Civilizations*, which had been assigned to us.) What were they doing? I had to wait to find out the answer. One of the men leaned over my desk and blacked out a line of the play, obscuring it completely; then he took hold of the section of *Ancient Civilizations* that pertained specifically to Hebrew civilization, and cut it out. To this day I don't know whether or not the author of that book, who was French, drew any connection between ancient Hebrew civilization and the modern state of Israel. The answer to this question remains a blank, just like the absent pages that were removed from the book.

At thirteen I appear among the girls looking puzzled and confused, as if I am afraid, or have found myself at a fork in the road branching before me and I don't know which one leads where. In stories there are always two paths—one to safety, the other to calamity—and blocking the way to safety is the ogre, whom those who are clever must get past by means of cunning and artifice. I don't know what it is I need, to begin with, in order to make a choice between the two paths. The possibilities have multiplied, the threads have become tangled, and it seems that they become more knotted each day, while I am as yet not even able to distinguish safety from calamity.

Three

H e stood behind the desk and smiled before saying a word—perhaps he won the day from that moment. The smile came as a surprise to all the girls in the sixth grade. They sat perfectly still, practically holding their breath in anticipation of what he would say, that young man whose smile and good looks and youth all belied that he was a teacher who would issue commands, convey information, and administer scoldings for incorrect answers or give a zero that would be recorded on the certificate—occasioning parental censure—and hand out various punishments. With two exceptions, female teachers were responsible for our instruction. Professor Younan, the mathematics teacher, was in his fifties, a stern-looking man. Professor Mahmoud was the Arabic-language teacher, and the girls used to make fun of his gleaming white sharkskin suit and his red suspenders—even his black hair, which was sleek as silk, did not rouse their admiration, for he slicked it down with a gel that left it oily and therefore subject to ridicule.

The girls' share of surprises on that October day in 1958 had not run out. A well-established rule dictated that the student asked and the teacher answered, or the teacher asked and the student offered a response for the teacher to assess: either he nodded once or twice, a gesture sometimes accompanied by the word, "correct," or else he frowned and jerked his head backward as if it had been struck by a stray bullet and his hand shot out with the index finger extended toward the student charged with having given an incorrect answer.

This teacher broke the rule. The girls were perplexed, waiting apprehensively, perhaps, until it would become clear to them what the new rule was to be, or how and according to what principle they were to behave in the event that the rules simply collapsed.

The teacher asked about the meaning of the word "history," and then listened to what all of them had to say. There were thirty of them, between the ages of eleven and thirteen. Not until the last five minutes of class did he speak. He said, "You have listened to one another's answers, and now the assignment I'm asking each of you to complete for the next lesson is to think about the question, with reference to the answers you've heard. It may be possible to benefit from what was said today; you may also ask your families, or consult a dictionary or other book. At the next lesson, I will hear from each one of you the old answer and the new one: they might still be the same answer or they might, following inquiry and research, be modified. Until next time, then." He smiled and said, "By the way, my name is Fawzi."

No place for singing, no place for laughing, no place for running or leaping about like popcorn on the fire. The subsequent class sessions seemed an intolerable burden. The bell rang, signaling the end of the day's lessons and of captivity, whereupon the girls made a run for the stairs. Shagar couldn't wait to get home and tell her family about the teacher, and to question them on the meaning of the word "history," and to think. How could thinking be homework? Homework as she knew it was solving arithmetic problems that gave you a headache; or it was a long, dull text of which the teacher required two, sometimes three copies to be written out: an exhausting exercise, which left an inflamed swelling at the tip of the middle finger of the right hand, usually discolored by traces of ink, that was eventually transformed into a rock-hard callous testifying to the quantity of homework, the burden of whose completion the fingers had borne. The teacher had broken the rule: he had said, "Ask, and think." A startling and fascinating new game, but how could thinking stand on its own, divorced from the solving of arithmetic problems whose numbers she stared down, clutching her pencil, trying desperately to write the conclusion to which her brain had led her before it evaporated?

The sixth-grade girls fell in love with the teacher with the innocence befitting young girls poised unsuspectingly on the threshold between their childhood and the world of adolescence. Among them were girls fixated on his green eyes, and others who wrote poems to his blue eyes (and the disagreement over the color of his eyes led to a rift in the class, which divided into two camps, each declaring the truth, which was refuted with absolute finality by the other), and still others who saw him in dreams whether waking or sleeping. Shagar encircled him with a halo of sanctity. She could not refer to him, much less discuss him at any length, without thinking of the subject of her discourse as some luminous angel who, by an unprecedented miracle, had descended from the sky, alighting not in the desert or on a mountaintop or on the valley floor, but right in the middle of the sixth-grade girls' lesson, transfixing the girls in their seats like stone statues in whose hearts the blood coursed with a most unusual animation, igniting them like living bodies that shimmered and glowed even as they sat silent as marble.

Fawzi taught them for two whole months, then was gone for a week. Then came the midyear holiday, and when classes resumed in the third week of January 1959, a different teacher came to give the history lessons.

Where had Professor Fawzi gone? None of the teachers or administrators or office staff would answer the question. Where did he live? Did he have a telephone? Inquiry was met with total silence, to which Shagar responded with anger, volatility, and rebelliousness against the teachers, the lessons, and her family, as if all of them had conspired against her. Had he died? When the husband of the science teacher died, the Arabic teacher had given them the news, saying, "You must show respect to her by your obedience and good behavior." After that the teacher had come to school clad in black. Death was clear; it was announced. The disappearance of Professor Fawzi was shrouded in mystery, as if it had happened in a detective story, only she couldn't jump ahead to the final pages to find out how he had disappeared, who was responsible, and why, thereby retrieving him, dead or alive. Had he left the school? Had they driven him out? Why? And why had no one told them anything?

By the end of the school year, it seemed to Shagar that Professor Fawzi had been lost, much as a person loses a precious ring and doesn't know whether he dropped it or it was stolen, and so there is nothing for it but to accept its disappearance, and to keep the memory of its beauty while enduring simultaneously the bitterness of its loss. The following school year, when she was chatting with one of her classmates at the edge of the schoolyard, her comrade whispered, "I know where Professor Fawzi went!"

"Did he die?"

"No, he was arrested! My brother told me that at the beginning of last year they arrested a lot of people, men and women."

"You mean he's in prison?"

"They're all in prison."

"Why?"

"Because they're *Shuyuʿi*. Communists."

"Meaning?"

"They're involved in activities that oppose the government."

"And who told you Professor Fawzi was with them?"

"You see, my brother mentioned him by name and said, 'I think he was arrested!'"

"He *thinks* or he's *sure*?"

"He said he knew him, and he thought he was arrested."

"Ask him, so we can make sure. But what does '*Shuyu'i*' mean?"

"I told you, opposition to the government."

"Against Gamal Abdel Nasser?" She nodded her head. "Are you sure they're against Gamal Abdel Nasser?"

"Would they have been put in prison if they were for him?"

At home Shagar asked about the meaning of *Shuyu'i*. "What does it mean to be '*Shuyu'i*'?" she asked. Her mother didn't know. Her grandfather Abdel Ghaffar said, "The *Shi'a* are followers of Sayyidna Ali." Her father moved his head upwards and back, gesturing with his hand, and changed the subject as if he had given her a full answer. She went back to questioning her classmate—the girl had nothing more than what she had already told her.

"Will you ask?"

"I asked, and I've already told you what I understood from my brother."

"Can you get Professor Fawzi's address?"

"That's a hard one!"

"Try!"

Two weeks later, her friend pressed a slip of paper into her hand and whispered in her ear,

"The address." At the end of the day, Shagar didn't board the school bus. She sneaked out with the girls who went home on their own. She took a taxi, giving the address to the driver. Abbasiyya. The driver let her off in front of a five-story building. She went up, checked the apartment number, and pressed the bell. A middle-aged woman opened the door.

"My name is Shagar Mohammed Abdel Ghaffar, and I'm one of Professor Fawzi's students. I've come to ask after him."

The woman hesitated for a moment, then led her to a spacious sitting room, attractively furnished. "Unfortunately, Fawzi isn't here."

"I know."

"What do you know?"

"I know he's in prison."

"Did they tell you that at the school?"

"No one told us anything."

The woman got up and went out, then came back with a glass of fruit juice.

"Is it true that Professor Fawzi is a Communist?"

The woman looked at her. At first she said nothing, then after a few moments of silence she said, "I don't know."

She seemed distressed. She asked Shagar how she had found the address, and Shagar told her. "Are you Professor Fawzi's mother?"

"Yes."

"What does 'Communism' mean?"

The woman stood up and extended her hand. "Thank you for inquiring. Goodbye."

Her father beat her. "You tramp!" he yelled at her. "Didn't anyone raise you to behave with common decency? Showing up uninvited all over the place, asking people about some boy, their son!" She couldn't forgive him for seeing Professor Fawzi as merely "some boy," and her having asked after him as a morally reprehensible act. He had tarred her luminous angel, while her mother, Sitt Gulsun, and her grandfather Abdel Ghaffar stood there watching this scene, and not one of them said a word.

Four

To the young, because they are young, everything looks bigger, taking on proportions relative to their age and to the space their bodies occupy, amidst other bodies heavier, taller, and broader than theirs. The tallest person is the oldest, and the uncle or aunt who has reached thirty is of such advanced age that it is difficult to grasp the concept of this "thirty," based on the five fingers, or even ten, that the child will hold out to indicate his age. As for the grandfather or grandmother, that's another story, combining reality and fantasy, the perceptible and the obscure, for the stories they tell of the past place them between two worlds, one foot here and the other there, with this mysterious "there" reaching into a past of which God alone knows the beginning and the end.

It seemed I was preparing myself for the sight of the school. The school so vast in my imagination was about to collide with the stones of an actual building, rising to a certain height and extending to a certain length, in a particular Cairo street. I couldn't find a place to park my car. I made the circuit of the neighborhood twice, then asked a passerby, who said, "You can park your car in al-Bustan Garage," and gave me directions.

I could have crossed Tahrir Street then proceeded to Mohammed Mahmoud Street, but I preferred to approach the school from Tahrir Square. This was not altogether logical, but it wasn't without a rationale. I wanted to see first the small gate designated for the kindergarteners: after all, it makes sense to begin at the beginning!

My father must have accompanied me through this gate on the first day of school. I remember that at the end of the school day, I stood waiting for them to call my name so that I could get into the designated line for those who would ride the same bus. On my chest, affixed to the school uniform, was a rectangular piece of pink fabric, fastened there for me by the teacher with four pins, one at each corner. The cloth panel bore my name, home address, and telephone number. At the time, it seemed a strange thing to me, a feeling that was defined for me when we left the classroom and I found that all the new children in the kindergarten had those big pink squares of cloth hanging on their chests. I stared at them but didn't laugh, knowing I had one just like it on my own chest. The children whose parents escorted them to and from school entered through this small gate, and left by it. Those of us who rode the school buses, however, didn't use it, because the buses let us off in the morning by the side of the schoolyard, and in the afternoon we would wait in the same place where we had disembarked to get back on the bus, which would go out through the rear gate that led to Sheikh Rihan Street.

Mohammed Mahmoud Street. All the cars crept along in one direction, toward Tahrir Square, while pedestrians came and went. The traffic didn't used to be this heavy. The American University was there, but I can't find a place for it in my memory. The Astra Café was across from it. I sat there in the early seventies, five years after I graduated from the university, with someone who wanted to recruit me into one of the new leftist organizations. He commenced his discussion by ridiculing and putting down all previous proponents of the left. The criticism came as no surprise to me—I agreed with some of it; what did surprise me was his superior tone, which suggested absolute self-confidence. I said to myself that if the man was a Lenin-in-the-making, I would regret having declined his offer.

The Astra Café went out of business—when? It was replaced by offshoots of the Coca-Cola culture: McDonald's, Pizza Hut, Kentucky Fried Chicken. The storefronts were in hues of screaming red and glaring yellow, offset by stripes in shades of red and white: the trademark of the American captain who presided over the "chicken that can't be beat."

I cross the street and find myself in front of the small wooden gate of Le petit lycée: the little school. I don't pause to contemplate the wooden façade of the door, or the vaulted archway, or my own feelings. I keep walking. A few more steps along is the other gate, the one designated for the girls from first-year primary through third-year secondary. We sneaked out through this gate two or three times to buy a hair ornament or a fancy notebook from the shop that seemed at the time like a distant frontier. I am startled now to find that the shop is merely one block from the school gate! I keep going without pause, as far as the intersection of Mohammed Mahmoud Street with Yusuf al-Guindi Street, at which point I turn right, following the school's enclosing wall.

It was neither a child's imagination nor a trick of memory: the school is immense, occupying a vast area, its buildings overlooking three streets. Its yard is a roofless atrium enclosed by the walls of the buildings. The portal leading to the administrative offices lies in Yusuf al-Guindi Street, in the center of the eastern wall. I continue to the intersection and turn right onto Sheikh Rihan Street. The gate of the Lycée des garçons: the boys' school—a huge wooden door, larger than that of the girls' school, but made from the same kind of wood and of the same design. Then the door of the theater. (The theater that belonged to the school was the site of the annual concerts, where I would be dazzled by ballet performances: dancers en pointe, the supple bodies bending and leaping and flying, the pink costumes, the lights, and the music.) Now the place has become a commercial theater. A large, wide-open gate, facing the garage door. I know that it leads to the schoolyard. I go in, but am stopped by a worker. I tell him, "I used to go to this school. I only want to look around the yard." He won't let me, saying that I must seek permission from the administration. I go back out, and a few steps farther on I find myself in front of the entrance to Ewart Hall of the American University. I don't go back to Yusuf al-Guindi Street to get permission from the administration to enter the school and reflect upon its details nearly 40 years after I left it and moved on to a different school.

Shagar didn't attend this school. What am I to do with this teacher I've invented? Should I make her fall in love with him and wait for his release from jail? Should I build a relationship between them and offer up a character embodying a typical Egyptian Communist? My son will say—and what he says matters to me—"This is predictable, that you depict a teacher and the heroine falls in love with him. Mama, your generation doesn't lack for romanticism, or melodrama for that matter—don't be angry—and being a leftist you'll make this handsome young guy a leftist, and the girl will fall in love with him and become a leftist in turn!" (I don't know whether this sense of sarcasm and aversion to any flight of fancy pains or reassures me about this generation that is growing up without any illusions to fall back on.) Should I drop Fawzi Kamel as a character from the narrative, and reconstruct his presence as merely a voice that guides the young girl toward recognition that a departure from the dominant pattern is possible? Should I keep him and have Shagar encounter him years later? If I do this, then what sort of character should Fawzi be? I knew quite a few leftists who spent the period between '59 and '64 in prison, and they differed in their personalities, their abilities, the clarity of their thinking; some were pretty, some ugly. Should I make him an erstwhile romantic who looks back on his youth with sympathy and sentimentality? An anachronism, a saintly man who has retained his luminous quality, a wingless seraph with dusty shoes and weary feet? Or should he be an old man lost in the crowd; or a party leader of dazzling tactical ability, mixing, in his rhetorical maneuvers, the discourses of revolution and containment, confusing himself and others; or shall I draw a tragic character whose life alternates between half-conviction and uncertainty—noble dream and frustrated dreamer, brilliant moments and painful failures? Why not make him a magnificent warrior to the end, and be done with it—or the other way around, make him an auctioneer recently come into prosperity, proud of his bell and his, "A la una, a la due, a la tre… "?

You won't make him one or another of any of these. You'll be surprised by him as he takes his own shape and imposes on you his own movement, his own fate; or you'll discover that he's gone, wandered off in the distance while you were busy writing—suddenly you'll remember and you'll turn around to look for him, but you won't find him. There are no premeditated decisions in writing. In the next chapter I'll come back to Shagar, and let him be what he will. At the moment I'm in Sheikh Rihan Street, just steps away from the school in which I spent nine years of my life. I left this school for another one in June 1960. On March 22nd of that year, the present Arab League building had opened up a few paces from the school, in Tahrir Square. I have no memory of this. The school buses took us from our homes to the school and let us off inside the yard, then collected us from inside the yard to take us back home again. I didn't know Tahrir Square. How can this be? Didn't I pass by it every day on my way to school? I lived in al-Manyal. Did the buses take a back route, or did they come by Kasr al-Aini Street, to make a right turn onto Sheikh Rihan Street several meters before the square?

For nine years I'll go by bus and pass close to the square, or cross it, or go around it, and spend the whole of every day—except for weekends, and holidays—from eight o'clock in the morning until two-thirty in the afternoon steps away from it and I won't know a thing in it or about it. Months after my graduation from the university I will read *The Open Door*. The first scene of the novel is set on the evening of February 21, 1946. Al-Zayyat wrote, "The movie houses were deserted; likewise the other public places, the bus, the tram. Police cars were cruising the streets carrying soldiers armed with rifles. There were not many passers-by... they talked amongst themselves."

Many are the voices that comment upon what happened that morning in the city center, and that relate the particulars to us: a demonstration against the English 40,000 strong, 23 dead, and 122 wounded. Ismailiya Square—later Tahrir

Square—was the stage for these events. Places suddenly acquire a new meaning when you get to know their stories—maybe not the whole story but a glimpse of a story, a piece of it that suddenly illuminates the place, so that you see it in a way that you never saw it before or understood it. When you figure it out, and you know it, it possesses you by right of the space it occupies in your mind and your imagination—or, more to the point, by right of the part it has played in making you who and what you are, and in shaping your response to this world. Just so are Helbawi House and the Abbas Bridge. But I am getting ahead of myself, for right now I am in Tahrir Square. I will read about the events of 1946 and in the year 1972 I will be in the square.

On the morning of January 24, 1972 I will go to Cairo University and find it surrounded by security forces, and I won't be able to go in to where a student sit-in has been staged in the large university hall. I will learn that the students were arrested at dawn and led off to prison.

In the evening, Mourid and I will go down to Tahrir Square: the students will be milling around the stone monument in the middle of the square, while other groups conduct discussions with passersby about economic and political conditions in the country, and explain the reasons for the sit-in. We head for the Izavich Café. There we find a number of our fellow writers and we hear talk of a national committee of writers and artists being formed. We sign our names on a petition sponsored by the committee that pledges solidarity with the students and their demands and condemns the arrests that took place that morning. We copy the petition, as do others of our colleagues. We divide up into small groups, each of which takes a copy of the petition, to gather the signatures of writers and artists. We carry out our mission and return to the square. The security forces, from a distance, are watching the students who are sitting and standing around the monument, shouting and chanting. We move on to the journalists' guild, where a number of writers, artists, and journalists are assembling. We count the signatures: between nine o'clock and midnight, our activity has yielded 105 signatures. What are we going to do with the petition? Opinion favors sending it to the president of the republic, the prime minister, and the head of the parliament. Three delegates are chosen, and I am one of them. We leave the guild hall on foot and head toward the telegraph office in Adli Street. The employee on duty asks us the sender's name, and we say, "This list—we want all 105 names to show." He says it's not possible, so we say, "The three of us, then—our names." He refuses. I show him my identity card and the employee records the pertinent information that is on it, then takes the text of the telegrams and the signatures that accompany it. We go back to the guild hall, and I leave with Mourid. On our way home we watch the students and the security forces. Before dawn, the forces advance on the students and clash with them; they arrest many of them, and pursue those who flee into the surrounding streets. In the morning, new students come to reinforce those who fled the night before; they demonstrate, and there are new confrontations with the police detachments.

There is more to the story, concerning my part in it and concerning the incident itself, but for now I move away from Tahrir Square, mere footsteps away from which I lived nine years without knowing the story of '46. The story of '72, though—that one I witnessed, and participated in, too. The workers' protests in '75 took place in the square, as well as the violent demonstrations of '77, and in the middle of all these events, also in '75, the funeral of Umm Kulthoum. A few meters from the heart of the square is the Mosque of Omar Makram. From the mosque, I will walk with the mourners time after time to say goodbye to friends and colleagues, and most likely my friends and colleagues will see me off from this very same place. The mourners will bid farewell to Umm Kulthoum from the Mosque of Omar Makram; I will hear about it and see it on the television screen while I am in the United States working on my doctorate. And from this mosque I will say goodbye to my lifelong friend, Latifa al-Zayyat. I take part in the ritual ablutions in the oppressive crypt of the Misr International Hospital. I go out with the body, and then we part company: she borne away in her coffin in the hearse, I in a car whose color I no longer remember.

Are my thoughts rambling? Where is Shagar in all this? I must get back to Shagar—I need to figure out what to do with her. She's graduated from school by now and enrolled in the history department of the School of Humanities at Cairo University. If Shagar were not a character in a story, I would have encountered her during my years of study at Cairo University, for the history department in which she studied is located on the second floor of the same building inhabited by the English department, in which I studied. We were students during the period between 1963 and 1967. Shagar will enter the gate of Cairo University and turn toward the tall palm trees on the right—they weren't as old then as they are now—and she will pass between the main building of the School of Humanities and the smaller building, which houses the English department on the first floor, and she will go up to the second floor to attend her history lectures. Almost every day she stops by the Central Library, the building facing her department, and spends hours there, sitting sometimes in the north-side research hall, sometimes in the south-side research hall, endlessly poring over catalogues. The workers know her, and none of them asks her for identification—they become completely familiar with her years before she is appointed to the department, and years before she is transformed from Miss Shagar to Doctor Shagar.

Five

Shklovsky says, in what is perhaps his most widely read critical essay, that habituation devours things, that when we have seen something over and over again we come to respond to it automatically, as if we had not even seen it; we carry out our actions robotically, as if we were not responsible for them. The details of our lives, to which we have become accustomed, do not arrest our attention as they did the first time; we go on and life goes on, passing us by as if it were nothing, all in vain.

Habituation—and Shklovsky says that this is one of the laws of perception—devours a person's life, "his works, the furnishings of his house, his spouse, even his fear of war." So why had Shagar not become habituated to that street, which she had traversed again and again for years?

A newly matriculated student on her way to the university. The statue, the acacia trees on both sides, then the monument, with the iron fence right behind it, and the row of palm trees, the clock tower, and the dome in the background. The opening scene. This is how Shagar sees it: self-contained. She passes it by in order to get to her college, as a young girl of seventeen when she walks as if she were flying, as a woman of fifty, when she leans for support upon the cane in her right hand, and throughout all the years in between. She watches, always she watches, whether the streets be thronged or nearly empty, whether it be summer or winter, morning or evening, whether the acacias are putting forth their blazing purple blossoms or whether they are stripped of them, whether she walks alone or accompanied by others, her route is still her route: the woman cast in stone at its beginning and the dome at its terminus. And when she leaves and crosses to the University Bridge, she is aware that the scene is behind her, she sees it at her back.

The scene was filled, perhaps as a woman is by the child in her womb or by the years she has lived or by knowledge that makes the eye sharper, more perceptive—or perhaps it is not so. In the first weeks, the place appeared to her as a captivating postcard, a picture, and she was surprised and delighted to enter it and become one of its components. Such is the innocence of the young, of course, their foolish fancies, which hover buoyantly above the earth and leave it to the feet to stumble about as they make their way cautiously toward perception, then knowledge. Take for instance that stone pillar that stands before the university gate. (Accuracy calls for use of the plural, for there are four iron gates: two that are big and wide and high, one through which cars enter and one through which they exit; people on the other hand—students, professors, and workers—use two small gates placed on either side. On days when there are protests, all are closed but one, the small gate to the right of the entrance. The students line up in front of it and entering is a slow process, because security agents inspect, one by one, the identity cards of all who enter.) We come back to the stone pillar, which, to the passerby and to Shagar as well, at the outset appears as merely one of the constituents that make up the scene: a small granite obelisk culminating in a flower or a flame, a carven object invoking ancient Egyptian history, and complementing or communicating with the granite creation of the sculptor Mahmoud Mukhtar, there at the beginning of the route. She knows it well, and she could have loved it before she knew it, then come to know it and to believe that knowledge is consummated such that you discover after ten years, twenty years, or thirty, that each new experience enlarges you, and enlarges the scene. (No, it's not just Mohammed Ezzat al-Bayoumi and Mohammed Abdel Maguid Mursi, and Abdel Hakam al-Garrahi and Khaled Abdel Aziz al-Waqad and that boy whose name we don't know—someone must know it—the boy who was shot near the wall of the School of Engineering and the following day *Al-Ahram* published a picture of that wall splattered with his blood.)

But why are events getting ahead of us? Shagar, as she takes in the university, hasn't yet seen the security forces, or the truncheons or the smoky tear-gas bombs or the stampedes. She hasn't yet seen that impoverished brown-skinned boy from the country, so young, standing outside the university wall in his army fatigues, sticking the barrel of his rifle into the space between two fence posts in the wall and aiming it deliberately at the demonstrators, as if he had learned his profession on stag-hunting expeditions in the company of a medieval European nobleman. She hasn't yet been struck by the truncheon that leaves its black-and-blue mark on the upper arm. Not yet; that is a future Shagar. The present Shagar is seventeen years old, a new student in the history department. Is it true that she joined the department under the influence of that teacher who taught her for three months? It is difficult to determine this, for a great deal can happen in a few days, so what can you make of five years in the life of a growing young girl who is one with the mice in her love of paper, which she consumes in her own way? In the school library, she had happened upon a book of ancient Egyptian legends, and from there she moved to the adjacent row of books. Then she joined the history department.

August '67, over lunch, her father announced the news, smiling: "The certificate, with distinction, and highest rank!" She didn't smile, nor did she say anything. She withdrew to her room.

During the academic year of 1967–68, Shagar continued to concentrate on her studies for the year preparatory to the Master's degree. She would go to the college, return from the college, prepare her lessons, go to the library, read, fill up index cards with notes and citations, turn in the required paper, achieving with the efficiency of a machine. But her soul? It had stolen away somewhere, retreated into the distance. She didn't get angry, she didn't cry, she didn't stop. In the newspapers and radio broadcasts, and on the lips of her family and the neighbors, a great deal of talk circulated concerning Sinai and the loss of the troops in the desert. She listened, and went on as if it were nothing.

Her professor said, "Why did you change your mind? You always wanted to specialize in Pharaonic history—what's happened all of a sudden?"

All she said was, "I'm going to study modern history—I think that's what I want." In succeeding years, Shagar would refer to this reversal as a "U-turn," for it was a total and unequivocal change, just as when you turn your car left and left again, and then head the other way. She brought three cardboard boxes and began moving books from her library into the boxes: books on ancient Egypt—its legends and architecture; books by Selim Hassan with their plain covers bearing only the author's name; the French and English books with their glossy covers adorned with pictures precise in their details of the carvings at the Valley of the Kings and the Valley of the Queens; the books she had been buying since she was fifteen years old; and the books she had photocopied at the university library and her grandfather Abdel Ghaffar had directed her to an old friend of his at al-Azhar who had fashioned for them strong, sturdy bindings of an olive color. She put them all in the box, and looked around her. Her task was not yet complete. The pictures. They were only copies on ordinary paper that she had taken to a shop in the city center, rolled and secured with fine ribbon. She got them back after two weeks: four large mounted pictures, each one in a large frame and covered with a pane of glass. She'd had difficulty carrying them down the main street, where three taxis passed her by, their drivers refusing to take her on with her burden. At last came a kindhearted driver who agreed to take her and even helped her carry the pictures to the door of her family's apartment. Above her bed, opposite the entrance to her room, she hung the picture of Maat, the goddess of balance and mistress of truth and justice. Maat was facing to her right, and when Shagar sat at her desk she could, by turning slightly to her left, see the countenance of Maat looking in a direction that revealed only the left side of her face. A tall, straight ostrich feather was fastened by a fine red band around the crown of her head, and behind her were hieroglyphic inscriptions.

On the left-hand wall, directly behind her when she sat at her desk, were two pictures. In one was an engraving of Isis on a sky-blue background. Her hair was a milky blue, and she was crowned with the disc of the sun and the horns of Hathor. Her face, shoulders, arms, and part of her crown were the color of sand with a tint of rosewood. In her right hand was the royal scepter. Next to the picture of Isis was one of Hathor the cow and the boy Amenhotep II. The young Pharaoh's body and that of Hathor the cow were the same sand color. His hair and the spots on the cow's body—the star-shaped spots representing the spirits of the dead—were green. The Pharaoh was crouched on his knees beneath the arch formed by the cow's legs, his head up-turned, nursing from her udder, against a back-ground of clear blue. Above the desk was a picture of Nut, the sky-woman. She touched the earth with the tips of her toes on one side and her fingertips on the other. With her legs and arms and her star-studded torso she formed an arch that was encircled by the body of her brother and husband. Geb rested in her embrace, and on his back his burgeoning vegetation grew.

She took them down from the wall, wrapped them in a sheet, and tied it. She fetched Ani's papyrus *Book of the Dead*—the copy that she always placed on her desk—and tossed it into the box. She asked her mother to help her move the boxes, then got a ladder and carried them one by one to the storage loft. Her mother asked her why she was doing this; Shagar muttered something incoherent.

She returned to her room, and looked around. Nothing now, except shelves on which were some dictionaries, a small empty library, and the desk, the bed, and the vanity. The room looked naked—desolate and cold. She switched off the light and lay down on her bed. She went to sleep.

A colored card the size of her palm rested under the glass top of her desk: the high scales with their two pans. Thoth stood supervising the balance, his papyrus in his left hand and his pen in the right. Shagar had forgotten to remove the picture. The following day she noticed that it was still in its place. She contemplated it, then decided to keep it there.

The research methodology professor in the Master's preparatory year: a loud-voiced man who constantly paced up and down in the study hall as if he were ablaze with the extraordinary ideas in his head. He didn't help the students understand that methods of research were approaches and tools linked to philosophical and epistemological constructs. For him, methods of research were limited to simple procedures: how to write footnotes, how to prepare a bibliography, how to divide the thesis into chapters and sections with prefatory comments and summary conclusions followed by indexes of sources and references. The professor said, "I shall require of each one of you a research paper, in which you must adhere to the rules I have taught you. You have a week to choose a topic and a month to complete the paper." During the succeeding eek the professor aimed his pen and began recording the names of the students and the titles of their papers.

"Shagar Abdel Ghaffar."

"The Massacre at Deir Yassin."

"This is not a topic for a history research paper, Miss Shagar. This is a topic for a newspaper article or a political analysis. If you want to do a paper on the Palestinian question, I suggest you study the role of the Arab High Commission or the Salvation Army or the Holy War—research the leadership role of one of them, and if you like the subject you can pursue it for the Master's thesis with a study of the role of these three organizations and others like them, the differences and the similarities. What do you think?"

"Can I write about the digging of the Canal?"

"In what respect?"

"The first concession and the second concession—an analytical paper."

The professor recorded the title in his notebook, and Shagar immersed herself in preparing the paper required of her.

Forgetfulness is a dodgy thing. It seems to a person that she has forgotten: she thinks that some desire, some idea, some reality, has slipped away from her, gone missing; the evidence is its total absence from her consciousness, she gazes at that river and sees upon it a thousand things—boats large or small, a number of people, a stick floating on the surface, or various insignificant things. Then one day she realizes that this thing has surfaced all of a sudden, as if it had been preserved there in the depths, submerged in the water, solid as a coral tree or a pearl resting in its oyster. Forgetfulness is a dodgy thing, Shagar tells herself as she organizes her papers and stands before the work that she has now completed, twenty years after the day in March '68 when the research programs professor told her that her topic wouldn't do.

At the end of November of the year 1977, she decided to begin researching the subject of Deir Yassin, and she gathered what material was available to her. She knew that there was a Zionist narrative, which she intended to present and disprove, and that there was another, an Arab interpretation, which she wanted to examine and elucidate. But as she assembled such documents, books, and articles as could be obtained, she began to discover new threads, which she followed carefully. They led her to an area of knowledge before which she stood amazed, wondering: Why has this been missing for all these years, who concealed it, and how, and why? Is it a naïve attempt to counter the Zionists' claims that the attack on the village was justified because it was a center for Iraqi soldiers? But in order to establish that, would the villagers have to be portrayed as sacrificial lambs, helpless in the hands of fate as they faced the butchers' knives?

The prevailing Arab narrative says: They were unarmed villagers set upon by the men of the Irgun and Lehi, who massacred 250 old men, women, and children, capturing the rest, and paraded the prisoners in a triumphal procession around the Jewish neighborhoods of Jerusalem, with the result that terror spread among the Arabs and they left, for fear that what had happened to the people of Deir Yassin would happen to them. Is this an accurate account? Were the inhabitants of Deir Yassin oblivious to the danger that surrounded them? That didn't make sense. As she sits at her desk—now here in Cairo—she can, merely by glancing at the maps and reviewing the course of events in the weeks preceding the massacre, see the perilous knife's edge upon which Deir Yassin was perched, for it abutted the western suburbs of Jerusalem, and overlooked the route between Jerusalem and Yaffa (or Tel Aviv). And it was surrounded by seven Jewish settlements: to the east, Givat Sha'ul, Montefiore, Beit Hakerem, Shkonat Hapoalim, Yefeh Nof, and Beit Vegan formed a barrier that separated it from Jerusalem; to the west, the Motza settlement separated it from the water main. The neighboring Arab villages were, to the south, Ain Karem and al-Maleha, and to the north, Lifta. Four months earlier the Zionists had launched heavy assaults on Lifta, which had then fallen. They had also attacked and taken over two Arab neighborhoods in West Jerusalem. The only road linking Deir Yassin and Jerusalem shut down, rendering travel to the capital impossible for the villagers, except by a circuitous route that took them south to Ain Karem, then east to al-Maleha, then north once again to Jerusalem—fifteen kilometers of rugged mountain track that took five hours on foot, instead of five minutes by bus on the direct route. (It was impractical for Hayat al-Belbeysi, the only teacher in the village, to make the trip from Jerusalem and back every day. She stayed in Deir Yassin.) With the fall of Lifta, only the southern access via Ain Karem and al-Maleha remained to Deir Yassin. How did the residents of Deir Yassin confront this blockade? Is it reasonable to assume that they didn't reckon with the imminent catastrophe?

The village had a history of resistance to the government of the British Mandate and to the Jewish settlers. In the period between 1936 and 1939, Deir Yassin and the mountains facing it constituted one of the insurgents' centers of operation. Some of its men undertook the ambush of a train carrying provisions and arms to the English. They cut the line, and the train was derailed. Despite the harsh laws imposed by the Mandate government (six years' imprisonment for possession of a firearm, sixteen years for possession of a bomb, five years with hard labor for possession of a dozen bullets, and fifteen days' imprisonment for possession of a club!), there were weapons in the village, which was subject to periodic searches: the British soldiers would come and close off the village, looking for the insurgents—entering houses, breaking jars of olive oil, pouring gasoline on the flour and sugar and rice. Then the British set up a checkpoint in the village where every afternoon at four o'clock the names of all the village men were read out in order to ensure that they were present and accounted for.

Just nine years—would that be enough for the villagers to forget about oppression and resistance? The index cards piled up and in her hands a miscellany of information accumulated, from which she was able to glean certain particulars, while others remained obscure or missing or confusing, as if she were following a thread that was suddenly cut, leaving her confronting the question: What next?

She was able to reach an initial conclusion about the linchpins of the attack on the village and the bases from which it had issued: four armed groups, two from Givat Sha'ul, or one from Givat Sha'ul and the other from the western suburbs of Jerusalem; the first attacked Deir Yassin from the north and the second attacked it from the east. Two other groups issued from Beit Hakerem—or possibly from Beit Hakerem and Yefeh Nof—the first to open up the village at a point on the southeastern side, while the second intended to circle around to attack it from the western side. The four groups consisted of Menachem Begin's men, the Irgun, and Yitzak Shamir's men, Lehi. The attack took place at dawn or perhaps an hour or two before dawn. What happened inside the village after that? A massacre! How? What are the particulars? And before the massacre, what happened? How can she put herself in the village?

She didn't find anything helpful in the Arabic documents; would she find it among the British papers? Or among Israeli writings? In the testimony of the villagers? How could she reach them, where might she find them? Deir Yassin was still closed. Nine years.

Six

68

When I began writing this text, it seemed logical to me to keep to the chronological order of Shagar's imagined life, and the details of my life as I have lived it, so that the two stories would proceed in parallel fashion without interference or confusion. But I realize now that I write by a process of association, and leave it to the pen to move like a shuttle between the past and the present. I notice also that every time I've approached Shagar and got better acquainted with her, the threads have become entwined. Yesterday, for example, I found myself thinking that Shagar, with her knowledge of history, could facilitate the writing of the special section on Helbawi's House, and the Abbas Bridge, and Moustafa Reda Street. Without her (Shagar, I mean), I am obliged to go back to the books and periodicals, or settle for the fragments of knowledge available to me about these places.

Helbawi House, called after its owner Ibrahim al-Helbawi, is the house in which I was born. My mother gave birth to me at six o'clock on Sunday morning, the 26th of May, 1946. (I've just looked at the calendar that shows corresponding Western and Islamic dates, and found that this matches the 24th of Jumadi al-Akhira, 1365.) My grandfather on my mother's side had rented this house from al-Helbawi's widow in the year 1941, after he and his brother decided to move because Allied soldiers had taken up residence in the house next to theirs in Helwan. Since my grandfather had six daughters and his brother had two, it seemed to them that the presence of British, Australian, African, and Indian soldiers in the neighboring house would not lead to peace of mind; hence this little family migration from Helwan—at that time a peaceful suburb—to the island of Roda, al-Manyal District. Perhaps my grandfather's choice fell to this house because of its proximity to where he worked, and to the home of his new in-laws, who, a few months later, would take in Bouthaina, his eldest daughter, to live with them.

Each morning in the fall, winter, and spring, as well as early summer, my grandfather would leave Helbawi House and walk a few steps to the bank of the Nile, and from there, for a few pennies, he would board a ferry that would take him to the other shore. A few more minutes of walking and he would arrive at the university gate, proceeding from there with a right turn toward the School of Humanities. In the year 1941, Dr. Abdel Wahhab Azzam held the chair of Professor of Oriental Languages in the School of Humanities at Fou'ad I University (now Cairo University), and in 1949, when my grandfather left Helbawi House to return to his house in Helwan, Dr. Azzam was dean of the college.

The young lawyer Moustafa Ashour would ask for the hand of Mayy from her father in the house at Helwan, and at the time of the wedding procession in 1942 he would take her from Helbawi House. Dr. Rashad Saqr, recent graduate of the School of Medicine, would enter Helbawi House to ask for the hand of Tahiyya, the eldest daughter of Abdel Fattah Azzam, but once engaged would not marry her until after his safe return from the Palestine War. Rashad Saqr would tell his bride, in Helbawi House, about a young officer with whom he had been besieged at Fallujah, by the name of Gamal Abdel Nasser.

Did my grandfather rent the house through the agency of a middleman? Did a friend guide him to it? Did he know al-Helbawi before the man's death? If so, did he respect him? Hold him in contempt? Feel sorry for him? Or keep his distance, mindful of the difference between them? These questions seem digressive, irrelevant, and yet I think they are not without importance, for al-Helbawi, whose name was on our lips each time we pointed out the house, and was repeated after that in reference to a neighborhood, no less, of the quarter in which we lived: there is a story behind al-Helbawi. And if matters were reversed, and it were Shagar who was narrating, she would recount to us the full story of Ibrahim al-Helbawi, the young man of rural origins who was able to become a star in the world of legal practice, and who at one time had been a member of the prosecutors' court in the trial of the peasant-farmers of Dinshaway in 1906 and, speaking on behalf of the occupying forces, had presented to the court the rationale for sentencing the peasant farmers to death. In the newspaper *Al-Liwaa'*, Sheikh Abdel Aziz Gawish bestowed upon him the nickname, "The Executioner of Dinshaway." The name stuck to him, even though he tried hard to atone for his offense by censuring the Dinshaway trial and volunteering to work for the defense in national litigations. Al-Helbawi died in the year 1940 at the age of 83; a year after his death, my grandfather rented the house from his widow, his third wife, I believe. Five years later, I was born.

Helbawi House, then, was the first—I don't remember it, for my grandfather left it when I was three years old. As for the house at Abbas Bridge, my mother says she moved there in July 1947, from the Shoubra apartment she had first entered as a bride. I was just over a year old. It was an apartment on the fourth floor overlooking the Nile and the Abbas Bridge, which I could see from the balcony and from the bedroom I shared with my older brother Tariq. The bridge opened twice a day to let the larger boats pass through. At three o'clock in the afternoon, I would see a line of cars waiting for the bridge to close. At three in the morning, it would open again, but I would be fast asleep and wouldn't see anything.

From the balcony, and from the window of my room, I saw the Abbas Bridge. In the early morning, when I was waiting for the school bus, on summer evenings when we were playing on the shore and buying roasted *termis* seeds and grilled corn, I would see the bridge, and I would see the big washing area that the vegetable sellers used: women in black garments, opening the public spigots over lettuce, radishes, leeks, watercress, green onions, and parsley, before taking it to sell in the nearby streets. I couldn't see the fisherman Amm Mahrous, who sold his own catch, but I knew he was somewhere along the shore, underneath the bridge. The washing area, the boats large and small, the bridge closed or open—these were scenes from daily life that we took for granted, and that sometimes caught our attention before we got used to them all over again. But one scene, a special occasion toward which we counted the days, came once a year; we waited for it. It came one day, and was gone, and again we had to wait. Thus the Day of the Nile Inundation: the water rose and changed color— we observed this, keeping an eye out until the appointed day: then we would stand on the balcony of our flat to watch the boats decorated with flags and colored lamps led by the *Aqaba*, the largest and most splendid ship of all. We stared off to our right until our eyes picked it out: a point of light in the darkness, gaining in size and definition as it approached. Now there was no need to twist our necks and strain our bodies to the right, for the procession was directly in front of us, gliding slowly along on the surface of the river, illuminating the water as it plied its nighttime journey. We craned our necks to the left in order to follow the boats, which had now passed the bridge and were growing ever smaller and smaller, until once again they were just a small spot of light, then a pinprick, disappearing into the darkness.

She too was a vanishing pinprick, a metallic spot, which, from my window, I followed with my eyes: my mother went on the Hajj, and I spent my time watching from the window, obsessed with waiting for her. I would hear the drone and look up: nothing yet. The sound grew louder, then that metallic bird would appear far-off in the sky. My mother had taken a plane. The plane would pass by, fade into the distance. She didn't come! There were many planes in the Cairo skies in those days. The word "Palestine" reverberated in the house. I didn't know what it meant. I wasn't more than two-and-a-half years old.

The incident at Abbas Bridge, when Cairo University students were blocked from behind by police officers and in front by the opening of the bridge, is a blank space in my childhood mind. The incident occurred on February 9, 1946, three months and seventeen days before I was born. At the age of ten I would have the impression, even after my family moved to another house, that I had complete and total knowledge of the bridge, and that I saw from it more than others did. It would seem to me that I knew the buildings of the medical college, and its hospitals known as Kasr al-Aini, which occupied the northern end of the island and which I passed every day on my way to school from our home at Abbas Bridge and subsequently from our new house in Moustafa Reda Street. I didn't know that in 1935 students of the college had hidden the body of their colleague, Abdel Hakam al-Garrahi, in the hospital so that they would be able to escort it in a public funeral procession. And when the Sudanese student Mohammed Ali Ahmad fell, the students of the college hid his body as well, and when the police had no luck in determining its whereabouts matters escalated into a battle between the students and the police, who tried to prevent them from staging a huge funeral for their martyred comrade. In my childhood the Kasr al-Aini building was a familiar presence. Later I would discover that a child knows things, and yet does not know them.

I am distracted by the subject of writing and of history, distracted by Shagar, so I leave off pursuing the family's move to a new house. Aristotle said something regarding this. He distinguished literature from history, as I well know. I'd better refer to his book. I leave the office and look in the library. I find a copy of Butcher's English translation published in 1955, and a copy of Shoukri Ayyad's critical edition of Abou Bishr Matta's translation from the Syriac, accompanied by a modern translation. I search for a specific paragraph, and find it:

> Based upon what has already been stated, it is evident that the work of the poet is not to narrate that which has happened, but rather that which might happen or is possible in accordance with probability or necessity, for the historian and the poet do not differ in whether their narration is in verse or in prose (for the reports of Herodotus might have

been rendered metrically, but would still constitute history whether composed in verse or not); rather they differ in that one of them tells what has happened, whereas the other tells what might happen. Poetry, then, is closer to philosophy, and is more exalted than history, because poetry comes closer to expressing the universal, while history leans more toward expression of the particular. The universal is that which one sort of person may happen to do or say in a situation conforming to probability or necessity.

Aristotle goes on to say,

It is incumbent upon the poet, or the "maker" (*poietes*) to be first of all a maker of stories, before he is a maker of metrics, since he is a poet by reason of the imitations he produces, and what he imitates is deeds. And if it should happen that he make verse on one event or another that has in fact come to pass, this makes no difference to his characterization as a poet, as there is nothing to prevent that actual events be consistent with the laws of probability or possibility, and by this reckoning he is their maker.

It is likely that Shagar would differ with Aristotle on his statement that the subject of history consists of the particular. Her objection does not, I think, spring from a bias toward her field of endeavor or an attempt to advance its cause, but rather from the fact that she, in pursuing the writing of history, considers the observation of events and particularities to be no more than a part of the task whose ultimate fulfillment can only be realized through the notion of universality that Aristotle described as "the law of probability." I interpret it by its inherent logic as a law that connects events and extracts from their ungovernable chaos and their cacophonous uproar a guiding thread, a light that enables human beings to understand their own stories. Am I confusing literature with history, or burdening Shagar with my own project? I don't think so. I will corroborate my own statements with what she has written: perhaps her study of Deir Yassin is a suitable example. Shagar did not present the attack on the village and the resistance of its inhabitants and the massacre that ensued simply as a factual event in and of itself or one connected to similar events in the years 1947–1948; rather, she presented it as a paradigmatic event, enabling her readers to consider the general as contained in the particular, and the connection between that incident and a series of other incidents whose sum total constitutes one of the essential characteristics of their modern history. The paradigm could fail to encompass the event, or could extend beyond it, or it might be an exact match. Deir Yassin was an example of the farthest extreme, but it was nevertheless consistent with the model. I put this aside for now, in any case, and get back to the houses I lived in. Why do I force them all—those houses, I mean—into one chapter? Why don't I leave them to appear in the text in the same order in which they appeared in my life? What is it I hope to gain by amassing them all?

In 1955, my father bought a house with a garden in Moustafa Reda Street, in al-Manyal District. We would no longer look out over the Nile and the Abbas Bridge, with a view of Giza on the opposite bank of the river, for we were to move to the interior section of al-Manyal, to a spot that could be described as the heart of the island. The distance to "the big channel," which separated the island from Giza, was virtually the same as the distance to "the small channel," which separated it from Cairo proper. Likewise our location was centered between the southern end of the island behind al-Roda Street, which ended at the Nilometer, and its northern end, where the buildings of the Kasr al-Aini medical college stood.

In the first days after our move, this house seemed to me and my brothers—Tariq, the elder, and the two younger ones, Hatem and Wa'el—a fascinating realm of the unknown, intriguing. The spaciousness of the house, compared to an apartment consisting of five rooms, was not the sole reason for this. There were also the colors in the panes of the two glass windows and the interesting way in which these played with the natural light in the morning and the lamplight at night: two windows of fitted glass, each one containing the figure of a shepherdess. The first shepherdess, clad in a green dress, bent from the waist over her water jug—only her left side was visible. The second shepherdess wore a violet dress—she leaned to the right, bearing in her arms a sheaf of wheat. In both frames appeared the same tree, with green leaves and red berries. In the first window was an ewe and her lamb with its nose raised to nuzzle its mother's neck. In the second were four sheep stretching their necks toward the sheaf of wheat held by the woman, and an ewe settling into motherhood, absorbed by her lamb as it suckled at her udder. In the daytime the sun's rays lit up the figures in the two windows, causing whoever was inside the house to exult in the splendor of the whole tableau. At night, the house lamps illuminated the windows, so that anyone passing in the street would be thrilled by their beauty.

The two windows looked out over the wooden staircase that led between the first and second floors. While for our elders it was nothing more than a means to go up or down, to us it was a playground where we ran and jumped, slid on the curved banister, and sprawled on the steps to converse in whispers or shouts and to laugh or quarrel; one of us might get angry or cry or fall abruptly silent because the din we were making had woken our father from his siesta, causing him to threaten us, "Just you wait until I get hold of you, you jackass kids!" We would laugh soundlessly, talking to each other in whispers for a few minutes, then lose ourselves in play once again, heedless of our father's nap and of the two shepherdesses with their colorful sheep looking out at us from their fixed positions in the stained glass.

This staircase was not the only stage for our daily operations—there was also the wide marble staircase at the entryway of the house, which we used for playing ball, and the high, nearly vertical stone staircase that connected the first floor to the basement, and a curving iron staircase, which you would find unexpectedly on a balcony onto which one of the second-floor rooms opened. (Later this would become my room, with my bed, my books, and my desk.) The garden, the basement, the roof, and every one of the staircases—all these we incorporated into our games. I would hide sometimes inside a large barrel or in one of the cupboards on the ground floor while playing hide-and-seek with my brothers. We would run on the iron staircase that took us to the roof, and our mother would shout at us, "Don't run! One of you is going to fall on those stairs!" We would answer her—still at a run—"We're not running!"

In the yard my brothers, at different stages, kept dogs, with various names from Guard to Rex to Jasmine to Lassie. I was afraid of them all, and would not play with them, feed them, or go anywhere near them. In the capacious chicken coop that occupied one side of the backyard, we would have chickens or geese or a turkey, or all of these at once. Occasionally we would have rabbits, which would dedicate themselves to digging their burrows until we discovered that they had reached the foundations of the house. Years later when my two younger brothers married and had children, there would be a goat for those children to coddle and tease every Friday when the family gathered at the house, which had by this time become known as "Manyal House," to distinguish it from the houses into which we had dispersed with our spouses and children.

But not one of all these marvels would ever

rival the gift our father brought us one day in 1959. We stood stunned, until our awe turned all at once to excitement. "His name is Garir!" said my father. Had we not all been so tongue-tied, I would have replied, "And my name is Radwa, and this is Tariq, who's the oldest, and this is Hatem, who's three-and-a-half years younger than I am, and that's Wa'el, our youngest brother." Our lexicon was inadequate to describe the horse's beauty or express our feelings. I would see that he was beautiful and enchanting, but I would never ride him. Tariq, on the other hand, would leap onto his back, and be out the gate with him, riding along the asphalt street until he got to the small channel. His skill and adroitness as a rider would earn him a reputation in Moustafa Reda Street and in all the surrounding streets.

From this house, which my father bought in 1955 and to which he brought Garir and dozens of objects large and small, his coffin would depart amid his wife, his sons, and his surviving brother, as well as his in-laws and his colleagues. I would find myself watching from the balcony and crying out as if I hadn't been born and raised in a middle-class family skilled at keeping its feelings under wraps, not bidding farewell to its dead with striking of cheeks and noisy outcry. In the evening Hatem asked, "Who was the woman who was shouting as we carried our father from the house?" and I did not answer.

Seven

Shagar was born on the 26th of May, 1946 in a house that overlooked the Abbas Bridge, but from the other direction, opposite our house, on the Giza side. (Her grandfather Abdel Ghaffar told her that her mother was six months pregnant with her when Umm Kulthoum sang "Ask My Heart" at the festival of the Prophet's birthday. Then she sang "Ask the Cups of Delight" in May—the month of Shagar's birth. Later the same year she sang "The Way Was Born," "The Path of the Mantle," and "Sudan." These were five poems by Ahmed Shawqi that had been set to music by Riad al-Sunbati.) In her childhood, before the proliferation of tall cement buildings, if Shagar stood in the southernmost corner of the balcony she would see the date palm on her right and, behind the palm, the pyramids of Giza. If she moved to the eastern side, she would see, behind al-Manyal on her left hand, the Mohammed Ali Mosque standing solidly in its place at the Citadel in the Muqattam Hills. (Her grandfather told her about the *mahmal*: the great procession that set off from the Citadel bearing the ceremonial covering of the Kaaba on its journey to Suez, and from there by sea to Jidda, on the way to Mecca. She gazes at the Citadel and her grandfather's voice comes to her, evoking the velvet-like cloth embroidered in threads of gold, the camels and the horses forging their way ahead to the rhythm of drumbeats and shouts of acclamation from the people.) From the rear window—the kitchen window—she would see the trees at the zoo, green in the daytime and shadowy at night. The roaring of the lions at night frightened her—though she knew they were confined in their cages, still she was frightened, wishing she were sunk in the oblivion of sleep, wishing she could shut her ears. The tolling of the university clock did not frighten her. She would hear the chimes and the intervals of silence in between, as well as what lingered afterward in the empty air, like the tail of the sound, or another faint answering sound, like the ghost, the phantom of a sound. When the radio announcer said, "The Cairo University clock has struck the hour of two o'clock precisely," Shagar recognized the clock she had known years before: she knew its chimes: four on the hour, a single chime on the quarter-hour, two on the half-hour, and three at a quarter before the hour; she learned three and four before learning how to count from one to twelve, as well as the meaning of a quarter, a half, and three-quarters.

She didn't notice the chiming of the clock as she sat behind a small, lonely desk in lecture hall 74 of the School of Humanities; to her left were the seats of the hall occupied by her family, friends, and colleagues. She didn't look in their direction. She looked to her right, toward the podium and the three professors. They wore black robes and before each of them on the baize-covered table was a copy of her thesis.

The committee members discussed it for three hours. They withdrew to confer, and reappeared after half an hour. She stood up; the audience stood up as well. The head of the committee first read the long introduction, and then said, "The committee composed of… and… and… has met at six o'clock on Saturday evening on the 11th of December 1971, corresponding to the 3rd of Dhu al-Qiᶜda, 1393. Following public examination of the student Shagar Mohammed Abdel Ghaffar, the committee has decided to award her the Master's Degree in Modern History, with Distinction."

She was lucky—Shagar often reflected on this. If she had defended her thesis two or three months later the administration would have obstructed her appointment, and might have even expelled her from the college. So said the president of the university. Were his words only a threat, his way of brandishing a stick at a young woman barely 25 years old? Was it a preventive measure, to constrain her future conduct?

She joined the student's sit-in from the first day, in the auditorium, and spent the four days there. The dome of the auditorium—the university's well established distinguishing characteristic, featured in cards and photographs—was no longer just an arched line, backdrop to a stage over which a woman made of granite presided. The students entered the auditorium and settled down in its spacious domain beneath its lofty dome, where they discussed and debated, agreed and disagreed, nullified official proclamations, and gave free rein to dreams—big ones—birds fluttering their wings, hovering and twittering in voices that rose toward the high dome. Shagar did not look at the ceiling. She did not see the dome from outside, now—she was inside the auditorium, immersed in discussion from morning until evening. She closed her eyes, overwhelmed by fatigue at the end of the day, and slept on two seats pushed together to form an improvised bed. She woke at daybreak, and went out onto the campus, which the blue of an overcast winter's dawn had penetrated. She sat down on the stairs. The clock tower and then the School of Humanities were to her left, to her right the College of Law, and between the two a flat expanse of green grass stretching almost as far as the iron gate and the monument commemorating the martyrs. Shagar stared, still drowsy from sleep. Then the light cleared. Alert now, Shagar began to write down all she had witnessed the previous day. She noted the cheering and the speeches and the telegraphed messages of support. Even the sharp disagreements that had arisen among the students of the ground floor and the ones in the balcony— these too she recorded: the tension in the air had been palpable. Some whispered that attempts at sabotage were being made, while others said the state security services were accomplishing their objectives. A third group insisted that these were natural differences, and that it wouldn't do to accuse those who disagreed—for whatever reason—of being saboteurs or agents. How had matters come to such a point? Chanting broke out all of a sudden, not the usual slogans that all the protestors had been repeating, but a challenge from the students on the ground floor to those sitting in the balcony. The students on the first floor shouted, "Medicine, Engineering, how much did you sell Egypt for, *how much*?!" The students in the balcony responded with an opposing cry, pointing their fingers accusingly, "Communists, communists, *we* are the Egyptians!" Shagar was startled by a skinny student who leapt up onto the chair he'd been sitting in and spat as high as he could in the direction of the chanters in the balcony.

At dawn on the 24th of January the security forces stormed the university and led the protesters from the auditorium to the police vans.

She spent only ten days in prison. At the end of the mid-year recess she went back to her work. The chairman of the department summoned her and informed her that the president of the university wanted to see her. She headed toward the building in which the auditorium was located, and asked for directions to the office of the university president. Up she went. She sat in the office manager's waiting room. "Come in, Miss."

He didn't invite her to sit down. He set his glasses on his nose and read from a paper in front of him. He took off his glasses, and looked at her:

"Miss Shagar Mohammed Abdel Ghaffar, teaching assistant in the history department?"

"Yes."

"You were with the protesters, were you not?"

"Yes."

"You were arrested on the 24th of January along with the student protesters?"

"Yes."

"How can we entrust you with the teaching of our students?" He went on: "You know that we can cancel the appointment of a teaching assistant at any time. The assistant is not a member of the faculty, he is a student researcher, nothing but a student researcher, a temporary employee, on probation."

She kept silent.

"Wouldn't it be better for you to attend to your studies and complete your Master's degree, instead of this nonsense?"

"I defended my thesis in December. Last month I was appointed to the rank of assistant instructor."

He raised his voice angrily: "You haven't gotten your doctorate yet, and you aren't a member of the faculty. I can dismiss you from the university!"

He stared at her. Then he pretended to be absorbed in some papers on his desk. Raising his head he said, "I expect to hear an apology from you, or else an explanation of what you've done!"

"Did you apologize?" her grandfather, Abdel Ghaffar asked her.

"No, I didn't!"

He laughed. "Stubborn girl, Shagar!" He laughed still more when she came home one day the following year holding in her hand a truncheon and a soldier's helmet. In her bag was a tear-gas bomb. She took it out of her bag and showed it to them. Her mother cried, "You're crazy!"

Sitt Gulsun's comment was, "Shagar will bring disaster upon you! If the university doesn't expel her, I'll eat my hat!" This observation was only the beginning of a lengthy monologue, which Shagar was at pains to ignore. She moved with her grandfather to his room, to tell him how the students left the university campus and clashed with the security forces.

"The kids decided to put on an exhibition of their loot, and they brought some of it to me to hold onto for them. One of the students grabbed the truncheon from its owner. The helmet rolled onto the ground in the commotion, and a student picked it up. And the tear-gas bomb—one girl managed to catch it before it hit the ground. That's today's take. The rest is coming!"

"And you left the university carrying these things?"

"I went out the back gate and took the bus. I went to the National Library, read for two hours, and then took the bus home!"

Shagar smiled, wondering, "Is this pure boldness or is it mixed with foolhardiness about the hunters' snares and rifles?"

She got away with it. Lecture hall 74 once again. The dissertation. The black robes. The defense. She got her doctorate.

She pores over the pictures. Pictures from the first defense—25 years old. Pictures from the second defense—28 years old. The intervening years don't appear in the pictures: the hair cut boyishly short, the slim body, the gaze—how to describe it? A great many color photographs are brought to her by students after they've given their defense. The same hall, the same black robe as well, only now she is the supervisor of the dissertation, or else a member of the student's committee. The body is no longer slim, the hair no longer black and cut short but rather gray and pushed back, arranged as befits a professor approaching the age of forty, in this picture. In her mid-forties, in that one. Fifty in a third. Looking at the most recent pictures, she is bemused, as if she does not recognize herself in them. Does she cling to the image of the girl, not wanting to accept this fifty-ish woman in her place? Because she is less beautiful, less graceful? What is the meaning of beauty? This filled-out figure, is it not worthy? She smiles: is no one, as life slips through the fingers, content? Not women? Not men, either. No one is proud of the graying hair, the wrinkles, the path descending toward death!

She goes back to the pictures from her Master's defense. The girl with the boyish haircut stands amid colleagues and friends after the defense. At the edge stands Yusuf. A country boy, clearly: tall, broad-shouldered, laughing. In the pictures from the doctoral defense, too, Yusuf laughs. In the last pictures his face appears harsh, pale, and distant, as if he were well on the way to dying. She hadn't noticed.

There are other colleagues in the pictures, too. They appear closer—they were closer. They grew distant. In the beginning, Yusuf seemed distant—he seemed boorish, outspoken to the point of rudeness. Then the passage of time brought its trials great and small, and a road that branched off from every question, and enticements that tempted her friends with delusions of grandeur dragged them down further and further, as she watched them recede, leaving her desolate and forsaken—and sometimes angry. Yusuf did not rise or fall; he held fast, like the wall of a house.

"What should I do, Yusuf?"

"Calm down a bit—we must think calmly."

From the train station she had made straight for his house. In her agitation, it had not occurred to her that she ought first to make sure of the papers she was carrying.

"Have you corrected the papers?"

"Not yet!"

He gave her a look of disapproval. He reached out for the bundle of answer booklets. There were 44 booklets, which they corrected together. Each one contained responses lengthy or brief.

"Are you sure the boy submitted a paper that was completely blank?"

She repeated what she had told him. "I left the house at six this morning, afraid I'd be late for the test. It was my first time offering a course at a university outside of Cairo. I got to the college a full hour before the test was to begin. I stood there in the examination hall for three hours, monitoring the test. There were about forty students, and I know them all—even the ones whose names I don't remember, I recognize their faces. This boy I hadn't seen before. It took me aback that he wasn't writing in the answer booklet; he ordered coffee, then tea, and he was smoking. He looked at the question paper, then at the answer sheet, and that was it."

"Did you make sure he was a third-year student?

"I checked his student I.D. Then, just to be extra sure, I leaned over one of the other students and asked her about him. She said, 'He's our class-mate, and he's at the top of the class. He was at the top in first year and second year!' The test period ended, and the boy turned in his answer booklet, so I flipped through the pages—he hadn't written a single word."

"The paper's been switched!"

"And the next step, Yusuf?"

"We've got to notify the police."

"The police?!"

"The student's up to some sort of chicanery, no doubt about it."

"Chicanery… the student?"

The next test. There was only a quarter of an hour until the end of the test period. The boy was smoking, with the blank test booklet in front of him. He got up to turn it in. The monitor reached out to take it from him. A detective placed his hand on the booklet and held it for safekeeping, while another did the same with the rest of the test booklets the monitor had been holding. Caught by surprise, she was petrified, and began crying and striking her cheeks in alarm. The students didn't understand what was happening, and milled around outside the hall until an officer ordered them to disperse. Before the investigation opened, the truth came out. There were two test booklets with the student's name and session number on them: the one he had been about to submit with no answers written in it, and the other concealed among the rest of the booklets with the monitor, its pages containing lengthy answers to every question. The object of the investigation was to determine who the student's collaborators were—one professor or another, one employee or perhaps two—and in exchange for what: sums of money, compensation in goods, or better employment? Also, how the papers were switched—and so forth.

The first rude awakening. Cruel. "Shagar, the university isn't outside society—what happens in society happens in the university, too!" Yusuf was right, and yet… the whistle-blowing, the authorities, the detectives, the police investigation!

Eight

S he didn't notice the notebook placed on her desk until four days after her grandfather's passing. When had he put it there? Had he intended to write more, then sensed the touch of impending death upon his shoulder, and so hastened to leave his gift upon her desk? Shagar began to read what was written there.

Dedication

I dedicate this portrait of my life's history to my granddaughter and the apple of my eye, Miss Shagar Mohammed Abdel Ghaffar, instructor in the history department at the Egyptian University, as a modest gift to her on the occasion of her receiving the Master's degree with distinction, and I ask God almighty to perpetuate for her always the blessing of knowledge, to be satisfied with her and grant her satisfaction, Lord who hears all prayers.

In the name of God, the merciful and compassionate, supreme over heaven and earth, and blessings and peace be on our Lord the true Prophet Mohammed. Now to the matter at hand: this is a record of the life history of Abdel Ghaffar Bin Ali Zein al-Abidin, poor servant of his gracious Lord. His mother was Saleha Bint Hasan al-Khawwas.

I was born about 1897 in the village of Zaribat al-Ashraf (now al-Adliya), near Belbeys in the Governorate of al-Sharqiya. This village was not our place of origin—rather, my father alighted there upon moving from the village of al-Zarabi in Upper Egypt five years before I was born. (My father left his first wife, two daughters, and three sons behind in al-Zarabi.) My father never told me the reason he left his native village and chose to settle in Zaribat al-Ashraf. Perhaps he meant to let me know the details of that story when I reached manhood, but it was not to be, for he died when I was not yet seven years old. He did tell me, though, about my grandmother Shagar, and his father and his maternal uncles who went to work on the digging of the Canal and never came back. My father headed east toward Ismailiyya when he got off the boat at the Port of Imbaba—whether in order to fulfill a pledge to his mother to visit the grave of his father and uncles, or for some other reason, I don't know. My father came to Zaribat al-Ashraf and settled there, then married a local girl, and I don't think he ever did manage to visit the grave, despite the frequency of his travels in that direction; most likely he found no sign to direct him to the graves of those who died in the forced-labor trenches.

The Reason for the Name Change from al-Zariba to al-Adliya

In the sixteenth century three brothers, descendants of the Beni Hashem of the tribe of Quraish, emigrated from al-Ta'if in the Hejaz to the city of Belbeys in the Governorate of al-Sharqiyya. The reason for their move to Egypt was a dispute that arose between them and al-Sharif Aoun, the governor of Mecca. The three of them, dissatisfied with his judgment, put it about that he was an unjust man who upheld neither civil nor sacred law. So they said, and the story was passed down through generations. They founded the town of Zaribat al-Ashraf, settled down there, and resumed their work in the cultivation and sale of henna in Egypt, the Hejaz, and Iraq.

In my childhood there was someone from the Hinnawi family—which had helped found the town—by the name of Mohammed Saleh, who rose to the position of head of the appellate court in Cairo. The Khedive Abbas II, son of the Khedive Tawfiq, owned about a thousand feddans of sandy clay, toward Anshas in al-Sharqiyya, and he wanted to increase his holdings in this region, so he instructed surveyors and his own employees to persuade the owners of the adjacent lands to relinquish them. Any among them who wished to attain the rank of "Bey" had to sign a contract for payment of one hundred feddans in the name of the crown prince Abdel Munᶜim. Whoever wanted the title of "Pasha" had to sign over two hundred feddans. As for any man who refused to give up his land, the Khedive's agents and employees would flood the land adjacent to his, and since all the soil in that region was sandy, the water would spread unchecked from one section to another, and the farmer would have such difficulty cultivating his land that it would lie fallow and he would be forced to relinquish it to the heir apparent or else sell it to him for a trifling sum. In this way the crown prince managed to gain possession of eight thousand feddans.

There is a family in that region who stood by their rights and refused to give up or sell out, even when it became almost impossible to farm the greater part of the land, so the Khedive ordered his workers to seize all of that family's acreage by claiming eminent domain. The family therefore brought the case up before the court of Zagazig, opposing the Khedive's special prerogative, but the court decided in favor of the Khedive, and so the family appealed the suit with the court of Cairo. The chief justice of the court was Mohammed Saleh al-Hinnawi. He studied the case and the initial decision, but he didn't accept the iniquity of it, and he decided to rule in favor of justice, even if it meant forfeiting his life. And indeed he bade farewell to his children the day before the hearing, because he knew with certainty that the Khedive would kill him if he ruled against him. Mohammed Saleh faced the court and ruled on the Khedive's special prerogative that the land must be returned to its owners, and that they must be compensated for the expense and inconvenience pertinent to the lawsuit. Two hours later a summons came from Abdin Palace for him to appear before His Excellency the Khedive.

The Khedive said to him, "You are the judge who ruled against me today?"

Al-Hinnawi replied, "I ruled in accordance with what would satisfy God and my conscience."

The Khedive then asked him, "What is your name?"

"My name is Mohammed Saleh al-Hinnawi."

"Where are you from?"

"I come from a small village next to Belbeys, called Zaribat al-Ashraf."

The Khedive replied, "Henceforward your name shall be Mohammed Saleh the Just, and your village shall be called al-Adliya [justice]."

The following day the newspapers' front-page headlines proclaimed that the Khedive had honored the judge who ruled against him. This announcement reverberated throughout Egypt, and the Khedival family took pride in it.

My Childhood

I no longer remember what my father looked like, but I do remember that he liked to eat dried dates and drink tea, and that he used to wear the *arabi*, a kind of large *gallabiyya*, with sleeves so voluminous you could store half a bushel of wheat in them. I often used to play with him, climbing into one of his huge sleeves and clambering over his body to emerge from the other one. Under the *gallabiyya* he wore long underwear made of Indian cotton. Also he was very generous, even though he was just a farmer, and of modest means. Each day when he came home, he used to charge me with gathering up our surplus bread from the low table where we took our meals, and wait for him in the street while he took it to the poor people at the mosque. My mother, on the other hand, used to object to our giving away the bread, so I got in the habit of stealing the leftover bread each night to give to my father.

My father died at the end of 1904, when I was about seven years old. People were dying in the streets because of an epidemic we referred to as "the plague," or "cholera." There were eight people in the family, two or three of whom died in a single day. They were taking the dead from their houses on carts and burying them just as they were, in their clothes, without washing the bodies or praying over them, in a large trench dug on the mountain. As a child I saw with my own eyes the ladders sent by the government. A great stepladder was set up along with three workers, each one carrying a tin bucket and a large pair of scissors. One of the workers would stand at the top of the ladder and cut the air with the scissors, put it in the bucket, cover it and pass it to the second worker, who would then pass it to the third, and so the plague would be covered by sand. This was the way to fight the contagion, according to the orders of English rulers, in that bygone era. God preserve us from the evil of enemy rule.

Social and Economic Conditions, 1904–1906

After my father's death, we moved to Belbeys to live with my maternal uncle, and my mother set up shop as a seamstress making men's and women's clothes, with a young girl assisting her in the shop. From the shop my mother earned enough money for our day-to-day livelihood. She used to give me a khurda-piaster, with which I would buy some *mulukhiyya* or else okra and tomatoes (or *banadora*, as we used to call tomatoes), as well as onions, and clover for the rabbits. One standard piaster was worth 8 khurda-piasters, each of which was 12 dirhams in value by weight, with "minted in Constantinople" stamped on one side. On the other side was "Abdel Hamid Khan Abdel Mugid." There was also the half-khurda-piaster, which was 20 khurdas, equivalent to 6 dirhams, and made of red copper; and the quarter-khurda-piaster, equivalent to three dirhams. Some of the vendors used to use these coins instead of counterweights when weighing out merchandise. My mother would give me the price of a haircut, 20 khurdas, half of which I would keep, giving the barber 10 khurdas, which was equivalent to 1/32 of a standard piaster. A customer would give the payment to the barber, who took it and put it in his pocket without seeing it, even if the customer's hand was empty. So God brought good fortune to them in their lives.

A large waterskin cost 20 khurdas and a small one cost 10; half a kilo of meat cost 1 piaster, a large chicken was 1½ piasters, a goose 2 piasters, 20 eggs were 1 piaster, half a kilo of butter 1½ piasters, half a kilo of clarified butter 2 piasters, 2½ bushels of wheat 60 piasters, 2½ bushels of fava beans 40 piasters, and 2½ bushels of corn 35 piasters. The rent for a two-story house with three rooms on each floor was 10 piasters per floor. A female water buffalo with her calf was 4 or 5 pounds—that is, about 400 or 500 piasters—a cow with her calf was 3 pounds, a sterile hinny 1 pound, a sheep 50 piasters, and a goat 35 piasters. Vegetables were sold by the basket and not by weight. A basket of dates was 1 piaster, half a kilo of honey a half-piaster, half a kilo of cane honey 1 khurda-piaster, half a kilo of tahini 3 khurda-piasters, and half a kilo of sesame oil was a half-piaster.

The midwives and barbers were the healers. There was one doctor in the region, whom the wealthy visited. He was a Turkish man called Baseem, and he charged 2 piasters for an examination. Cutting out and sewing a caftan cost 2 piasters; a *gallabiyya* together with its undergarment was 1 piaster. Soap was very scarce, and only the well-to-do used it. The salt company was the first to manufacture soap in Egypt, and the sale of salt was contingent upon that of soap, so whoever wanted to buy a measure of salt had to purchase a quarter-piaster cake of soap as well; anyone who didn't buy soap wasn't allowed to buy salt, either. The great majority of people didn't use soap. The women and girls would take clothes that needed washing to the irrigation canal, bringing along a wooden pestle. They would place the clothes in the water, then remove them and place them on a big rock, where they would set to pounding them with the pestle until the stains were gone and they were clean. No bleach was used except on the wrappings for the turban.

In 1905 the sweet potato made its appearance, and it had a profound impact, being considered among the most important fruits of the earth, because it fed the poor at little cost. In 1912 the mango was introduced, whose trees came from India. Apples were sold from handcarts, at 1 piaster for slightly over a kilo. Other fruits were for the most part sold by the basket, not by weight. Grapes were sold in the orchards twice a year by *wazna*, the *wazna* being a large basket holding about 25 kilos, one *wazna* for 5 piasters. A basket containing about 12½ kilos of dates was 1 piaster. The transactions of wholesalers and sellers of houses and land were by "bag." A person might say, "I bought such-and-such a house for 10 bags," the worth of a bag being, by convention, 2½ pounds. Another might say, "I married off my daughter so-and-so for 10 bags and bought such-and-such a feddan for 3 bags," or he might say, "I bought this Arab stallion for 4 bags and I wouldn't sell him even if I were offered 6 bags for him."

The gold pound-coin, stamped with the image of the British king, was worth 97½ piasters, while the pound stamped with the image of the queen was worth 97 piasters, and the Napoleon coin, which was known as the French pound, was worth 67 2/10 piasters.

In 1906 the Khedive Abbas used to go every Wednesday to his farm at Anshas, and some weeks he announced that he would stop by the Belbeys station and then return to Cairo. He had a private train with just one car, whose engine he would drive himself, since he knew a great deal about mechanics and steam locomotion. The driver and fireman would accompany him, but he was the one who would pilot the train, wearing his khaki suit and his lofty tarbush, similar to military dress. On the day he went to Belbeys station, our master's, the sheikhs from the *kuttab*, would bring us outside to wait for him at the station, and the moment we caught sight of him we would say in unison, "Greetings to our Khedive Abbas." He would put his hand in his pocket and shower us with two-piaster silver coins, and we would compete for them, some of us getting one or two, others none at all. Then we would return to school, and divide our profits with the sheikhs.

An Anecdote from My School Days

I entered the *kuttab* at the great mosque and studied there for four years, from 1904 until 1908. I memorized half of the Qur'an, and learned to read and write. Each student had a tin tablet on which he wrote in black ink with a bamboo or reed pen. Every Saturday we paid the fees, which came to one half-piaster and a loaf of flatbread, except for the indigent among us, who would bring a loaf of flatbread but no money. The school's weekly proceeds were two baskets of bread and about 50 piasters, which would be divided among our masters the sheikhs.

I was forever running away from the school, because our masters the sheikhs used to beat us savagely, using the *falaqa*, a kind of thick pole with a rope tied to the middle of it. They would secure the student's feet in the loop of rope and wind it around him. Two other students would use the pole to lift up his feet before our master, who would proceed to beat him with a reed cane 40 or 50 times, so that the student taking the beating would be unable to stand on his feet or walk for about six hours. They used to say that the cane wielded by the teacher at the *kuttab* was from heaven, but I say it was from hell.

My Life during Illness

I was four years old when I fell ill with a fever. My mother tried to get me to take castor oil, but I refused, and the neighbor women gathered around and tried to persuade me, but I wouldn't accept it. I said, "I won't take the syrup unless you bring me a rabbit," so one of the neighbors hurried to her house to get a rabbit. Then I said, "I want another rabbit, to play with the first one," so the same neighbor went and got it for me. I said, "Bring me a white she-camel." My mother was angry, and was thinking about ways to force me to take the syrup, when the midwife who had attended my birth arrived—we regarded her as the family physician. She wrapped me in a blanket, carried me to the basin at the mosque, and tossed me into it. Then she fished me out, wrapped me back up in the blanket, and brought me home. The basin at the mosque, which was used for ablutions before the advent of faucets, was something like a pool, and its water was changed once a week. Its water was not sanitary, since the worshippers washed themselves in it, and some of them were not clean. In spite of this, I recovered from my fever and didn't get sick again after that, so it seems that this method made me immune to infections of all kinds.

An Anecdote from the Early Part of My Working Life

In 1908, when I was eleven years old, one of my mother's relatives, who worked at the Agricultural Bank of Egypt in Belbeys, took me to practice writing and arithmetic. He was a very generous person, for he allowed me to fill out applications for the peasant farmers seeking loans from the bank, in exchange for one half-piaster per application. My daily take was between one and two piasters. I turned over these sums to my mother. A year later, this same relative helped me obtain employment as a scribe at a watermelon farm in the region of Beni Saleh, on the estate of Her Highness the Princess Neʿma Hanim Mukhtar (she was the daughter of Khedive Ismail, and was called Mukhtar after her husband Mukhtar Pasha of Turkey). My daily wages were two standard piasters and a watermelon, which I would sell for a half-piaster. After that I moved

to a job in Burdin, which is located between Belbeys and Zagazig. It comprises 4,000 feddans of
land, which were within the holdings of Khedive
Ismail. After his death, these holdings were divided equally between his two daughters, Amina
and Neᶜma Mukhtar, with 2,000 feddans appor-
tioned to each of them.

In 1915 I moved to Cairo and worked at a
shop owned by the brass merchant Hagg Sayyid
Ali on Beit al-Qadi Street in Gammaliya. Cairo
wasn't crowded, and transportation was simple.
Donkey drivers stood waiting in the squares to
convey people to their jobs for a small sum. The
soap-manufacturing company had box wagons
drawn by horses or mules, and the cost for one
person to go from Sayyidna al-Hussein to al-
Ataba al-Khadra was two millemes; from Sayyidna
al-Hussein to the Citadel was three millemes;
from Sayyidna al-Hussein to Sayyida Zaynab, five
millemes; and from al-Ataba al-Khadra to
Sabtiyya by way of Bab al-Hadid, five millemes.

Umm Kulthoum

I listened to Umm Kulthoum for the first time in
1917—that is, nine years before she went to live
in Cairo. The brass merchant Hagg Sayyid Ali
for whom I was working had been blessed with a
son after seven daughters, so he decided to celebrate the observance of the feast of the Prophet's
ascension to the seven heavens with a night that
would be the talk of the town—relatives and
neighbors. Hagg Sayyid sent me to the village of

Tamay al-Zahayra to meet with Sheikh Ibrahim al-Sayyid and negotiate with him to come to Cairo along with his daughter, Sheikha Umm Kulthoum, to hymn the Prophet's life story at Hagg Sayyid's home in the city. So I traveled to Sinbillawin and from there to Tamay al-Zahayra, and I contracted with Hagg Ibrahim for his daughter to celebrate the night in exchange for three pounds, which included both fee and travel expenses. I returned to Cairo with the contract, signed by Sheikh Ibrahim.

On the night of the 27th of Ragab, Sheikh Ibrahim arrived, and with him his son and his daughter. When Hagg Sayyid saw Umm Kulthoum his face turned red with fury. He took me aside and scolded me, saying that the night was going to turn into a farce and a scandal, with people thinking he had cheated them out of a professional singer by bringing them this child, and no one would believe that he had paid three pounds for her! To salvage the situation, Hagg Sayyid told me to go look for Sheikh Ismail Sukkar, who was among the foremost singers, but I found him in the process of getting ready to go to Helwan to celebrate the night at the palace of Ezzeddine Bey Yakan. I went back to Gammaliya to tell Hagg Sayyid what had happened. He cursed me, and I knew that as soon as the night was over he would fire me.

Umm Kulthoum appeared. A young girl, thirteen or fourteen years old, wearing a man's coat, her head covered with a kufiyyah secured by a camel-hair cord. A clamor rose up among the audience, of surprise and incredulity, but no sooner had she begun to sing than they fell rapt under her spell, and they called for encores. I said to myself, "My boy, even if you do lose your job, this is the night of a lifetime—we'll play today and pay tomorrow." By the end of the night Hagg Sayyid was so happy that he gave me 50 piasters, just like that, for no particular reason!

From that day I became a lover of Umm Kulthoum's singing, and whenever possible I went to the places in which she performed. This became a source of contention between my wife and me. She said I was frittering away money on nonsense, but I was angry that she would refer to Umm Kulthoum's singing as "nonsense," and I told her she was a fool. In 1926 the record company Odeon issued fourteen recordings of Umm Kulthoum's songs, and I couldn't wait another moment. I bought a gramophone and all fourteen of the recordings, but my wife, instead of rejoicing over this beneficence, shouted in my face, "And you bring it to the house to involve me in this?" And with that she left and went home to her family. I tried to reconcile with her, but she was determined that she wouldn't come back to our house unless the gramophone left it. And so we went our separate ways.

Incident: "It's a Direct Object, Mohammed Effendi!"
In 1919 I was working in Gammaliya and living in the same neighborhood, and I had friends among the students at al-Azhar. I participated

with them in the strike from its first day, which was Monday, March 10th. It was the second day of the revolution, for the students of the colleges of law and engineering and the school of agriculture had started the strike before us, on Sunday.

During the following days, the students of al-Azhar emerged from the halls singly or in small groups, then gathered in the squares and surprised the British with demonstrations. One day I carried on my shoulders Sheikh Abdel Aziz, who stood out because of his loud voice and his ability to improvise catchy slogans. He started chanting, and we chanted behind him until the British appeared and began to open fire. There was confusion in the ranks, and I lost my balance, so that we fell to the ground, Sheikh Abdel Aziz and I. Another comrade lifted onto his shoulders a young demonstrator, someone from the Effendi, who raised his voice in a chant, "We'll ransom the Wafdu with our own souls!" Sheikh Abdel Aziz shouted in his thunderous voice. "The Wafd*a*, Mohammed Effendi, the Wafd*a*! You have to get your grammar straight: the Wafd*a*, direct object with the *fatha* ending—it's a direct object, Mohammed Effendi!" I grabbed his hand and nudged him, saying, "Hey, is this the time to correct grammatical endings? Let's go, on your feet—we're going to get trampled to death here!"

"I can't," he replied.

I picked him up, and he resumed chanting even as I was running with him to take cover from the gunfire. His leg was broken, but even after I brought him to the bonesetter, he kept repeating indignantly, "We'll defend the Wafd*u*. A direct object with a *damma*. God be praised, Effendis of the new era. Go easy there, sir, the pain's bad, very bad!"

Two Incidents I Didn't Witness with My Own Eyes, But Heard About from a Reliable Source

This was told to me by Hagg Mohammed Abdel ^cAal, a wholesale dealer for whom I worked during the years 1932 to 1942. He said, "The estate of her Excellency the Princess Amina Ismail and her son Prince Tahir Pasha used to obtain its palace supplies from my shops on a monthly basis. At the beginning of each month I would make out a bill and direct it to the estate, so that I could get paid. One time I went to collect the balance of the bill, and the chief clerk told me, 'His Excellency Prince Tahir is with the equestrian club. Wait until he arrives, and he'll pay the bill.' So I waited. Meanwhile, King Farouq showed up in a small car, which he was driving himself, and he was wearing dark glasses. As he entered the grounds, the secretary went to meet him. 'Who are you?' the king asked him.

"'I'm the secretary,' was the reply.

"'What's your name?'

"'Mahmoud.'

"'I'm thirsty, Mahmoud,' said the king. 'Bring me a glass of water at once.'

"The secretary hurried off to the palace—which was about a hundred meters from the estate office—to get the water. In the meantime, the king went into Tahir Pasha's office. I watched him through a window, and saw him pick something up off the desk and put it in the back pocket of his trousers. Then he went out, got back in the car, and returned to his palace. A moment later, the secretary came running with a carafe of water and a glass, trailing three servants. They asked me what had become of the king, so I told them, 'He went into Tahir Pasha's office, took something off the desk, and put it in the back pocket of his trousers,' so Mahmoud Effendi went in to see what was missing from the desk. He came back out and said that the king had stolen a statuette of the Khedive Ismail, a small figurine of pure gold set with precious stones, which had been part of Princess Amina's share of the inheritance when her father's estate was divided. It was worth 4,000 pounds.

"When Tahir Pasha arrived, the chief clerk told him what had happened. 'The bastard!' Tahir exclaimed. 'He's asked me for it several times, but I never agreed to give it to him.'

"He went straight to the palace, where he went to the king and demanded the figurine, but the king said, 'This is a statue of my grandfather, and I have more right to it than anyone else!'

"Tahir Pasha replied, 'It's true it's a statue of your grandfather, but my mother received it as part of her share of the division of the estate.'

"'In the royal family,' the king answered him, 'I am the only heir!' So Tahir Pasha went home empty-handed."

Another Episode Concerning King Farouq

Hagg Mohammed Abdel ʿAal told us this story as well. He said, "The estate of Her Highness Princess Amina Ismail and her son Tahir Pasha was very close to the palace. One time the king gave a big party at the palace, to which he invited luminaries both Egyptian and foreign. Princess Amina had a complete set of gold-plated silverware, engraved with the crown and the name of Khedive Ismail, which she had received as part of her share of her father's inheritance. The king asked for this set to use at the party, promising to return it afterward, so the Pasha sent it over. The silverware set remained in the royal kitchens, as Tahir Pasha forgot to ask for it back, and in fact he forgot that he'd lent it to the king in the first place. One day Tahir Pasha ordered an inventory of the kitchens, and the silverware set could not be found. The Pasha notified the prosecutor's office and accused the secretary, who was entrusted with the keys to the estate. The secretary was arrested, sentenced to prison, and dismissed from his job. The secretary was a friend of mine, and I knew he had been wrongly accused, as I had visited him on occasion at the appellate prison in Bab al-Khalq. When it pleased God to reveal the truth, one of the king's cooks went to a goldsmith, and with him was the gold-plated silverware set inscribed with the crown and Khedive Ismail's name, which he wanted to sell. The goldsmith notified the Gammaliya police department, and the cook was arrested. He confessed to the theft and was sentenced to prison. The chief clerk was released, after spending a long time in prison despite having committed no crime."

Nine

My paternal grandfather didn't leave me any notebook that I would wrap in velvet and keep in my closet, for I was born three years after he passed away. My father, when he took us to Belbeys, would stop at the edge of the village where the cemetery was, to recite the Fatiha over his father's grave, and we would recite after him. We used to go once or twice a year. I remember the gate to the house: a wooden gate, very old, with a latch. A dusty courtyard, roofed over. Rooms on the first floor virtually abandoned. Some relatives of ours occupied the second floor. I recall two palm trees in a spacious open area, and a smaller house in which my father's paternal uncle lived.

My father would take us to Belbeys in his black Hillman automobile, and the journey would take an hour. The trip to my maternal grandfather's house in Helwan took about the same amount of time, perhaps a little more. A taxi would take us to Bab al-Louk Station, where we would board the train. It would stop at Sayyida Zaynab, Mar Girgis, al-Maᶜsara, Turra, the Turra Cement Factory, al-ᶜAin. Mere names from the world of my childhood that only later would acquire meaning. We would get off the train at the last stop. At the door of the station we were greeted by the smell of horses and a line of carriages, each with its driver stationed at the front of the vehicle with the reins in his left hand and a crop in his right. We would get into one of them, and my mother would say, "House of Azzam, Khusrou Street, please, yaa osta." The driver would raise his whip and bring it down on the backs of the two horses, which would jerk abruptly into motion and set the carriage rocking, but it would soon settle into the rhythm of the horses' canter. My mother would sit in the larger seat, with Hatem and Wa'el beside her. The "grownup children"—Tariq and I—would sit on the smaller bench seat opposite her. We couldn't turn around to look at the driver behind us, so we concentrated on the hoof beats of the horses on the pavement, measured in time with the rumbling of the wheels and the snapping of the whip, interrupted occasionally by a sudden whinny.

Asma and Ruqayya would be at the house. Asma, my grandmother, was petite, with golden-brown skin, whereas Ruqayya, her sister-in-law, was stout and white-skinned; she loved cats. "Sitt Ruqayya," Asma called her, and Ruqayya never called Asma anything but "Sitt Asma." They cooperated firmly over the food for each meal, preserving both amity and respectful distance, intimacy and formality; and it had been thus for the more than sixty years that they had lived together under the same roof. Someone in need might come to the house and stay there for weeks or months. In the summertime, Umm Duqduq would sit cross-legged on a small carpet at the threshold of the door, "for the fresh air." She was blind, or nearly. Silent there, thinking about something or other, she would flood the stairwell with the fragrance of coffee with a little grinder she would fill from time to time with a handful of the roasted beans. That done, she would turn her attention once more to the remnants of fabric she had collected, ribbons and strips that she would roll into a large ball, with which she would occupy herself later, using the pieces to produce a brightly colored rag-rug.

"Umm Duqduq, tell me the story of the major general."

"Bless the Prophet."

"Blessings be upon him."

"Once upon a time, oh best beloved, in ancient and far-off times, there was a He-Mouse and a She-Mouse. And on a day among days, He-Mouse and She-Mouse found an egg. He-Mouse declared, 'This egg is mine,' but She-Mouse said, 'No, it's mine.' They fought, then went to the Monkey seeking a just solution to their quarrel. Monkey broke the egg in two and lapped up the contents. Then he gave half the shell to He-Mouse, the other half to She-Mouse. 'What'll we do, what'll we do?' He-Mouse and She-Mouse said, 'We'll make a boat.' They went down to the Nile and made a boat from the eggshell.

"Along came Chick, who said, 'Whose boat is this, so fleet and fine?'

"'He-Mouse and She-Mouse's boat,' they replied.

"'And I am Yellow Peck-Peck Chick,' said she, and with that she hopped into the boat with them.

"Along came Rooster, who asked, 'Whose boat is this, so fleet and fine?'

"'He-Mouse and She-Mouse's and Yellow Peck-Peck Chick's boat,' they replied.

"'And I am Rooster, father of Little Rooster who crows on the fence,' said he, and with that he hopped into the boat with them.

"Along came Sheep, who saw them and said, 'Whose boat is this, so fleet and fine?'

"'He-Mouse and She-Mouse's and Yellow Peck-Peck Chick's and Rooster-Father-of-Little-Rooster-Who-Crows-on-the-Fence's boat,' they replied.

"'And I am Sheep, with the wool that's sold at the market,' said he, and with that he got into the boat.

"Along came Camel, and he asked them, 'Whose boat is this, so fleet and fine?'

"'He-Mouse and She-Mouse's and Yellow Peck-Peck Chick's and Rooster-Father-of-Little-Rooster-Who-Crows-on-the-Fence's and Sheep-With-the-Wool-that's-Sold-at-the-Market's boat,' they replied.

"'And I am Camel of camels, Porter of porters,' said he, and with that he hopped into the boat with them.

"Along came Flea, who asked them, 'Whose boat is this, so fleet and fine?'

"'He-Mouse and She-Mouse's and Yellow Peck-Peck Chick's and Rooster-Father-of-Little-Rooster-Who-Crows-on-the-Fence's and Sheep-With-the-Wool-that's-Sold-in-the-Market's and Camel-of-Camels-Porter-of-Porters' boat,' they replied.

"'And I am Major General Flea,' said he, and with that he hopped into the boat, and they sank. The flea climbed out soaking wet, and flew to his wife, Mistress of the Full Moons, and he found her lighting the stove to heat water for a bath. 'I'm cold,' he said. 'Warm me up.' Getting close to the fire to warm up, he popped and died.

"His wife began to lament. Along came Crow, who said, 'What's with you, Mistress of the Full Moons, carrying on like this?'

"And Flea's wife answered him saying, 'Mistress of the Full Moons laments Major General Flea who fell into the fire and roasted!'

"'And I, Crow, will fly no more,' said Crow.

"He went to Date Palm, who asked him, 'What's with Crow, that he flies no more?'

"He answered her saying, 'Crow has given up flying, and Mistress of the Full Moons laments the Major General, who fell into the fire and roasted!'

"'And I, Date Palm, will bear fruit no more!' said Date Palm.

"The water saw the Date Palm and asked her, 'What's with Date Palm, that she'll bear no more fruit?'

"Date Palm answered, saying, 'Date Palm has given up bearing fruit, Crow has given up flying, and Mistress of the Full Moons laments the Major General who fell into the fire and roasted!'

"And I, Water, will flow no more!'"

Zakiyya Umm Duqduq would continue her tale, and I would follow the thread, or jump up suddenly to join in play with the rest of the boys and girls.

I don't remember my grandfather in this house, his house. I saw him there, perhaps, but have forgotten it. By the time I grew up a bit, he had traveled to India to become the first Egyptian ambassador there since India's independence. In all likelihood he was appointed to this post with leave from the university, where he was a professor of Oriental languages, fluent in Urdu as well as Persian, which was his primary specialization.

My grandfather died when I was twelve years old. The clearest image I have of him in my mind is perhaps from the year immediately preceding his death.

The summer holiday. The house at Abouqir owned by my grandfather's paternal uncle, in which his daughter and her husband—my grandfather's brother—stayed in the summertime with their children. A wide wooden balcony overlooking land planted with date palms, and beyond the date palms the sea. It was the time of night when we could not see the great nets laid among the trunks of the palm trees to catch migrating quail. A circle of children sitting cross-legged on the ground listening to a man seated among them, a man of towering height with a handsome face, wheat-colored skin, and a moustache flecked with gray. In his sweet and gentle way, he was telling them about the Rabbit Arnabad. (Was it a tale from *Kalila and Dimna*, or a story woven of its own fabric?) He went on for a long time with the tale, until one of the children was overtaken by sleep, and then he said, "I'll finish the story for you tomorrow." Did he finish it? I don't remember. I remember my maternal aunt standing on that balcony saying that she couldn't believe she was about to turn thirty, and I looked at her and thought "thirty" seemed as far-off and lovely as the light of the stars in the sky. My grandfather passed away at the age of 61. I never heard him recite the poetry of al-Mutanabbi. And it wasn't I who told Tamim that he had studied his poetry closely and written about it: Tamim found the book in the library, read it, and then transferred it to his own room. Like his father, Tamim writes poetry, and my grandfather used to compose poetry as well—but he was a university professor, and I know what it means for a person to be a teacher: it is as if something about the profession constricts the spirit. I cannot imagine my grandfather howling like one possessed by a poem that had taken him over—I picture him only calm and steady. Was he always that way, or is it just that I only knew him after he became a grandfather? I asked my mother. She said, "He used to recite poetry." I remember him taking his walk in front of the house, or shaving his face every morning—he recited verse in a low voice as if he were singing it.

In our house the rotation starts with Tamim, standing and delivering a recitation, shouting, swaying, arms flying, hands gesturing, fingers forming pictures in the air all over the place:

> I want this time of mine to obtain for me
> That which time obtains not from itself.

Then it is his father's turn:

> Meet your destiny only without seeking
>   it,
> So long as body and spirit keep company,
> For happiness sustains not that in which
>   you rejoice
> Nor will grieving restore to you that
>   which you have lost.

And now their voices join as one:

> Let then the camels of this world bear
>   you away.
> Forsooth, all partings are alike to me,
> No recompense within your caravans
>   receding,
> No price for my life if I should die of
>   longing.
> Those who partake of passion are undone:
> Knowing not the world they fall,
>   uncomprehending,
> Their eyes dissolve in tears, likewise their
>   souls,
> As they yearn for naught but ugliness
>   with its fair face.
> How often have I been slain, how often
>   perished in your midst
> And then risen: no more the grave and
>   shroud.

The witness to my burial before they spoke
Was a multitude, but then they died
before those they buried
Man achieves not all he hopes for
Winds blow contrary to the will of ships.

The voice rises, transported, possessed, in total disregard for a sleeping neighbor—or for a woman, one who loves poetry, preoccupied at this moment with other concerns. They would not hear of being alone with their pleasure in the verses: they want her to pay attention, to turn toward them, to take part in the recitation. The woman is sitting on her chair, gazing at them: the boy her son and the boy his father, both adults now, standing together, within the domain of a poem, connected. Usually the verses were those of al-Mutanabbi. They might recite someone else's—Abou Tammam or Imru al-Qays, among others—but in the end they would come back to Ahmad Hussein al-Mutanabbi.

Tamim:

> We make ready the sword and lance,
> But death slays us without a fight.

Mourid:

> We keep close the swiftest steeds
> That yet cannot outrun time's steady gait.

Both together:

> And who in bygone times loved not the
>   world?
> Yet never can such love be fulfilled.

The allotment of your life is one beloved,
The allotment of your dream a thing
    imagined
With grievous losses has fate assailed me
    until
So covered with its arrows is my heart,
Each missile striking breaks upon the last
Powerless; I have become insensible to
    calamity
For attending to it nothing have I gained.

"Ahmad Hussein—the devil take him!" A final comment brings the session to a conclusion. Mourid goes to the kitchen to make a cup of coffee, but Tamim remains there, standing before me, demanding that I listen to "Just these two lines!"

I want from the passing days that which they
    will not
And I complain to them of our separation:
they are its army
The way of all creation is to refuse a love
    enduring;
How can life, then, restore to me love lost?

Mourid's voice issues from the kitchen:

All but incurable, he whose malady is the
    wide-eyed gaze,
Of which so many lovers before me have
    perished.
Let him who wishes look upon me, for the
    sight of me
Is a warning to all who think passion a simple
    matter.

Mourid returns with his coffee. The session is not over, for now they recite a new poem:

> Like the sight of a beloved's ruined house is
> > the promise you both made me
> To commiserate, as tears are alleviated by
> > their flowing, but in this you failed me
> And what am I but a lover; and every lover
> Has two intimates of whom the more vexing
> > is censure
> Thus might one not of his own people be clad
> > in the vestments of passion
> Man seeks companionship in those who
> > rebuke him not
> I have collapsed the collapse of ruins, indeed
> > have I stood there
> In the posture of a miser who has lost his ring
> > in the dirt
> In despair did the moralists of love guard
> > against me
> As the prudent man guards against a breaker
> > of horses.

Then:

> And if I should repair to a distant land
> By night would I travel: I would be the secret
> > kept by the night.

Did the ancient Greek rhapsode mentioned by Plato in one of his Dialogues recite poetry in this way? Poetry comes by divine inspiration—so says Plato—and thus the poem generates its own magnetic field whose mesmeric forces are transmitted from the stanzas of the poem to the rhapsode and thence to the listeners. But was my grandfather, who dedicated long years of his life to the study and analysis of al-Mutanabbi's poetry, captivated like Mourid and Tamim in the presence of his poems, or was his devotion after his own fashion, both different and peculiarly his own? In his introduction to the complete works of Aboul Tayyib al-Mutanabbi that he edited, my grandfather wrote:

> In my youth I was interested in Aboul Tayyib, on whose life and poetic works I wrote a thesis, and I became reacquainted with the man whom I was extolling. I started reviewing the precious manuscripts in Egypt's National Library, measuring one against another. Then I was called to Iraq... and there I published a book on the history of al-Mutanabbi, out of a desire to participate in the celebration that gripped the Arab countries from the banks of the Tigris to the shores of the Atlantic Ocean.

> The biggest celebration was in Damascus, where delegations from the Arab countries had gathered in summer 1354 of the Islamic calendar. I gave a lecture at the University of Damascus. It was my good fortune to have taken part in this celebration as well.

> When I returned to Old Cairo, I proposed to the Arabic-language department in the School of Humanities that they honor Aboul Tayyib by publishing an accurate, unabridged edition of his complete works that would constitute a basic reference for researchers of his

poetry, and an authoritative source for scholars of his narrative. My suggestion met with approval, and I was charged with the publication of the proposed edition. The Committee for authorship, translation, and publication was commissioned to print the book, and the committee made ready to do so. I was told, "Let's see what you can do with this." Thus I applied myself for several years to this arduous and protracted task.

Abdel Wahhab Azzam dug for traces of Aboul Tayyib in the libraries of Cairo, Baghdad, Damascus, Istanbul, and Paris. He compared the various versions, scrutinized the commentaries of Ibn Jinni, al-Wahidi, al-Mi^carri, and al-^cAkbari, so as to make corrections to the main body of his work, to draw parallels among the narratives and use them to verify information; he concluded with an analysis of a new edition of the complete poems. In the addendum to the introduction he wrote for the book he says, "The task of editing the work was concluded at Roda Island, Old Cairo, at noon on Monday, the 5th of the month of Safar, in the year 1363 by the Islamic calendar." The published book bears this date in the Christian calendar: 1944. My grandfather aged nine years in the course of completing al-Mutanabbi's collected works.

Upon publication of the collection, Abdel Wahhab Azzam was 47 years old, a professor of Arabic literature and Oriental literatures at the Fou'ad I University (now Cairo University). He published his translation from Persian of the Shahnamah, finished his study of *Kalila and Dimna*, and completed a number of other books, including both edited volumes and original works. He had six daughters and three grandchildren: Zaynab and Fatima, children of Bouthaina, the eldest of his daughters, and Tariq, child of the next eldest daughter, Mayy—my mother.

At the age of 21, Abdel Wahhab had married the daughter of his paternal uncle, Asma, a girl not yet 15, who had learned the fundaments of reading under the tutelage of a sheikh whose services her father had procured to instruct her in the Qur'an. (Did Asma marry late, or was this regarded as one of the innovations of her time? Her mother had married at the age of 11, and lived to see her granddaughter's granddaughter, not because she lived to old age, but rather because she became a grandmother before she was 30.) Throughout the 1919 revolution, Asma went back and forth between her father's house and her uncle's house, where her cousin, the bridegroom, lived. As my grandmother told it: "We used to sleep with all our clothes on, for fear the English would raid the house." Why were they afraid the English would raid the house? Did my grandfather take part in the revolution? I don't know, but his village, al-Shawbak, as well as al-Badrashayn —which was bound to al-Shawbak by ties of proximity, sociability, and kinship—had tales to tell of the revolution. Abdel Rahman al-Raafiʿi writes,

> The worst of the atrocities was that which occurred in the village of al-Aziziyya and al-Badrashayn (in Giza) and the settlement of

al-Shawbak (in al-Ayyat). It was detailed in official records, and a historic case was argued in the administrative council of the District of Giza. The substance of it is that, on the 25th of March 1919, at approximately four o'clock in the morning, when most people were asleep, about 200 British, armed to the teeth, descended upon the villages of al-Aziziyya and al-Badrashayn, and one unit surrounded each village.

The historian Abdel Rahman al-Raafi^ci continues his narrative, going on to describe how the soldiers stormed the villages and attacked their inhabitants, women and men, drove them from their houses, and then set fire to them. "Any of the villagers who tried to put out the fire was shot and killed by the soldiers."

From here al-Raafi^ci proceeds to recall what happened at al-Shawbak:

> On the 30th of March at al-Shawbak, in al-Ayyat, atrocities took place that exceeded those at al-Aziziyya and al-Badrashayn, for in the afternoon of that day soldiers arrived in an armored convoy, from which descended a force bristling with weapons, and proceeded to storm the village and its houses. They took from the houses whatever their hands fell upon, be it jewelry or money or poultry, they violated the women; they killed Abdel Tawwab Abdel Maqsoud when he tried to defend his wife's honor and dealt likewise with the chief guard of the village; the wife of Suleiman Mohammed al-Fouli was killed trying to avoid being raped; and when they saw

how the villagers resisted attack, they opened fire indiscriminately. Twenty-one villagers were killed, twelve wounded, and they set the houses on fire, destroying 140 houses in a village whose homes numbered not more than 210. And worst of all that befell this village was that they arrested one of its elders, Abdel Ghani Ibrahim Tolba, together with his son Saïd and a village resident by the name of Khafaga Marzouq. They buried them waist-deep in the ground—on the pretext that they were going to interrogate them—and then they executed them by firing squad just like that.

Abdel Rahman al-Raafi꜄i appends to his own account the opposing narrative entitled, "Report of the Military Command." He says,

The military power's announcement concerning these atrocities consisted only of what was stated in its report of 1 April 1919: "False information has been propagated with respect to events alleged to have taken place at al-Aziziyya, and it was requested that a true accounting of these events be sent; accordingly the commanding officer on the scene at the time has made a report. He states that evidence had surfaced, the substance of which was that the villagers at al-Aziziyya and al-Badrashayn were known for sheltering armed Bedouins, and based on this premise an investigation of the two villages was undertaken on that day, 26 March, and a quantity of weapons was found at al-Aziziyya. During the investigation, the instigators of the trouble attempted to escape by jumping from rooftop to rooftop, resulting in the collapse of a roof beneath their weight. The roof fell onto household fires or oil lamps, which was the cause of the conflagration in the village.

The report also describes in the following manner what happened at al-Shawbak:

There was a train that was being used for reconstruction projects. As it made its way south on the afternoon of 30 March, a group of villagers were meddling with the tracks in the vicinity of al-Shawbak, and five of those who were engaged in trying to destroy the line were killed. After that the train was fired upon from the direction of the village, so the soldiers evacuated its residents.

At the end of his report, al-Raafiʿi invokes words used by members of Giza's administrative council, including those of Mohammed Effendi Mansour Atallah, who recorded the following rebuttal:

Until the third day after the incident at the village of al-Shawbak, residents were finding the bodies of their dead among the wheat fields, or floating on the surface of the waters of the canals; moreover, the livestock destroyed by cannon shot or bullets fired by some of the men of the English army were of a value beyond calculation. As for the village's corn harvest that was drying in the sun on the rooftops, the British sprayed it with gasoline and burned it, resulting in a massive loss amounting to the villagers' entire harvest.

My grandfather did not suffer the woes that beset his extended family at al-Shawbak. The

English didn't set fire to his house or burn his family's provisions or kill their livestock. The English raided the house and found a pistol. They arrested my grandfather and charged him with possession of a firearm, then released him when the testimony of a Libyan friend, al-Dokali, exonerated him. Al-Dokali claimed ownership of the pistol, and since Libya was an Italian colony, he obtained the privilege of foreign protection, according to which possession of a weapon did not fall within the jurisdiction of the law. Notwithstanding this incident, I don't think my grandfather was in the vanguard of political activism. He was a scholar, intent upon his research and his papers. He went to the university and taught his students, met with his colleagues—professors and writers, returned home to his house in Helwan or al-Manyal, played with his daughters, then went into his office to carry on with his studies. The scene in which he sat reading or writing was a familiar part of daily life for my mother, but one I can only see in my mind's eye.

In my childhood my grandfather was merely my grandfather: a kindly and handsome grandfather, a man of towering height whose tarbush raised him still higher and further reduced my own diminutive size. He smiled, teased, brought us sweets, and sent treats for Ramadan on the last night of Shaᶜban. We rejoiced at a visit with him. When we readied ourselves for the trip to the airport to meet him on his return from India, we bathed, dressed in our finest clothes, and sang on the way to the airport, as if we were going to a festival. We sang on the way back, too, because we hadn't left the festival behind us but were bringing it with us in the car, or at least we were accompanying the car that bore it, either behind or in front.

Ten

My grandfather died in January 1959. Four and a half years after his death I enrolled in the School of Humanities at Cairo University. He wasn't present in my imagination as I entered the campus and the humanities building, or as I moved along the corridors, passing from one lecture hall to another, these places in which he had spent long years of his life. He was absent from memory, perhaps, or perhaps the aspirations of a young woman relegated him to other realms of the mind. Until my graduation from the university I hadn't read any of the books he had written, translated, or edited. I am mindful now of a curious parallel trajectory: I loved my grandfather, and I loved the university, but each of these two narratives stayed on its own distinct and separate track.

I studied at Cairo University, but I was appointed to a position not there, but rather at Ain Shams. Why? Because the department chair at that time, Dr. Rashad Rushdie, said, "I don't want this girl." So the girl went to work elsewhere.

Was it a long journey, or a short one that passed in the blink of an eye?

To begin with, a young woman enters the lecture hall, where the students are close to her age—in fact she looks younger than they do. At the age of 21 she looks 17. She is capable, nevertheless, of conveying to them such knowledge as she possesses, and of making those instantaneous connections from which she learns as much as they do. She teaches English to students from other departments: Arabic, history, geography, psychology, sociology. After a few years, she teaches translation and a course in literary criticism to the students of her own department. Later she will teach poetry. She completes her doctoral degree, approaches the age of 30, and in due course reaches 40, 50. The faces of the students are exchanged for others; the lecture hall does not change.

Lower humanities. You go down a few steps below ground level: a small wooden door on the right opening onto a great auditorium, relatively dark despite the fluorescent lights, which are turned on in the daytime; a wooden platform whose paint chipped away many years ago, leaving its panels colorless but for a dull shade of ash; upon the platform is the lecturer's desk—her desk, and beneath it the students' seats: rows of wooden benches with writing tablets affixed to them; the drone of the fans suspended from the ceiling—sixteen of them in all—merges with the clamor of students outside the auditorium, ascending to or descending from upper humanities at the end of some lecture or other. We are surprised by a little bird that has lost its way; half a minute—it will escape through the window. But the poem will not escape her, most of the time. She casts her net over it, as if she were a hunter by trade. Only in the beginning. Then the poem draws near. The students reach out their hands, catch hold of the tremor in its body, consider the gleam in its eyes and eyelashes. Is it a deer in flight? How then did we possess it? How did it come to rest so close by, and so tame? When did the auditorium disappear? We see now only a careworn mariner who suddenly holds the hand of a young wedding guest innocent of the tale. The ancient mariner tells it: the slain seabird, the ship becalmed upon a trackless sea: "... a painted ship/ upon a painted ocean." Sun and moon. A woman playing at dice laughs aloud. The bodies of the dead sailors. Throats of ash. Thirst. A boisterous wedding, a ragged ancient mariner, a youth, and a story.

Third-year students like the course on the Romantic poets. Fourth-year students shy away from the course on literary criticism, and understand theory only with difficulty, approaching it with considerable struggle. Not for them the slain albatross stirring fear and fantasy, nor the west wind binding cycles of nature and the blossoming of revolution, nor the bard, like a prophet possessed, turning the world upside down by glorifying the powerless and sweeping the powerful, like so much refuse, into a corner.

The auditorium resumes its ordinary shabbiness, with the yellowish light from the fluorescent fixtures, the small wooden door, the dreary fans—

if we turn them off we suffocate, but when we turn them on they make such a racket that we wonder: "Is one of these fans about to crash down on our heads, and who will it land on?" Yet with all its shortcomings, lower humanities sometimes seems like an unattainable goal: "The auditorium is taken," says the staff person who does the scheduling. "We gave it to the students in the Arabic-language department, since there are more of them." So we are packed into a small lecture hall. The lucky ones settle on the wooden benches, while the unlucky ones sprawl on the floor, or stand leaning against the walls and the door. Some of the young men manage to sit on the windowsill.

The same class, the same students. The Shafiq Ghurbal Auditorium, where dissertations are defended and visiting professors lecture. Spacious. Relatively clean. A layer of green baize covers the lecturer's podium. A microphone that places me in no need of Hamlet's question, "To be or not to be." Do I use it, with all its static, or shout out my lecture in a voice that won't reach the back row of students? A course in African-American literature. Can the auditorium clear from the faces of the boys and girls the strain imposed by the stifling ugliness of the place, or is it the awareness that they are journeying through an experience that is coterminous with their own, inasmuch as they can relate to it? They can identify with the oppressed. This is reflected in the gleam of their eyes and in their questions and in their eagerness to know more. "Sometimes I feel

like a motherless child/ A long way from home."
She recites the words of the plantation slaves' folk
song. They like it. They listen intently to the
story of the escape route known as the "Underground Railroad." No railroad, no trains, no passengers, but rather a coded system of flight from
the South to the North. The slaves' myths, their
folklore, the Civil War, the Emancipation Procla-
mation, the poems, stories, and essays all excite
their interest. I mark the examination papers at
the end of the semester, and the responses corroborate the accuracy of what I inferred in the
course of my lectures: oppression and the struggle for liberation are for the emotional life of this
generation the tautest of bowstrings. In 30
years—the age difference between them and
me—none of that has changed!

Why is it that I write only these fragments
from my life at the university? Is it laziness, in-
adequacy, or evasiveness? Or the wisdom inherent in the detachment that makes writing
possible, since the experience of the 30 years I've
spent in the university—or, more precisely, 31
years, plus the 4 years I spent studying at Cairo
University—seems to me like a sea in which I
could drown. What writer has ever been able to
put her entire life into one text?

But I want to tell about the incident of the
laundry.

It brought me up short at the college entrance—its main entrance, leading to the library
door—an imposing structure of metal and glass.
A small space. Beyond the glass hung jackets and

other articles of clothing. A smiling woman sat behind a gray steel desk. I didn't understand. I went in and inquired.

"This is a dry-cleaning establishment," said the woman. "We opened this week."

"A laundry?"

"Are you a professor at the college, ma'am?"

"Yes."

"Perhaps you'll bring us your laundry, professor? We do washing, ironing, and dry-cleaning. We have rush-order service, and our prices are reasonable."

I forgot there was an elevator and that our department was on the fourth floor. My feet carried me to the stairs and up I went.

"Good morning, doctor," the office boy said.

"Good morning. What's happened?" He just looked at me, uncomprehending.

"The laundry on the first floor?"

He smiled. "The dean rented the entryway to a laundry."

I turned and looked toward the second floor, where the dean's office was. The dean wasn't there. I went to the assistant dean of the college. "What's going on?"

He didn't understand, so I clarified my question. He laughed. "Oh, the laundry! We wanted to increase revenues for the college, specifically income for the student affairs office. We rented out the entryway to a laundry, and also the big hall in the other building, the one used by the committee for testing the blind students. We thought we would make use of it at times other than the examination period."

"But, sir, this is a travesty!"

He smiled kindly. "Why a travesty?" he said. "You studied abroad, professor, and you know about these things; no doubt you saw concessions inside the university there, and..."

"In the university where I studied there was a large store that sold everything from notebooks and books to combs and toothpaste, but..."

He interrupted me, "See, there you go! Nothing to be perturbed about!"

"Sir, when a university is very large, with a sizeable campus and a specially designated building—sometimes even more than one building—for student activities and services, then it can have shops offering this sort of amenity. Our university, sir, barely has enough room just for its students. In lectures the students sit on the floor or stand to listen to the lesson. The university has no cafeteria, either for the students or for the professors, and the library is a book closet, not a library. Sometimes when two sections are getting out of a lecture at the same time, it's like Resurrection Day. Furthermore, putting a laundry at the main gate of the college, right in front of the entrance to the library, is completely out of place—it's so ugly!"

I left the assistant dean's office and went to the other building. The merchants' signs—for shoes, socks, shirts—were hung outside the hall. I went in: there was a variety of goods: spices, dates, peanuts, cassette tapes from which one sound emanated, audible outside the confines of the hall. I saw all this with my own eyes. I left and went to the lecture hall.

The faculty council meeting was noisy. Some could not restrain themselves from making sarcastic jokes. The rest were angry. The dean held forth at length in defense of his decision. He concluded his speech by saying, "I wanted to extend a service to the college and to the faculty!" We did not thank him for his good intentions. He said nothing about our lack of gratitude, although his face registered signs of regret and surprise as the council secretary recorded our decision to shut down the laundry and the market immediately.

The dean left and someone else came, who also left and a replacement was appointed in his stead, the electoral process for the dean's position having been done away with just like that, by ministerial decree. We were not informed, but read about it in the newspapers like anyone else: an effort toward instituting equal opportunity for all citizens. I can attest that none of the deans from that time on, whether elected or appointed, was tempted to revisit the idea of renting the college entrance to a laundry.

Eleven

Shagar thought only that it was a personal gift that her grandfather had generously bestowed upon her before his death. She wrapped it in a piece of velvet and put it away. But she was left with a lingering sense that the gift had some greater significance that she had not apprehended. She finished her doctorate, became a lecturer, an associate professor, and then, at last, full professor. On the day when she read the academic committee's report promoting her to full professor, she went home and opened up her closet. She took out the velvet-wrapped parcel, opened it up, and held the notebook in her hands. She was seized by an overpowering sense that there was some connection that bound this notebook, her grandfather's gift, to the professorial status at which she had just arrived. She wrapped the notebook up in its velvet covering, and put it back in its place.

It seemed to her, as she was leaving the office of the university president on that day in 1972, that she was at risk of being dismissed. She was not dismissed. Should she consider herself lucky

that she was able to preserve her position, or regard this as no more than she was entitled to,
considering all that she had worked and striven
for? But if she looked around her, she saw that
the axiom, "He who seeks shall find, and he who
sows shall reap," was no longer anything but a
naïve proverb used in didactic readers for children in first grade. They would have only to grow
up a bit to discover that this was merely another
one of the many deceptions found in abundance
in schoolbooks written by men, be they kindly, or
simpleminded, or professional con artists. How
had she sown and reaped without a stone falling
on her head and killing her or leaving her crip-
pled for the rest of her life? She was lucky, no
doubt about it, for this sort of thing—that is, a
boy or girl on the rise being struck by a stone—
was becoming so commonplace as to seem like
the rule rather than the exception.

A child needs a measure of care, needs someone to take her by the hand, look after and support her like any green shoot threatened in the
beginning by its own fragility. This was one of
life's lessons that she absorbed as a young girl
whom others looked after, and she adhered to it
when she grew up and was in turn charged with
looking after her students. Less than two months
after her meeting with the president of the university, she completed a detailed plan for her research, as well as a list of proposed sources and
references, and a request in the name of the dean
of the college that her dissertation be registered.
She presented the plan to her professor. He read

it and approved it. "I agree to supervise," he said, and signed his name. The following week she presented the plan to the department council, after which the papers proceeded by the standard route to the college council, then the university council.

She wrapped herself up in her research and forgot about it. Or it seemed that she forgot. She completed the dissertation. She didn't consider—either during the defense or in the moment when it was announced that she had obtained her academic degree, or in subsequent years—that she was indebted for her dissertation project to her meeting with the university president, and perhaps also to fear, a fear that drove her to make haste in finishing and perfecting the work so as to ensure her ongoing relationship with the place. Shagar meditates on the young woman as she descends the staircase after her meeting with the president: she is angry, taken over by a spirit of obstinacy and the desire to prove her own ideas with a rebuttal of such stunning eloquence that it would raise her own status and diminish her adversary—he appeared to be her adversary. "Afraid?" The girl did not pose the question to herself, and, if anyone else had asked it, it would have struck her as an unfair question, a stupid, injurious question. But she was—Shagar now thinks likely—afraid.

In September 1981, when she was dismissed from the university, she didn't panic; after all, she was no longer under pressure to write a thesis or a dissertation. There was nothing in the decision that threatened a transformation in the course of her life.

In prison there was ample time to consider the particulars of a life dispersed randomly in the press of daily concerns. In prison there is time, because the days, and the nights as well, take their time: each hour has its own sphere, through which she passes in stoic endurance, and into which the succeeding hour does not crowd. Perseverant, country hours that know none of that feverish haste, the constantly ringing telephone, or the harried pushing and shoving in the city's streets and its overflowing buses, its chaotic rhythms. She contemplates her relationship with the university, her students. With the boys and girls in the classroom, and also that special relationship: it begins diffidently, feeling its way. Timorously? Perhaps. But slowly, by degrees, it finds its way, and begins to run along its course—like a river? Like a river at times, and at times like a modest rivulet flowing noiselessly, yet carving its path with determination. She conjures them up, one by one, the girls and boys with whom she engaged on an individual basis, and supervised their theses. It's a different kind of acquaintance, outside the classroom, reaching as far as the home, and the far-flung country out into which the girl or boy proceeds, dispatched to his or her course of study. It begins on either side of that small desk in the history department. The rudimentary idea, the driving desire behind a big research project that would put the ocean into a bottle. "But…" she says, reining in the dream a little—or a lot. And now the research plan, the bibliography, the daily workshop, the anxiety induced by small problems. Then the bound thesis, the black robe, the applause, and the shared moment of achievement.

It's different in the classroom. Usually she doesn't know the names. She confuses the third-year students with the fourth-year students. She greets one of them warmly, thinking that he graduated some years ago and has come to visit the department. The boy smiles, and she discovers that he is in the fourth year, attended the day's lecture, and has come to ask her about something. Sometimes it's the other way around: "You're in the third year, right?"

The girl laughs, "No, doctor! I graduated three years ago, and I've come to see you!" After a few moments of confusion, the awkwardness passes. Are the boys and girls an anchor? A sail? A rudder? A compass? The wood of a ship that buoys her up and preserves her from drowning? Does she escape to them, there in the classroom that encloses her history lessons? Or does she attend to them because when she is on the point of despair their eyes give the lie to reality, in favor of an alternative truth, so she knows that there is a hidden way, obscure and unseen now, whose sudden appearance will not take her by surprise, for she has seen it and felt it and experienced it on every day that she has stood before them and given herself to them and they have given themselves to her? Enough melodrama, Shagar. You keep looking the other way, Shagar. You're clinging to visions of a resplendent savior the embodiment of whom is miraculously distributed among several hundred students! You love them, they love you, and that's beautiful, but what does that love have to do with the fantasy you're laying upon them like some kind of glamorous mantle? They're no magic cloak, Shagar, but flesh-and-blood human beings, good and evil, noble and debased—time will bend them, and they'll bend. Don't you ever learn, Shagar? You saw Khalil, the brightest and finest, going downhill at a run, and you closed your eyes—he's just confused, you said, it will pass; an isolated case, you said: a boy who began with a promise, then didn't fulfill that promise. There are dozens of others besides him, holding fast to their learning, their integrity, like a burning ember, steadfast and capable. And the incident of the "salt of the earth," what have you got to say about that?

It was one of those events in history, her personal history. She called it "Salt of the Earth."

The thing didn't strike her at first. The resemblance between the answer booklets seemed to her to be of the usual kind: notes written by a student of average ability, and copied by his classmates, then memorized and written verbatim in the response booklets. In such cases she gave a marginally passing grade, even if the answer was correct, explaining that something different was expected. Some of them believed her; others preferred to abide by the precept that years of schooling and dozens of teachers had ingrained in them: that they should collect whatever she gave out in the classroom, hold onto it like a temporary deposit, and spew it back to her on the day she asked for it at their examination. She marked 30 answer booklets, and paid no attention. Then she was arrested by the repetition of one sentence that appeared on two consecutive lines. Was it absentmindedness on the part of the writer? The same repetition appeared in the next four papers. How? She went back and inspected the booklets she had already corrected. Had the entire class cheated? Had there been some paper from which the students had copied word-for-word and been under so much pressure from the test that they would copy even a repeated sentence or a grammatical or spelling error? The problem wasn't confined to the students in one examination hall or to one question. Sometimes doubt is a sin, in the words of our ancestors. Better check again. She went back over the papers, tracing the origin of the crime. My God—the *crime*? She hadn't chosen to be a police officer or a spy, surely? Had the students betrayed her? She shuddered at the thought. Should she confront them? Confront them *how*? She still hadn't decided by the time Monday came around, the day of her weekly lecture to the fourth-year students.

Was she raving? Possibly she was stringing their own precious beads, which must have slipped from them as they ran for the bus or to a tutoring session or to a job that paid their living expenses. She remembers that she spoke about the university: the mission, the dream of its earliest pioneers, and the generations for whom they had paved the way. About the dead body of Abdel Hakam al-Jarrahi; about the students of Kasr al-

145

Aini; about the goddess Maat, whom she had loved and whose image she had hung above her desk; about the similarity in the test papers. She was confusing matters, switching from one topic to another as if she were delusional. She said— and it was as if she were not standing at the professor's podium, as if they were not children sitting in their classroom seats—she said, "I'm afraid. I want to hear from you, I want some reassurance."

Silence.

Then, one after another, the boys and girls raised their hands and asked to speak. First a girl: "You're saying that close to a quarter of the response papers prove that the students got the answers by cheating. I'm sorry to say that the proportion is inverted, for cheating is the rule: the proctors stand by the doors, 'keeping watch,' so that they can warn the students if one of the professors is approaching."

Another girl: "The proctors help the students cheat—one of them might be asked to take a 'crib sheet' from a student to one of her classmates in a different test section."

Now a boy: "People are weak by nature, and when we find that others whose level is below ours and who don't try as hard are getting higher grades, and that cheating is the norm, then we cheat."

Another girl: "The tests have been like this since we were at school, and when we enrolled at the university we found the same thing going on!"

Another boy said that crib sheets, foolscap, notes, and sometimes books were used in cheating, and that this was done openly. Finally one boy said, "I cheated during this test and others. And I'd be lying if I told you now that I'll avoid cheating from now on. I might be able to swim against the current, and I might not. Our society annihilates us in a thousand ways on a daily basis, so we learn gradually how to get our own back from it. You said that you thought about leaving the university, and I say to you that if you do that you wrong all of us, not because you deprive us of the benefit and the pleasure of studying with you, but because your presence here preserves something of value for us, a light that assures us the darkness is no longer total, and chaos, wickedness, ignorance, injustice, and corruption, even if we can't get away from them entirely, aren't the law of the land. People naturally need a star in their sky. You said that you hung a picture of Maat over your desk when you were a young student. The picture inspired you and you moved forward on your path. Don't cut off that power source, Dr. Shagar. I might look to you and move forward as you did, or even if I can't do it one of my classmates might be able to." The rest of the students applauded him. She was perspiring heavily—she wanted to say "Thank you," but her voice was stuck somewhere, no doubt held back by her tears.

Before she left the hall, a girl approached her and held out her hand, in which was a small piece of paper with something printed on it. She said,

"This is the 'crib sheet' from which we got the answer to the first question. It was written on the computer and then the font was reduced. There's a place that specializes in preparing this type of crib sheet for various subject areas."

Why did she find herself, as she left the classroom, absolving her students of their responsibility in this... had she really exonerated them? Did she love them so much that she would collude with the mothers who persuade themselves that it is others, always others, who corrupt their children? Was it a melodrama, a sentimental scene in a second-rate film? The prodigal son returns, weeps on his mother's breast, she forgives him, and everyone lives happily ever after?! Why did the incidence of cheating surprise her every time, as if she didn't know that it had become the norm? No, not yet the norm, but a common occurrence, a widespread and widely accepted phenomenon, almost normal: at primary, middle, and high school, at the academies and universities. Did she think that corruption extended to every place except her classroom and her own students? Had corruption struck even at the salt of the earth?

She sat down at her desk and wrote a memorandum to the dean in which she explained what had happened. She said that cheating was well established and that there could be no reasonable doubt, in the evidence of 126 response papers representing 28 percent of the total number of papers. She called for nullification of the test results and the opening of an investigation.

A new battle, and a losing one as usual! The

dean would not agree to rescind the examination results or to open a formal investigation. He responded to her memorandum with a letter in which he denied that any cheating had taken place, declaring that the proctoring of the examinations was on task and that the examination process at the college was a paragon of discipline. He concluded his letter with an implicit rebuke. No, not implicit—his meaning was plain as day. He said, "The problem is that the professors set questions that are predictable, and the students learn the professors' notes by heart, which is one of the reasons for the similarities among the responses." In other words, the letter said that she was wrong, inadequate, and deluded, and that all was as it should be. "Something is rotten in the state of Denmark!" My God, was she, at the age of 50, to be compelled to live the experience of the adolescent Hamlet? What Hamlet and what sort of travesty was this? She wouldn't leave the theater with the bodies of the heroes strewn about the stage at the end of the tragic duel. The youth were being hijacked—what was the meaning of this?!

And Karim?

She didn't witness his birth, or hold him in her arms during his first weeks, nor did she help his mother change his wet diapers or wash his bottom or bathe him or dry him or sprinkle talcum powder on his body. He rode the elevator with her and stood on tiptoe to reach for the buttons, asking her which floor she wanted.

"The fifth floor. And you?"

"The fifth, too."

"How old are you?" He held up his hand, spread his fingers like a fan and tucked in his thumb. "You mean four."

"Yes, but I don't like to talk a lot. When someone talks a lot they can make mistakes, and maybe get someone upset, and maybe..."

The elevator arrived at the fifth floor. As she was extracting her key from her bag, she asked him, "Are your mommy and daddy coming up after you?"

"No, they're at home."

"You live here?"

"Yup. Do you live here?"

"Uh-huh."

"So we're neighbors. Well-behaved people should be nice to the neighbors when they see them and say, 'Good morning,' and check on them if they're sick, and nice people, if they have something good to eat, should offer some to the neighbors. Wait a minute." He dashed to his apartment, and pounded impatiently on the door. She stood waiting for him as he went inside; he came back carrying a piece of cake on a plate. "Yesterday was my birthday."

"Happy birthday! Can you come in, so that I can give you a birthday present?"

"Maybe I can come see you after I ask Mama. But you can't give me a present because my birthday was yesterday. I mean, it's over. You have to wait until next year—if you still like me then—because people only give presents to people they like, and if they don't like them they don't have to give them presents ever. So next year, you say 'Happy birthday, Karim,' and give me a present, and I say, 'Thank you.' The present could be a flower, or it could be a toy, or a pen, or a kiss. How come you're laughing?"

"Because you're a smart boy, and nice, too. Can I ask you something? You said that people give presents to people they like. And you gave me a present before we got to know each other..."

"I thought you were nice. Later if you turn out to be mean, I'll stop liking you and stop giving you presents. Like in the movies, when I like someone who seems good, and afterwards it turns out he's bad, that's it, I don't like him."

"Can you ask your mommy if it's all right for you to come visit me?"

"I'll ask her, but I have to know your name."

"Shagar."

"Shagar?! That's a really pretty name!"

"Karim is a beautiful name, too."

"No, it's not."

"Why not?"

"Because at my nursery school there are five of us called Karim. The teacher says, 'Be quiet, Karim.' But I was already quiet. Or she says, 'Karim doesn't know how to draw,' but I do know how to draw—my drawings are beautiful! And she talks about Karim Ali Ahmed or Karim Nabil Tadrous or Koukou—'cause Koukou's name is Karim, too. If my name was something like the word for 'green,' Akhdar—I mean, like, 'Be quiet, Akhdar,' then it would be me who was talking. She'd say, 'Akhdar gets a zero,' and it would be me who didn't do the work. 'Akhdar is great,' would mean I was great. Everything would be clear, right?"

"Right... although Akhdar is a strange name."

"I asked Mama, 'Why didn't you name me Abdel Maqsoud? There isn't a single boy in the class whose name is Abdel Maqsoud! But Akhdar is better than Abdel Maqsoud. Anyway, I like green—I'll show you one of my pictures—and besides one time I dreamed I bought a pair of green shoes. It was before Eid and I said, 'I want a pair of green shoes,' but we couldn't find any, so I cried and cried, and then Papa bought me a big box of crayons, so I drew a picture of a boy wearing green shoes. Mama and Papa laughed, and said the shoes were three times as big as the boy's head. Look, I'm not going to visit you right now, because Mama's going to say it's lunchtime and then time for nap. Six o'clock is better, okay?"

The imagination fails, and even minds demonstrably possessed of high intelligence will sometimes fail to observe what is right there in plain view. The idea—even the ghost of such an idea—has not crossed her mind the entire three months, from that first week of September, until they released her. She went home, washed her face, changed her clothes, and knocked on Karim's door. She was greeted by his mother, who called to him, but he didn't respond. The mother went to get him, but came back without him, saying he was sleeping. She waited for him at home, but he didn't come. She went to him again. She called his name. No answer. She went into his room, where he was sitting at his desk. He didn't turn around.

"Why don't you want to say hello to me?" No response. "Aren't we friends? Why don't you want to talk to me?"

"I don't want to talk to you!"

"Why not?"

"Just because. I don't have to."

She approached the desk, and he moved his chair away from her. She put down the box of chocolates she had brought. It was wrapped in shiny paper, and tied with a fancy white bow.

"Please take your present away. I don't want it."

"Why not?" He didn't answer. She got up and left the room. She asked his mother whether she had told him she was in prison, and his mother reacted with consternation.

"Absolutely not! I told him you had gone on a trip!"

She understood. This made matters seem simpler at first, then more complicated.

She stood waiting at the entrance to the building as he got off the school bus. He went inside without stopping to greet her. She followed him toward the elevator and rode up with him. She spoke the words she had prepared during the previous night: "I wasn't on a trip—I was in prison. And in prison I was forbidden to talk on the telephone or write letters. If I had been allowed to, I would have called you and let you know..." She forgot the rest of what she had planned to say. The elevator arrived at the fifth floor. He got off, and she stayed where she was until she heard the doorman call, "Close the door!" Shaken from her reverie, she closed the elevator door and headed for her apartment.

She didn't have to wait long. That afternoon there was a knock at the door. Standing in the doorway he asked her, "Can I ask you why you were in prison?"

He was seven years old then. She had to answer his question. Was her answer, however simplified, the beginning of awareness of injustice? She shudders now to think of it, as if she had brought the boy to the edge of a dangerous precipice. Unsettled by this shudder, this thought, she addresses them both, speaking aloud like a crazy person: "What are we supposed to do? Protect the young at any cost, even if it means concealing the truth from them? You're a fool, Shagar. Your profession has corrupted you—idiot! Do you imagine yourself to be the source of enlightenment, as if life were nothing but a stupid test, giving your own words back to you like an echo?" Life is thrown up in front of the young, in the streets, destroying some, blowing up in their faces like a land mine, and either killing them or warping them; the rest, the luckier ones (whose parents provide them with good education, food, housing, and jobs)—they can look the other way. But do they really turn away from the land mines, or do they simply consider them an inevitable reality? A reality that requires them either to participate in its creation and propagation, so that as long as the law is to kill or be killed, one might as well save one's own skin, and live—live like a king, if possible. This was what Khalil said. But what about Karim? Would he kill, or be killed?

Twelve

On the 19th of November 1977, Anwar al-Sadat traveled to Israel. The following day, the morning of Eid, five security officers came to our house and took Mourid, and deported him from Egypt.

Two months later, I traveled to meet Mourid at his brother's house in Doha. Tamim had his first passport, with its accompanying picture: round-faced. He wasn't smiling—he appeared anxious or upset. The two bottom corners of the picture showed a pair of hands helping the infant boy to sit up straight. He was a child six months old, or perhaps a little younger, probably able to sit up on his own. Perhaps I was afraid he would fall from the photographer's chair, and so I crouched behind him and supported him with my hands. I sent the picture to Mourid so that he could acquire a separate passport for Tamim, which would enable me to accompany him to Doha during the mid-year break from classes.

Tahrir Square. The *Mugammaᶜ*. A woman in her thirties climbs the staircase amidst a throng of others ascending and descending. She inquires, waits in a long line. Gradually she approaches the iron bars of the window. She arrives. She extends her hand, in which are two passports, to the clerk sitting behind the window. Her own passport is green, bearing the imprint of the eagle above the words, "Arab Republic of Egypt," printed in Arabic and French; then there is a passport of a lighter green, inscribed with a crown above the words, "Hashemite Kingdom of Jordan," in Arabic and English; and finally there is a photocopy of a third passport. The clerk returns the papers and the two passports to the woman. She must write, in lieu of a request for residency, a different request. Such-and-such an office, the clerk told her. The woman buys white paper and fiscal stamps, and heads for such-and-such an office.

"Your business?"

"A document confirming sponsorship of the baby and guaranteeing his support. A statement is required." The woman does not see the paper, she does not recognize the letters, she makes spelling errors. She tears up the paper and starts over. She makes a mistake writing her own name. A new piece of paper. She writes the wrong date. She starts over for the fourth time. At last she writes the statement, and the clerk stamps it. A third office. The clerk asks, "Date of arrival in Egypt?"

"Whose arrival?"

"Your son's."

"He's six months old. He was born in Egypt and has never left."

"Date of his father's last trip to Egypt?" He searches through the photocopied papers. "Here it is: May 17, 1977, to get a residency permit— there had to be a record of his last trip."

"But my son was born a month after that date!"

"It doesn't matter."

He records the date on the passport and the permit for a year's residency. The woman takes the passport to a clerk who writes, "The declarations are accurate," and signs. A final clerk affixes two stamps: a small one and the one of the eagle to which is appended the name of Passports, Immigration, and Nationality Administration: "Foreigners' Registration Office."

Now it is possible for her to take her son to visit his father. The woman puts the papers in her bag and leaves.

June of '77, five months before Mourid's deportation and three days after the birth of Tamim. A photograph: Tamim, with me holding him, swaddled in white and encircled by my arms. Nothing can be seen of him but his black hair, which covers a bit of his forehead. His eyes are closed. The Nile is plainly visible behind me, filling the background of the picture. In front of me is the hospital, which I have left just a few minutes before, but it doesn't appear in the picture. The same street on which I was born 31 years earlier: it extends all along the western bank of Manyal al-Roda Island, from the hindmost buildings of Kasr al-Aini Hospital at the northern end of the island, to the Nilometer of Roda, at its southern tip, accessible by either the University Bridge or the Abbas Bridge. A difficult birth, it took two nights. Then Tamim arrived. Mourid went to register his birth certificate. He came back, looking surprised and confused. Taking a seat beside my hospital bed, he said, "I gave the documents to the clerk, along with the marriage certificate and the hospital form, and I informed him that the mother was Egyptian. The clerk said, 'I'll record the mother's name and nationality on the certificate, but this means absolutely nothing. Whether the mother is Egyptian, English, or Israeli doesn't concern us at all—what matters is the father!'"

We met Mourid in Doha, in Budapest, in Amman, during the summer holidays and at the mid-year break. I also met him in Algeria, the Emirates, and Morocco, at cultural events in which we were jointly invited to participate.

Seven years after his deportation, Mourid would be able to return to our house in Cairo, not to live with us, but for short visits, determined each by a prior permit granted by the authorities in charge of security. Upon his arrival at Cairo Airport, an airport official would stamp his passport and make a note upon it saying, "One week, non-renewable," or, "Two weeks only." We would meet him at the airport. See him off at the airport. Wait until we could go to him during our summer holiday, or petition once again in the hope he might be permitted to visit us again. This situation lasted for another ten years.

In January 1995 Mourid was granted permission to live in Egypt. He came home to 6 Ramez Street in Muhandiseen, the same house from which he had been deported seventeen years earlier. We had grown older—Mourid had turned 50 the year before, and I would reach that age the following year. Tamim had grown as well: he was in his third year of high school, and was preparing for his certificate exam. In a few months his father would accompany him to the examination hall, then return after some hours to take him back home.

Tamim passed the exam with a score of 91.6. The posting of the highest scores by the placement office was announced, so he went, along with his classmates. He stood in line, purchased the forms he needed, and returned home triumphant. Two days later it became clear that the forms he had acquired did not pertain to him. There was a special placement office for foreign students. Where? In Manshiyat al-Bakri, across from Abdel Nasser's house. We went there. A detailed set of stipulations was written in a clear hand on a piece of cardboard hung on the office door. We bought the proper forms. Status: a foreign student, his mother Egyptian, who has completed the three stages of education in the Egyptian school system. The requirement? Besides the placement forms, the parents' certificate of marriage; the mother's identity card or passport; an affidavit of employment if she was employed; documents proving completion of primary and middle school, as well as the secondary school final exams. We submitted them. We attached a letter from Ain Shams University declaring that Dr. Radwa Ashour was professor and chair of the English department in the School of Humanities.

The placement results came out. Tamim was accepted into the school in which he wanted to enroll at Cairo University. Classes began at the end of September. October: we inquired at the college about his papers. They hadn't arrived. November: they hadn't arrived. At last, December: they arrived. At the Office of Student Affairs, the clerk in her *hijab* stood up from behind her desk and produced several files. She extracted one of them: Tamim's file.

"Foreign student?"

"His mother is Egyptian."

"Widowed or divorced?" Then she repeated, more sharply, "Widowed or divorced?"

"I don't understand."

She shouted at me, "Madam, are you a widow?"

"No."

"Divorced?"

"No."

"Then the boy's a visiting student—foreign. It makes no difference if his mother's Egyptian."

I took a deep breath. "There's been a decision on the part of the Higher Council of Universities, issued last May, to the effect that students whose mothers are Egyptian should be treated the same as Egyptian students."

"I was never informed of any such decision!"

Number 2 Darih Saad Street. Office of General Administration for Foreign Students. I made the acquaintance of one of the higher-ups. He told me he had attended a doctoral defense I had supervised. He ordered coffee for me. He gave me a copy of the Council's decision. He said, "I think they pulled back from the decision without recording this in the documents, and instead substituted a waiver for resident children of Egyptian mothers exempting them from ninety percent of the expenses, contingent upon evidence of financial need."

"And this means?"

"It means documentation to the effect that the family's material circumstances don't allow for payment of the expenses!"

In these years suspended between disasters public and private, we lived as other people did. Our life was not devoid of pleasures both great and small, for life takes care of itself when all is said and done. A few days after the massacres at Sabra and Shatila, Tamim attended his first day of school at the Hurreya School in Giza, wearing a white shirt, gray trousers, and a dark red tie. I gaze at him with my own eyes and with his father's eyes, and experience a twofold joy, complete and absolute. Going every morning to a place where there were children, teachers, and supervisors was nothing new to Tamim. He was a year and a half old when we enrolled him at the Mani Néné preschool, a private facility in Budapest, which he attended regularly from January to August 1979. In September, the university turned down my request for an extension of leave to be with my husband. We returned to Egypt. Tamim entered another preschool in Cairo. At the end of the academic year we returned to Budapest. We enrolled him in a new preschool whose name he confidently pronounced, Budapesti Harisniya Gyar Ovuda (the sock factory preschool of Budapest). He attended this preschool regularly for two years in a row. His father would take him at eight in the morning, and bring him home at four in the afternoon. Tamim would come into the house with an assortment of stories, or a song, or a flower to present to me, or some walnuts in his pockets. He would turn and head for the balcony, squat down, take out his loot, and removing his shoes, set about cracking the walnuts with one of them. If I tried to dissuade him, he would insist that this was how to crack a walnut, and that this was how all the children at the preschool went about it. How old was he when he said to me, "Truth is like a hazelnut: you have to wear yourself out until you get to it"? I understood where he had gotten this idea only after he came into the house carrying those spiky objects.

"What are these, Tamim?"

"Hazelnuts."

"Hazelnuts—where?"

"They're hidden inside. I have to get them out."

During the holidays we would go to the Buda Hills, forests of oak, evergreen, white poplar, chestnut, walnut, and other trees for which we couldn't find anyone to tell us the names. We would run and jump and play with a ball, then sit on our mat to eat whatever food we had brought with us. Or we would go to the restaurant where the horses were, in that Hungarian village. We would apply ourselves to the soup, which they would present to us in a bowl large enough for ten people. Tamim would hurry to finish his meal, because he was impatient for the horses—he wanted to feed them or pet them or watch them run. At this restaurant, in the summer of 1984, Tamim—who was then seven—got the egg he wanted. We were having our lunch, when a villager passed by crying his wares: "Eggs! Eggs that bring good fortune to their owners!" In the man's hand was an egg with a miniature horse-shoe affixed to it with fine nails.

"I want one!" cried Tamim. Mourid paid for the egg. Tamim held out his hand and took it. "Allah!" he exclaimed, "Luck is with me—they'll let Papa come back to Egypt!"

We hid our emotion behind a discussion of the egg. We said that it was beautiful and amazing. We said, "Look, Tamim, look how the man made it: he drilled this tiny hole to empty the egg, and then he fastened the horseshoe on without breaking it—how did he do that?!" None of us forgot what Tamim had said that day, and when Mourid was permitted to enter Egypt two months later, the egg took on a new status, not because we—or Mourid and I, at least—believed that it had brought luck to Tamim and to us, but simply because Tamim had said what he said—and indeed our wish was fulfilled.

The threads entwine, all of them are inter-twined. Even the days in the hospital in Budapest were not without a gentle and profound joy. The nearby hospital for the first two weeks; then the other, more distant hospital for the succeeding three weeks. A clinic for the treatment of respiratory ailments, everything there depressing beyond the oppressiveness of disease. My only companion in the room was a Russian-made radio, which Mourid had bought for me specifically so that I could pick up broadcasts of the Egyptian news, and follow reports of the campaign of September 1981. Mourid would take Tamim to his preschool at eight o'clock each morning, then come to visit me, and we would drink our coffee. He would go to work, then leave his office at three and set off for the preschool to fetch Tamim. At four I would begin watching for them. They would arrive at four-fifteen or a little later. From the window I would see the white Lada, with Mourid in the driver's seat and Tamim in the back. The car would slow down, stop, they would get out, and I would redirect my gaze to the door of my room.

In Cairo, Tamim came to visit me when I was lying in Badran Hospital, then later in Magdi Hospital. He liked to lie in my bed. He was three. Then he turned four, and was no longer interested in the bed, but in the metal cart pushed by the nurse who conveyed meals to the patients. She would set the tray down beside me, which held Tamim's interest. "Can I eat with you, Mama?" Visiting hours would end, and they would leave. From the window I would see them turn together and wave. Then the car would take them away. I can see the whole scene that I watched from the window, as well as an orange

Gerbera daisy in a pottery vase that Mourid had brought me. (The daisy lived for a whole week, and the vase moved with us from the hospital to our house in Budapest, then to the house on Ramez Street, and now it's with us in our present house.)

It wasn't all sorrow and grief, but rather a life full of interwoven, prickly strands, containing the meat of the hazelnut. My friends were in prison: Latifa, Amina, Awatif, Farida, Shahinda, and Safinaz; a number of my acquaintances and dozens of leading cultural and political personages of Egypt. The officially recognized detainees numbered 1,500; my name did not appear among theirs, although it did appear on the list of professors dismissed from the university. Matters in Egypt had assumed a gravity more severe than the pain that spread from my back to my left shoulder and my neck each time the needle was inserted into my lung to draw off the fluid that had accumulated there. But life, I repeat, takes care of itself. In the hospital, in September of '81, while I was suffering from pleural effusion in my right lung, Mourid and Tamim came every day, and it seemed that I was making a good recovery, for the doctor permitted me to spend the weekend at home. On Friday evening I would go home, and early Monday morning Mourid would take me back to the hospital. Sometimes, when I could manage it and when the doctor gave permission, I would walk in the garden of the clinic, and gaze at the oak and chestnut trees, becoming familiar with their trunks, their leaves, the acorns and chestnuts. Life seemed familiar and solid, in spite of everything.

Tamim loved airports and traveling. So he said, and sometimes I would comment, but at other times I would keep silent. He rode an airplane for the first time when he was seven months old. Mourid's mother accompanied us on our journey to Doha. Our trip was smooth, in contrast to the journey to Budapest the following September, when security procedures had been tightened. A few days earlier the first Camp David Accords had been concluded. The employee at the security check said, "Passengers are not allowed carry-on luggage." I was holding a small bag with a change of clothes for the baby, a little woolen blanket, a container of milk and a bottle. I informed the employee of this.

"Carry-on luggage is strictly forbidden!"

"What am I supposed to do?"

"It's simple: carry everything in your hands."

"How?"

"In a nylon bag."

I would have to wait to go through passport control before I could get to the duty-free shops and acquire a nylon bag. I stuffed the container of milk and Tamim's change of clothes into my purse and slung it over my shoulder. I carried Tamim and his bottle in one arm and our passports and tickets in the other hand. Then I headed for passport control. I handed over the documents. The bottle slipped, fell on the floor, and broke. For months afterward, Tamim would never tire of the story of the broken bottle. He was fifteen months old and could form meaningful sentences.

He was not quite six years old when he took a plane by himself. I said goodbye to him calmly, knowing I wouldn't see him again for two months, during which I had to correct my students' papers and finish up with the administration of the exams. I filled out the forms and helped him check in; I kissed him: "Say hello to Papa for me." He waved to me, walked away, then turned around. He waved again, smiling—he was in high spirits.

I had never been afraid of flying, but I grew afraid. Was it age? (With age, human beings cling more tightly to life, which makes sense, despite the obvious paradox: is not old age by definition a life threatened with extinction?) It must be age, I said to myself, resisting the premonition that the plane was going to kill me. Was it the awareness that tomorrow, or one day soon, some airplane would bear Tamim away to some country or other in which he would be a stranger because he was Palestinian, and then there would be another plane, and eventually there would be a multitude of planes etching, in their lofty trajectories through space, a map of parallel tracks? Was this not the law of dispersal imposed upon the mothers of every Palestinian I knew, upon Mourid's mother and her four children? Or was it the accumulation of anxieties I had never allowed to surface in their time, with the result that they now exacted their toll on me with redoubled force? That hour I spent waiting at the airport, waiting calmly as if I wasn't suspended upon this curious string manipulated by an officer who might or might not let Mourid enter the country, as if I was not wracked by apprehensions that intensified as soon as Tamim reached the age of 14, as they would hold him up for some time while they searched their lists and made sure; or we would be returning together from a trip, I would present both passports at the same time, and the officer would stamp mine but tell Tamim to wait. I would wait with him, and the officer would say, "Go ahead, madam," with superficial courtesy, so that I would be obliged to respond in kind, moving along to stand on one side of the barrier, while Tamim stood on the other. And we would wait.

Before me on the desk now are fourteen old passports—mine, Mourid's, and Tamim's—each one bearing a stamp that says, "Canceled." I hold them in my hand and I resemble one of those tour company employees at the airport, who meet a tour group and collect all their passports in order to expedite the necessary procedures.

During the time we lived in Budapest we went to Vienna several times, because the two capitals were only about 260 kilometers apart, a distance that could be covered in three hours by car. We would go to Vienna for a short holiday, sometimes for medical treatment, or to meet friends—that sort of thing. Jordan would no longer renew passports for citizens affiliated with the PLO. They did not renew Mourid's passport. He carried an Algerian passport, which the Algerian government had granted him. The name on the passport was Mourid al-Barghouti. Occupation: poet. Birthplace: Deir Ghassana, Algeria! I carried an Egyptian passport, and, because according to legal convention a woman is subordinate to her husband, the Egyptian passport authority had (it was, after all, the least they could do) recorded under "Remarks": wife of Nawwaf Abdel Raziq al-Barghouti, nationality Jordanian. Nawwaf is Mourid's name as registered by the village mayor in 1944, because when the midwife went to inform him that Abdel Raziq and Sakina had had a son and he asked her the name, she hesitated, saying it was a strange name. She tried to remember it, but she couldn't. The mayor solved the problem for her. "His brother is Mounif," he said, "so we'll call him Nawwaf." The mayor registered the birth of the baby and brought the certificate to his mother, who took it from him, thanked him, and put it away, out of her children's reach until the day when Mourid, at the age of 11, came home from school and told her that the director had requested the birth certificate because it was required for admission to the exam certifying completion of primary school. Only then did Mourid discover his other name. It was this midwife and this mayor whom I never met that determined the name to be recorded on my passport and Tamim's.

The Zionist occupation of the greater part of Palestine led to the annexation of the west bank of the River Jordan to the east bank; thus the Hashemite Kingdom of Jordan came into being, and so Mourid, and after him Tamim, became Jordanians. Jordan's refusal to renew the Palestinian passports resulted in Mourid's carrying an Algerian passport specifying as his place of birth Deir Ghassana, although to the best of my knowledge there is no such village in Algeria. But individual freedom has its advantages, and in Europe, where relationships were unconstrained, the passport officer at the border checkpoint between Hungary and Austria wasn't about to spend a lot of time on us. Nothing unusual: an Algerian befriends an Egyptian woman who has a child by a previous marriage or relationship with a Jordanian. The repetition of the name al-Barghouti might give him pause, but he doesn't make an issue of it. He's afraid of seeming ignorant, for it might be a common Arabic name, like Mohammed—as Jan is a common Austrian name! In the event that the officer should complicate matters and we should face difficulties, then on our own heads be it: since our travel to Vienna was a luxury, we could forgo it. But that Mourid should come to see his wife and son and stay for a few days in his own house: this is not a matter of luxury, on the one hand, or of self-induced calamity on the other: here our fate was in the hands of others, and for the most part we were helpless to change it. We would go to meet him at Cairo airport, wait in the depressing corridor to watch from nearby as the passengers emerged from the arrival hall. We would wait an hour, two hours, which seemed bearable, perhaps because we were used to it, but also because what mattered in the end was that Mourid be permitted to enter.

In 1986 we waited ten hours, from 1 o'clock in the morning until 11 in the morning. We left the airport at 4:30 in the morning without Mourid. The reason: the visa issued by the Egyptian consulate was meaningless, and it was necessary to obtain the standard agreement of the internal authorities at Lazoughli, Cairo's head-quarters for National Security Investigations. We went back home. Tamim asked repeatedly, "What are we going to do, Mama?"

"By tomorrow morning the problem will be solved, Tamim."

He got into bed, and then called me. "Mama, do you think Papa will get in?"

"Yes, Tamim, in the morning, inshallah, they'll let him in."

"Sure?"

I didn't answer. "Are you sure?" he repeated.

"Yes, Sweetie."

I smoked a cigarette, thinking: How do I start? Whom do I call, and when? How do I explain my absence from the fourth-year oral examination board, when the exam is set to take place at the college in the morning? I looked at my watch: six o'clock. At eight I called one of the people who worked in Cairo's PLO branch office. He upbraided me for not having called the office before Mourid's arrival so that they could see to what needed to be done. (Only on one occasion had I resorted to contacting the office to facilitate Mourid's entry, and I hadn't got results—whether because of indifference or neglect or ineffectiveness, God knows.) I called a friend of ours, who promised a solution to the problem. "Give me ten minutes," he said, "and I'll call you back."

I called the head of the department. "It's an emergency," I told her. "Please get one of my colleagues to take over for me until I get there.

My friend called back, as he had promised. Then he called again and said, "In half an hour Mourid will be on his way home—don't go to the airport."

At eleven o'clock Mourid arrived at the house. I made coffee and we drank it together. Then I rushed off to the college. I said to Tamim, laughing, "This is a rare chance to be alone with your father!"

In 1993 it seemed as though we were making progress, in spite of everything. The ten hours of waiting became five! Mourid was invited by the General Organization of Cultural Centers to participate in an Arabic poetry festival. The plane was due to arrive from Amman at two o'clock in the afternoon. I said to Tamim, "There's no need for you to miss school. When you get home at 3 or 3:15, go buy some flowers for your father, and when you get back either you'll find us at home or we'll be there within fifteen minutes. Your father has been invited officially, along with Saadi Yusuf and Ibrahim Nasrallah. The entry procedures won't take more than a few minutes." At the airport, two employees from the Higher Council for Culture were waiting to meet the guests. The plane landed safely. An hour passed, two hours. One of the two employees went into the customs area, then came back. He called the Council. Back he went again. I called Tamim.

"What's the problem?" he said.

"Maybe it's your Uncle Saadi, because he's Iraqi, maybe it's Papa—I don't know."

The Council employee appeared with a piece of chocolate. "Mr. Mourid sent this to you," he said. "He knows you came straight from the university!"

He called the council and asked to be connected to the minister's office. He hung up and stood by the phone. Ten minutes later his call was returned. He went back to the customs area. An hour later he reappeared—this time he was beaming.

"What is it?" I asked him.

"We've discovered what the problem is. Mr. Mourid's name in his passport corresponds to one in the computer, the name of someone who is forbidden entry. The resemblance between the names is the cause of this delay!"

I made no comment. We kept waiting until our Three Musketeers appeared: Ibrahim Nasrallah—they let him in, but in solidarity with Mourid and Saadi he refused to enter. Three and a half hours later they let Saadi in—for Mourid's sake, he waited with Ibrahim Nasrallah. Finally they let Mourid in, and the three of them emerged. We got home to Ramez Street a little before nine o'clock.

And because we swallow all this and refrain from choking on it, it stays down.

Reality is more complex than what meets the eye; this account abridges it. How many times did

the plane convey us gently and easily to our re-
unions? The Hungarian Air flight—the only direct flight between Cairo and Budapest—became
as familiar as a bus, or the train to Alexandria. It
took off, with us on board, at 3:30 in the morning.
We would arrive at the Budapest airport in the
early morning. Mourid would pick us up in his
car. We would traverse the streets of Pest, then
the Danube, on our way to Buda on the west bank
of the river. We would climb toward the Rosza-
Domb, then bear right toward Vérhalom Street.
Mourid would slow down and stop the car in front
of a grocery. Tamim would go in and come back,
delighted, with the rounds of bread that he had
loved since the time he attended the Hungarian
preschool. From the grocery we would proceed
to a residential compound, and pass by the gate-
keeper's kiosk. On our right were two tall white
poplars and a children's swing set. We would turn
left, Mourid would park the car, and we would un-
load our belongings and take them with us up to
the third floor, open the door on the familiar furnishings. This was also our home. To the right of
the entryway was a small kitchen that overlooked
the poplar trees and the swing set. I would call
Tamim for lunch or dinner, or Mourid would call
him: sometimes "Tamim!" but at others "Tam-
tam" or "Tamatim" ("tomato"), which later
evolved into "Tamatish," and subsequently
"Mukarrar," or "Maᶜqoud," after a visit to Algeria
during which Mourid discovered that tomato
sauce is known in Algerian dialect as "mukarrar
maᶜqoud al-tamatish." In this way the three

words were used interchangeably as new names for Tamim. Mourid would shout at the top of his lungs, "Ma^cqoud! Mukarrar!" and Tamim's voice would be heard beneath the window, "Yes, Papa!" In a moment of anger or frustration, I might exclaim, "Ya zift!" Tamim would answer, "Yes, Mama," and dash up the stairs, fearful all the way of some rebuke. He would ring the bell, and when I opened the door he would find us laughing. Suddenly grasping the absurdity of responding as he had to "You rubbish!" as if it were yet another of his new names, he would join in the laughter.

At the age of 3, Tamim received his first oud, purchased for him by his father in Tunisia. And in Budapest, from a dark-skinned gypsy who had set up shop at the entrance to the produce market, where she spread out her goods made of straw and cane and wood, we bought a small chair for Tamim. He would sit upon it, holding the oud, improvising those early, rather curious epics into which he inserted all that was familiar to him, from macaroni to Palestine.

We would try to forget that this was a visit of only a few weeks' duration, to end when the holiday was over. We invited friends and family. Among those who would visit us were Hussein Muruwwa in 1983 and, in the following year, Naji al-Ali. Tamim would sit on his little chair and perform for Abou Nizar Hussein Muruwwa; on the page of a small notebook, Naji al-Ali drew Handhala holding a flower, with the caption, "Good morning, Tamim!" They left, and in the news some time afterward the BBC announced the assassination of Hussein Muruwwa at home in Beirut. I heard the news in Cairo; Mourid heard it in Budapest. The announcement of Naji al-Ali's assassination in London we heard together when we were listening to a broadcast in Balatonföldvár, a village on the shores of Lake Balaton in Hungary. Each time, gunfire muted by silencers. Emile Habibi and Latifa al-Zayyat died of old age, bedridden by then. In Budapest Latifa had brought Tamim a small red piano. He sat cross-legged in front of it and plunked on the keys—he was eighteen months old. "Dance, Latifa!" he said, and she laughed. She got up and took two steps, sat down, and laughed some more. Some years later, Emile Habibi laughed loud and long with us, clutching his stomach, his corpulent body shaking. "For the love of God, Tamim, enough!" But Tamim kept on telling his endless Egyptian jokes. In the early 1990s, I would meet Emile at Cairo Airport. We would shake hands, each of us aware of the gap newly opened between us since his acceptance of the prize he had been awarded by the state of Israel. He received it on May 15th, Israel's "Independence Day." Amidst the flashing of Israeli journalists' cameras, Emile mounted the podium to shake hands with Shamir and receive his prize. Exactly five hears later, also on May 15th, Damascus would bid farewell to the body of Saadallah Wannous. We had walked together in the Buda Hills, Saadallah and I, each of us talking about the pleural effusion that had afflicted us both.

Threads separated, paths divided. All of them died. We left Budapest.

Thirteen

The doorbell rang. I opened the door to find Thurayya, my neighbor. I invited her in, but she remained where she was, standing at the door.

"I'm going shopping. When are you traveling?"

"Tomorrow evening."

"Have you heard the news?"

"No."

"Bashir al-Gemayel died. They said yesterday he was wounded in an explosion at the Phalangists' headquarters. I heard the news this morning—they said he died."

She left, and I closed the door. It was almost eleven o'clock. Mourid was at his office and Tamim was at preschool. I didn't turn on either the radio or the television to hear the details. I carried on with my travel preparations.

The following day, a Thursday, Mourid took us to the airport in his Lada. Our plane lifted off at 10:30 p.m. Tamim felt the separation from his father keenly, and I tried to distract him by talking about the new school he would be going to, about our friends and family who were waiting for us in Cairo, and about our next visit to Budapest. "In the winter vacation you'll play in the snow with your friends." He stayed quiet until he fell asleep. I reclined my seat a little and closed my eyes. On my way to Cairo after staying for two years in Budapest, where I had gone immediately after undergoing two major operations. The first year there was wide open: for recuperation, for writing, for our life together as a family. The second year was heavily freighted, an over-packed suitcase weighed down and filled to bursting with its excessive load: an afflicted right lung, the hospital, and the hospital again; arrests in Egypt, expulsion from the university; the assassination of a president and his successor's assumption of office; the release of prisoners and the government's decision to reinstate the professors who had been dismissed; the invasion of Lebanon and the siege of Beirut; the ousting of the Palestinian resistance. Ships, trucks, tears, and handfuls of rice cast in farewell. Another surgery. Mourid waving goodbye to us; at the end of it all, the flight.

The plane landed in Larnaca. Forty-five minutes later, it resumed its journey to Cairo, where we arrived at 2:30 in the morning; we got home at 4. Tamim kept repeating, "I miss Papa." We sat together in the living room, waiting for daybreak. Gradually the light crept in through the wooden shutters on the windows and the birds began to chirp. The place seemed less desolate then, and so we went to bed.

I slept fitfully; when I woke up I occupied myself with opening and unpacking our luggage, and shopping for the food we needed. In the evening, my mother came to visit, along with some friends. I didn't buy the newspaper, nor did I turn on the radio. Saturday morning I had to go to the doctor—a week before we traveled I had undergone a small operation, so it was necessary to have a follow-up examination and get the bandage changed. After that we went to our house in al-Manyal. There I glanced at the front-page headlines of *Al-Ahram*, but I didn't read the particulars. I think it was only on the following day, Sunday the 19th, that I learned what had happened: that is, the Israeli occupation of Beirut and the massacres. I don't know why I associate the memory of what happened during those days in Beirut with all the minutiae surrounding our trip, as if my inattention Wednesday, Thursday, and Friday were one of those lapses that can be neither forgotten nor pardoned, but stays front and center in the memory. I am aware that there is a bitter irony here, in that my attention or lack of attention to what happened could make not the slightest difference, since ultimately the outcome was absolute powerlessness either way: frustration, and nothing but frustration. Yet *attention* means that you are involved in the event, that the person who has been killed is yours and that you belong to him. Then again, no—not altogether. What I mean is that there are no words for what I felt then and still feel. Perhaps it is similar to what my mother-in-law felt each time she thought of her son Mounif, the eldest of her children, flung down on the sidewalk of some street in Paris, bleeding to death. She tries to remember what it was she was doing at 11 o'clock on Monday night. Was she asleep? How could she have been asleep? The idea nearly drives her mad, sleep becomes a guilty act, and the fact that she didn't know doesn't mitigate, but rather intensifies, the guilt.

When Thurayya came to the door on Wednesday morning, bringing me the news of the assassination of Bashir al-Gemayel, Ariel Sharon, the fat man who loved dogs but hated Arabs, was standing on the roof of a tall building near the Kuwaiti Embassy in Beirut, looking out over the city and the camps. Afterwards he called Begin and said, "Our forces are approaching their target. I can see them with my own eyes." Sharon wrapped up the telephone call and then went to Bikfayya to extend his condolences for Bashir al-Gemayel's death. I don't remember what time I went to sleep on Tuesday night, or when I woke up on Wednesday morning, but I know now that the Israelis, all through Tuesday night and into Wednesday, were transporting their matériel and their paratroopers via concentrated airlift connecting their airports with the airport in Beirut. At dawn I was asleep. The Israeli forces surrounding West Beirut, from Dahiya to the south and Marfa' to the north, began to invade the city. Wednesday to Thursday I was getting ready to travel—washing and ironing our clothes, and buying the little chocolate bars with the curious designs on them that Tamim liked, which I would give him when he went to school. Beirut fell. The Israeli tanks were in Hamra Street, in the Fakahani, in Corniche al-Mazraa. On Saturday the Israeli forces had taken over all of Beirut, and enabled the Phalangists and Saad Haddad to spend 40 hours in Sabra and Shatila. They used bullets and hatchets and axes and knives. They killed. They slaughtered. They raped. They bashed in heads. They chopped off limbs. They defiled the corpses. They plundered what they could of money and jewelry. Saturday: mission accomplished. They left the camp. Sunday: bulldozers. Bodies. Flies. Paramedics in masks. The camera lenses of the news agencies. Grieving women. Foreign diplomats proceeding with leaden feet through the alleyways.

Thursday night into Friday. The plane is in the air. Total darkness outside the window, punctuated by flashing indicator lights. In Beirut the electricity is cut off, and total darkness descends upon the city, interrupted starting at midnight by rocket fire directed at the camps. At 11 o'clock—an hour after the plane's departure from Budapest—the commander of the Phalangist forces that have entered Shatila sends his report to the Israeli commander: "So far we have killed 300 civilians and terrorists." This is the harvest of the first six hours. The final tally was impossible to calculate with such accuracy. Lebanese government sources were able to count 212 corpses buried in mass graves, but failed to ascertain the identities of the bodies. Three hundred and two bodies were identified and burned with the assistance of the emergency team. Two hundred forty-eight bodies were buried with the help of the Red Cross. About 1,200 bodies were identified by their relatives and buried in family graves. There were other bodies—they can be numbered in the hundreds—beneath the rubble, and bodies buried by the Phalangists and Saad Haddad in mass graves in the course of the slaughter, whose exhumation was not afterwards permitted. And more than a thousand men—the French newspapers set the number at two thousand—were transported in lorries which took them to parts unknown. They disappeared forever. In 40 hours the camp lost nearly a quarter of its inhabitants. Throughout those 40 hours, the Israelis would have been following what was happening through their binoculars, from their posts overlooking the roofs of the three adjacent buildings. One of their officers would later testify, "We were watching like theater-goers with front-row seats."

The Israeli government would find it necessary to issue a press release exonerating Israel of responsibility for what had happened. The statement was published as a paid advertisement in the *New York Times* and the *Washington Post*, under the headline, "Blood Libel":

> On the New Year (Rosh Hashana), a blood libel was leveled against the Jewish state, its government, and the Israeli Defense Force (IDF).
>
> In an area where there was no position of the Israeli army, a Lebanese unit entered a

refugee camp in order to apprehend terrorists hiding there. This unit caused many casualties to innocent civilians. We state this fact with deep grief and regret.

As soon as the IDF learned of the tragic events, Israeli soldiers put an end to the slaughter, and forced the Lebanese unit to evacuate the camp.

The civilian population of the camp gave clear expression of its gratitude for the act of salvation by the IDF.

Any direct or implicit accusation that the IDF bears any blame whatsoever for this human tragedy is entirely baseless and without foundation. The Government of Israel rejects such accusations with the contempt they deserve.

In fact, without the intervention of the IDF there would have been much greater loss of life. It should be noted that for two days and nights the IDF carried out actions against terrorists in West Beirut and no complaint whatsoever was voiced concerning civilian casualties.

It is now clear that the PLO cynically violated the evacuation agreement. They left behind 2,000 terrorists; they concealed heavy weapons—artillery, tanks, and mortars—and immense quantities of ammunition.

They did this in order that West Beirut should continue to be a center for PLO terror against Israel and other free nations.

The people of Israel are proud of the IDF's ethics and respect for human life. These are the traditional Jewish values on which we have educated generations of Israeli fighters and we will continue to do so.

We call upon free men of good will to unite with Israel in its struggle for truth, in its fight against international terrorism, spearheaded by the PLO, and in its quest for security, peace, and justice.

"The white man's burden," once again! The Israeli Army (the Defense Force, so they call it) is a rescuing army. "The Israeli Army's arrival (in Beirut) brought peace and security, and prevented a slaughter to which the Palestinian residents of West Beirut were vulnerable." Sharon to Draper, the American envoy. "Our arrival in Beirut prevented a disaster." Chief of Staff Rafael Eitan, to the Israeli Press. The classic occupation scenario wasn't enough: they also had to posit an ethical image of themselves. Perhaps the need for this was all the greater because they were Jews, carrying the legacy of the victim in search of justice. It was essential that the mirror reflect the righteousness and noble character of the face. The familiar old face. It would be a catastrophe if a sudden glint of light should fall upon the mirror and the face should fail to recognize itself, alarming its owner or causing him to turn his back or reach out to break the mirror because it was contemptible, a liar. In the Knesset, Sharon declared, "Any attempt to link this unfortunate episode with our army, including the call for a commission of inquiry, is madness, and violates the rights of the Israeli Defense Force, those in charge of it, and the whole nation of Israel." You could say that this statement was to be expected, since Sharon was the minister of defense, the one most directly responsible for the destruction of Lebanon, the invasion of Beirut, and the massacres of Sabra and Shatila, so of course he would defend himself and the military authority he commanded. But this takes on a deeper meaning in light of what Israelis wrote in their condemnation of the massacre. A soldier said, "Seeing the piles of corpses in the camps of Beirut made me ashamed, for the first time, of my association with the Israeli army." A journalist said, "This butchery made the Lebanese war the greatest disaster to befall the Jewish people since the Holocaust." A writer said, "Mr. Begin, in one stroke you lost millions of Jewish children who were all you possessed on this earth. The children of Auschwitz no longer belong to you. You have wasted them. You sold them for nothing." They were all able to condemn the slaughter—perhaps it made it easier for them that the hands that committed it were not Israeli, and that the invasion was of a neighboring land called Lebanon. As for the original sin that had enabled them to establish their state, this was what the mirror could not bear—here the mirror must keep its counsel, or at least admit a few dark spots, if it dared go to such lengths. Few were the Jews who were able to cry out like the child in Hans Christian Andersen's story, and reveal that the emperor strutting in his imagined finery was actually naked. This was what the American Jewish writer Noam Chomsky would put his finger on when he described Elie Wiesel as a "terrible fraud"—for Wiesel, winner of the Nobel Prize as well as several other international prizes, who wrote volumes against silence and described in detail the ordeal of the Jews in the Holocaust, of which he himself was a survivor, did not see the contradiction in his own total silence in the face of what was happening to the Palestinians, or in his affiliation and his work, in the 1940s, with the Irgun, of all the Zionist organizations the most racist and the most guilty of terrorism. Hundreds of Jewish intellectuals would hold fast to the notion of the ethical legacy of the Jews. They would go on referring to their ancient identity, disregarding the newest ingredient of the word "Jew": an ingredient created out of Deir Yassin, Bahr al-Baqar, by the breaking of bones, by Qana: a newly forged identity, which the mirror could not afford to reflect, except as a blank.

Five years ago in Cordova, at the entrance to the Great Mosque, I saw an Israeli man and his wife, and although I don't understand Hebrew it appeared to me that they were quarrelling. I wondered whether the ugliness that showed in their faces was a projection of my own feelings toward them, or whether they actually were that ugly: features combining the coarse and the sour and something else equally repellant that I can't put my finger on. Within the mosque-church, I saw a whole group of Israeli tourists, none of them quarrelling—they were listening to a tour guide. I watched them for a few moments, then moved away. No, it wasn't just my sense of injustice: there was something in their faces, their movements, the look in their eyes—what was it? Perhaps it was this mirror, perhaps it was the lie or the betrayal of the ancient vision of justice juxtaposed against the specious claim that it still existed. Or perhaps it was something else. I remember now an essay by Jean Genet, "Four Hours in Shatila," which I had translated from French into Arabic in collaboration with Dr. Amina Rashid in 1983. Genet says:

> Before the Algerian War, in France, the Arabs were not beautiful, for they tended to be awkward and slow-moving, their facial features uneven. Then almost at once victory made them beautiful. But even before that, a little before victory became such a resplendent thing, when more than half a million French soldiers were falling and dying in the Aurès and throughout Algeria, it was possible to observe a curious phenomenon at work upon the faces and bodies of the Arab workers: something like the advent, the presentiment of a beauty that was still fragile but was going to dazzle us once the scales at last fell from their skin and from our eyes. We had to accept the evidence: that they were politically liberated so as to appear the way we must see them—very beautiful. Just so the freedom fighters, having escaped the refugee camps, from the law and order of the camps imposed by the need to survive, and having at the same time escaped from shame, were very beauti-

189

ful. And since this beauty was new, which is to say unspoiled—in other words, innocent—it was fresh, of such vitality that it at once discovered what placed it in harmony with all the beauties of the world, delivering itself from shame.

At first glance, what Genet says seems like simply a rhetorical expression of his own partiality toward and affection for the Algerian rebels and the members of the Palestinian resistance. But I think that his words constitute a universal human axiom. Some 70 years before Genet, the Irish poet Yeats observed the same phenomenon when he wrote his famous poem on the uprising of 1916: these were ordinary people, whom he knew—that man a lout, a drunk, this woman shrill, a public scold; they are borne along on the course of daily life, partaking of its "casual comedy." Then all at once the poem tells us, "A terrible beauty is born." Seized by a vehement love, they make ready; their hearts are "enchanted to a stone/ To trouble the living stream"; they are killed, "All changed, changed utterly/ A terrible beauty is born." This beauty that Genet saw, and likewise Yeats before him, is opposed by an ugliness caused by connivance and lies. It is as if the mirror rebels against the silence imposed upon it, and so it leaves to the face, the expression, the movement of the body, and the rhythm of speech the task of exposing that corrupt thing within, which once upon a time was blooming and vital and innocent, but is so no more.

Fourteen

Tamim told me, while I was discussing with him the significance that *ka* and *ba* held for the ancient Egyptians, that the Arabs, in pre-Islamic and early Islamic times, believed that the spirit of one who was murdered became a bird that hovered around its family crying, Give me to drink, give me to drink," until the family exacted vengeance for the killing. "The Arabs," Tamim said, called this bird *al-hama*—that is, "crown bird"—perhaps because of their belief that it emerged from the head of the murder victim. The bird might also be referred to by a term, *al-sada*, that could mean either "echo" or "thirst."

I checked *The Encyclopedia of Animal Life*, by al-Damiri, which confirmed for me the accuracy of what Tamim had said. I learned that *al-hama* or *al-sada* was a reference to the male owl, one of those nocturnal birds that leave their nests only at night. It has associations, in some tales, with a murder victim, but in other stories is not restricted to this context. According to al-Damiri: "The Arabs maintain that if a person dies or is killed his soul takes on the image of a bird that cries over the grave, bewailing the loss of its human body." The expression "the flight of *al-hama*" recurs in some verses of ancient poetry, linking decapitation with allusions to birds. I also learned that *al-buwwa* is a name used to refer to a smaller type of owl.

We found it arresting, the resemblance between this belief and the interpretation of "the spirit," or *ba* according to the ancient Egyptians, who represented it in the form of a bird with a human head, and sometimes human arms as well. This *ba* accompanied its owner to the grave, but did not remain confined with him; rather it migrated freely between the grave and the world of the living, visiting the family of the dead person or the places he had frequented, satisfying its need to eat, drink, and mate in the daytime, and returning at night to its master's grave, where it would be united with his body in order to secure its immortality.

I became acquainted with the *ba* while searching for the meaning of *ka*, and I discovered that references to the one were always associated with references to the other, sometimes occurring within discussions of the ancient Egyptians' conception of the human personality. I didn't find what I was looking for, but I learned a few things —for instance, that human personality consists of five parts: its body, its *ka*, its *ba*, its name, and its shadow. It does not seem as though the conclusions we have reached, or what the scholars have discovered up to this point, allow for a complete understanding of these categories, perhaps because we have no corresponding concepts. And unfortunately the meaning of *ka*, which is what I had been looking for, remains for the most part obscure, a source of confusion.

Some of the ancient reliefs represent one Pharaoh or another with an analogous figure behind him. Perhaps these reliefs are what account for the translation of *ka*, in early studies, with the Arabic word for "double," *qarin*. Khnum, the god of creation, has a rotating wheel like that of a potter, his tool for fashioning human beings. He uses this wheel to create two corresponding forms: the body of the newborn, and his *ka*, which will accompany him from the day of his birth until after his death. During his life, a person is "master of his ka, coming and going with it," though it remains unseen. The *ka* has the characteristics and physical features of the person, with the same height and girth, the same walk and way of laughing, and wears similar clothing. It might leave the person when he sleeps, to go wandering here or there, during which time it might meet and converse with other *ka*s. In contrast to the *ba*, which takes the form of a bird, the *ka* is represented by two hands raised above the head, and this is because the god of the sun brought forth the world by spitting from his mouth the first married couple among the gods. He placed his arms behind them, so that his *ka* crowned them and flooded them with life. To each, then, his *ka*: god, king, and ordinary human being. Ra has fourteen and the Pharaoh has more than one, but every other human being has just one. It is born with him and it attends him during his lifetime, but when he dies it does not die with him. It accompanies him to the grave, and lives with his mummy or his funereal statue. The family members bring it food for its sustenance from among their own provisions, so that it might continue to live, for in its life rested the assurance of the resurrection and immortality of its master.

Some scholars interpret *ka* as a person's life force, his strength of spirit and his creative power, but what is strange is that the *ka* does not reside in the person's body, but in his name. The *ka* occupies the name, and the name embodies the *ka*. Some texts draw a connection between the *ka* and the name, which does not die away, despite the death of its owner. These texts point to those whose memory remains on earth even though they did not construct for themselves pyramids of copper or tombstones of iron. They left no progeny to inherit their legacy or bear and reiterate their names. Instead of all this they left their writings, their sacred and scholarly texts, to bear witness to the power of their *ka* and the perpetuation of their names even after their relatives were overwhelmed by forgetfulness, the priests overseeing their graves had died, and the graves themselves had been reduced to ruins.

I don't want to go into new details concerning the name, the shadow, and the relationship of each of these to the perplexing *ka*, about which I took to reading while writing this novel. Some have found it simplest to translate *ka* with the word *qarin*, but what is the meaning of *qarin*? I consulted *Lisan al-Arab*, and found that Ibn

Mandhour al-Misry had devoted thirteen pages to *qarana*, the root of *qarin*. There are dozens of meanings associated with the word and its derivations. Among these are "companion," "captive," and "prisoner of war." In the Hadith:

> The Prophet Mohammed is said to have passed by two persons tied to each other (*muqtaranayn*); he asked them, "Why are you tied to each other by a *qiran*?" and they said, "We have made a vow," meaning that they had pledged to be bound to each other by a cord.

And *qarn* is the cord that binds them... In holy writ: "And others bound in fetters (*muqranayn*)"... And *qarn* means "contemporary" with; you say, "He is of my *qarn*," in other words, "He is my age." Al-Asma°i said:

> One is *qarn*, who is alike in age, and *qirn*, who is alike in courage... And the *qaran* is the cord that yokes two camels... And he said:

> Tell Abou Masma°, if you should meet him,
> That I am at the door, like one bound in
>   fetters (*fi qaran*)

> ... And the *qarin* is your companion, who is as one with you... And the *qirn*, your equal in courage and in battle, and the *qarn* is a citadel, and its plural is *quroun*... And the *qaroun*, the *qarouna*, the *qarin*, and the *qarina*: the soul.

Is the *ka* the embodiment of the soul?

What is Shagar's position on all of this? And why do I want this novel to have the same title

that Shagar chose for her book on Deir Yassin?
The name is not an exact match. The title of her
book is *al-Atyaaf* (the specters), a definite noun.
For mine I've substituted *Atyaaf* (specters), with
no definite article. I close the sixth and final volume of *Lisan al-Arab*, where the word *qarana* is
located, and open the fourth volume to see what
else Ibn Mandhour might have to tell me. There
are five pages in which the meanings and etymol-
ogy of the root *Ta-wa-fa*—from which comes the
word *atyaaf* ("specters")—are explicated. From
this I quote the following:

Taafa bi-alqawm: "to move around and among
people... turn around and move away." And
someone *'aTaafa* something if he has surrounded
it; in the Holy Qur'an: "... *yuTaafu ʿalayhim*: they
will be surrounded by vessels of silver..." And it is
said: *'aTaafa bihi*, meaning "to hover around
[something]": and *'aTaafa bihi wa ʿalayhi*: "to
come to [someone] by night." And al-Farraa'
said: "*Taa'if* and *Taif* are the same, the shadow of
something that has possessed you"... And according to Mujahid's interpretation of holy writ:
"should a Satanic visitation (*Ta'if*) touch them,"
this means "Anger,"... and Abou Mansour said:
"The *Taif* in the speech of the Arabs means 'madness'... Anger has *Taif*, because the mind of
whomever anger has provoked wanders far, such
that it becomes like that of the lunatic whose reason is gone"... And *Taafa* in a place means, "to
make a circuit or a tour" of it; and *Tawwafa*: "to
go or travel in it"... And Abou Haitham said,
"The *Taa'if* is the servant who waits on you with

gentle solicitude"... And the *Taa'if* of something is a *part* of it... And the *Taai'fa* is a band of people, but the term may be applied to one person who is, so to say, in a class by himself.

And the *Tawf*: a piece of wood that is drawn through the water and may be ridden; its plural is *'aTwaaf*. Abou Mansour said, "That upon which one crosses the great rivers, composed of cane and reeds, one held tight upon the other, then secured with strips of cloth, so as to keep it from falling apart, after which it may be boarded and the crossing made."

And the *Tuufaan*: the water that spreads everywhere; it has been called "the torrential rain that in its profusion floods the land," and the *Tuufaan* has been called "the great death." And in the Prophet's Hadith, related by his youngest wife Aisha, "The *Tuufaan* is death." And it has been said that the *Tuufaan* is anything that is copious, that surrounds and encircles all, such as an inundation that overwhelms many cities. And widespread killing, sweeping devastation may be called *Tuufaan*... likewise the overpowering blackness of night.

Under *Taif* Ibn Mandhour writes, "*Taif* is an apparition that comes in sleep... And *'aTaafa*, in language, is to be comprehensive; and *Taif* is the imagination itself.

I don't think Shagar made any reference to *Lisan al-Arab*. The typewritten manuscript bears the title *Deir Yassin: Investigation Concerning a Massacre*. But on that morning, as she sipped her coffee before going out to meet with the publisher, she changed the title to *Al-Atyaaf: The Story of Deir Yassin*. Was the reason for this that Aziza, Naziha, and Basma Zahran had come to her in a dream the night before? Or was she making a connection, consciously or unconsciously, between the night visitors and another journey that had long preoccupied her in her youth, at the crossing of a shrouded underground river from one bank to the other?

Fifteen

What is Shagar doing? She is writing a history book. The words do not match up. They lie. How is she to interpret the voices and images that have pursued her—the words of Hayat al-Belbeysi, Basma Zahran's headscarf, and Omar? He came to her in a dream. He wasn't a two-year-old boy, but full-grown, like her. "The dead don't grow up," murmurs Shagar. The elevator is out of order. She descends the stairs she has climbed to the department that handles imported audiovisual material at the Ministry of Culture. They check the tapes carefully. On the ninth floor of a building on Kasr al-Aini Street, they are handed over to her. She signs for them. She writes to friends she knows well, and to others of whom she knows only their name and occupation. The postman brings her photocopied documents or a book or a chapter from a book. A page from a newspaper comes to her by fax, one a handwritten testimonial, another typewritten: their words have been translated into Standard Arabic. Why? The audiotapes: the transcript of their words is in their everyday vernacular—she clutches these more eagerly.

It's a curious business, Shagar. You pursue the specters. You bring them home. You listen. You haven't yet given yourself up to old age, Shagar. Have you become your own great grandmother, harboring their speech in your breast, or recounting some small part of it to the children gathered at the dinner table?

She descends the stairs. She goes home. She listens. Helpless lambs facing the butcher's knife? That is a lie:

We formed an emergency council to organize our defense of the village. We set up fortifications. We organized a night watch: we took it in shifts to stand guard—from 6 o'clock in the evening until midnight, and from midnight until 6 o'clock in the morning. We dug trenches at the entrance to the village from the eastern side, toward Givat Sha'ul. We brought large rocks from the quarries. We blockaded the road that led to the school. We assigned to Ali Qasim, one of the early freedom fighters in the 1936 uprising, and Salah Abed, who had worked with the British border patrol, the task of training our young men. We sent a contingent of them to Egypt to buy weapons. They went, and came back with twenty-five rifles and two Sten submachine guns.

Khalil Sammour

The price of a rifle went to 55 pounds, equivalent to the monthly salary of the higher-ups in the Arab mandated government. The price of one cartridge of rifle ammunition (five shots) was 50 piasters, the equivalent of a whole day's wages for an ordinary Arab worker. The women of the village donated their jewelry for the purchase of arms.

Hussein Atiyya

I took a thousand Palestinian pounds with me to Egypt. I contacted the brokers, and they took me to Mansoura. I bought five rifles with ammunition. The Egyptian secret service arrested me. They confiscated the weapons and ammunition. I was released following calls to the leadership of the Egyptian army, and the army undertook the transfer of arms, which were delivered to me in Rafah. I put them in the box of a truck carrying produce to Jerusalem, and from there to Ain Karem, and from Ain Karem to Deir Yassin on the backs of mules and donkeys. I delivered them on Sunday, April 4, 1948.

They came back from Egypt. Battles were raging in al-Castal. Children were able to follow their ups and downs from the rooftops of the houses. Al-Castal fell. We tried to regain it. Reinforcements for the Jewish attackers arrived from the Haganah. They surrounded us. Tuesday the sixth of April al-Castal sent out for help from the neighboring villages. Twelve youths from Deir Yassin set out to take part in the defense of al-Castal.

Israeli officer Uzi Narkis

I reached al-Castal on Thursday, April 8 to supply the forces with provisions and ammunition. I asked if everything was going well. They told me that conditions were excellent and spirits were high. We had forced the Arabs to withdraw without any losses on our side, but there was one casualty on the other side. I went to check it out. I still remember this body: stretched out on its belly in a field, wearing a light-brown outfit. We didn't know whose body it was, but he had a copy of the Qur'an with him. I took the Qur'an and left.

Zaynab Atiyya (Umm Salah)

When the young men of our town went to al-Castal, we sang for the freedom fighters, and we were overjoyed by the news of the victory of Abdel Qadir al-Husseini. We only found out that he had been martyred, and that al-Castal had fallen, from one of our own boys by the name of Yusuf Ahmed Alia. He told us, "Just as you sang, you'll weep—not tears, but blood."

Hajj Mohammed Mahmoud Asaad

We were surprised by the news that Abdel Qadir al-Husseini had fallen... The elders of the village assembled the youths and the men who bore arms... They were distributed around the most important positions in the village, particularly the eastern gate, which bordered the settlements of Givat Sha'ul, Montefiore, Beit Hakerem, and Beit Vegan.

Umm Eid

Thursday night my husband Mohammed Eid heard the announcement of Abdel Qadir al-Husseini's death via transistor radio. He took a bath and went to bed. I went to take the kerosene stove outside after cleaning it, but at the threshold I sensed a movement and I was afraid. I ran back inside the house. I banged hard on the door and woke my husband. He calmed me down. I nursed the baby and went to sleep.

Aziza Ismail Atiyya

I didn't sleep. From the roof of our house I saw people gathering in Givat Sha'ul. My husband wasn't at home—he was with his brother Ahmad at the guard post at the quarries, by the eastern entryways to the village. The children were sleeping. I couldn't sleep. I picked up the baking tray, locked the sleeping children in the house, and headed for the village's central oven. It was about two in the morning.

Umm Aziz

No one slept that night... I went with several women of the neighborhood, as was our habit, all of us bringing dough to bake our bread at the communal oven. I baked the first batch of seven loaves. I put the second batch, seven more loaves, in the oven. They stayed inside the oven. I didn't take them out.

Ismail Mohammed Atiyya

At 2:30 in the morning I saw searchlights, from vehicles that were coming and going from the settlements, across from our house, which overlooked the valley and the open space to the southeast of the village. We went to the main road to investigate. The movement stopped. All seemed calm, the darkness total. We went back to the central guard station in front of our house.

Hussein Atiyya

We heard footfalls coming from a northeasterly direction. We were standing on a hill overlooking the main road, in the direction of Givat Sha'ul. The movement stopped and silence fell. Then we heard gunshots behind us in the center of the village, at the guard post of our cousin Ismail Atiyya and his son Mahmoud.

Hajj Mohammed Mahmoud Asaad

At 3:30 we heard gunshots and the voice of Ismail Atiyya shouting, "My fellow villagers, the Jews have attacked us, the Jews have attacked us!"

Hussein Atiyya

Immediately afterwards a second Jewish group came at us from the north, from the area of the school. The battle started between us and them, with skirmishes in the neighborhoods central to the village. We moved to Hajj Ahmad Radwan's house, which overlooked the east gate of the village. We assembled on the roof of the house. We saw an Israeli armored vehicle approaching with ten fighters behind it, then another group of attackers catching up to them.

Ezra Yakhin, the Israeli officer in charge of escorting the armored car

The car hit a ditch. We had to fill it in before we could resume our progress. Then we encountered another ditch, and at the entrance to the village was yet a third. We decided that there was no point in continuing.

Abou Tawfiq al-Yasini

They kept coming until they reached the school, where we had piled a lot of rocks, so that they couldn't advance any farther. One of them left the vehicle and started picking up the rocks. One of our boys took aim and hit him. His comrades drew him under the vehicle and then pulled him inside.

Abou Mahmoud

They operated a megaphone from the armored car that was stuck in the trench. They tried to intimidate us so that we would leave the village and run away. The megaphone started repeating, "Give up the fight, withdraw! Throw down your weapons and run for your lives!"

Jumaa Zahran

I left the house for the dawn prayer around four o'clock. I heard a popping sound, but I didn't know where it was coming from because of the darkness. The weather was cloudy, and a drizzle of rain had started. When the battle started, at around five o'clock, I was unarmed, because the weapons were with my father Hajj Mohammed, my brother Ali, and my nephew Mohammed Mousa. After the first exchange of gunfire, my father was killed. I took an Italian rifle from him. I was surprised by some Jews in front of our houses, so I took up a position behind the wall and started shooting. I was set on by one of the attackers who wanted to take my rifle. We fought hand-to-hand—I got the upper hand, and shot and wounded him. He aimed a hail of bullets at me, but I withdrew to the high ground in the western part of the village. The combatants from the village were assembled there. After that I didn't see any member of my immediate or extended family, or our house, ever again.

Abou Mahmoud

They threw a grenade into Zahran's house, which burned down the house and everyone inside it. Twenty-eight members of the family were killed on the spot.

Jumaa Zahran lost his wife Basma Asaad Radwan, and his five children: Fatima, Safiyya, Shafiqa, Fathi, and Rasmiya. The eldest of them was eight years old, the youngest not even a year.

Jumaa lost his father, Hajj Mohammed Zahran, his mother Fatima, and his father's wife Hamda.

Jumaa lost the wife of his elder brother Mousa and their four children.

Jumaa lost his younger brother Mohammed Zahran and his brother's son Mohammed Ali.

Jumaa lost the wife of his uncle Ahmad Zahran and their four children, the eldest of whom was ten, the youngest two.

Jumaa lost his cousin Mahmoud, a youth of eighteen.

Abou Yassin

I was thirteen, and we were asleep—my brothers and sisters and I, and our mother. My father was dead. We woke up in the middle of the night to the sound of gunfire and machine guns coming from all over. My brother went to see what was going on—he came back right away and got my siblings and me so we could make a run for it. My little sister was on my back, and the bullets were flying over our heads like rain. They got us to the Ain Karem road, but my mother and brother went back. The teacher Hayat al-Belbaysi was with us at the time. She stopped and said, "By God, I'm ashamed of myself. It's my duty to go back and help the wounded, at least." She went back—she didn't go the rest of the way.

The resistance began at the northeast gates of the village and at Hajj Ismail Atiyya's house, which overlooked the valley to the southeast. Hajj Ismail and his grandchildren managed to repel the group of attackers as they tried to storm the gate facing the valley. They were forced to retreat. Then this contingent of villagers threw themselves into the confrontation with the group advancing from the east.

The resistance formed up on the high ground to the west, which had a prospect on the whole village. Fire poured onto the attackers from four positions: from Ali Qasim's house at the westernmost point of the village, from Mahmoud Radwan's house, from the house of his brother Hassan Radwan to the northwest, and from Abou Ali Salah's house, the last of the village houses at its farthest point in the northwest quarter. (The resistance at this last house persisted until a Haganah unit arrived with two-inch mortars and leveled the house.)

Hajj Mohammed Mahmoud Asaad

Ali Qasim was able to drive off the group of attackers from the west before he was gravely wounded and taken to Ain Karem.

Hassan Radwan

I woke to the sound of gunshots and shouting, so I went out to investigate. I took a rifle from my neighbor's son. I stationed myself in front of the house, behind a wall looking out over the whole village, as well as the main road from Givat Sha'ul. My rifle was a British one that had been brought from Egypt, and it held five rounds. In my house were about 30 cartridges, the ammunition for which I had bought from here and there, sometimes from other villagers. At sunrise I saw the Jews coming from the east, from the Zahran family houses. It was about 5 o'clock. I started firing on them, and they returned fire... At about 7 o'clock I joined Jumaa Zahran and Khalil Sammour and his brothers Abdel Majid and Abdel Hamid.

At 7 o'clock in the morning the attackers sent for reinforcements, which came from Givat Sha'ul: weapons, ammunition, grenades, explosives, two units from the forces of the Haganah, and two mortars.

Reuven Greenberg, of the men of Etzel (Irgun)

The Arabs were fighting like lions. They were better, more accurate marksmen than we were. The Arab women were running from their houses under a hail of gunfire, collecting weapons from any of their fighters who had fallen, and taking them back to the houses.

Joshua Goldshmid, operations officer for Etzel
We thought of retreating. The resistance was strong, and we were unable to evacuate our wounded because of the heavy fire. I suggested that we concentrate our strength on attacking each house in force: bombard it with gunfire, and under cover of our firepower the explosives men could advance and detonate it.

Patchiah Zalivensky, leader of the Lehi forces (Stern Gang)
Each phalanx advanced on its target. We blew up the doors using sticks of gelignite. Then we tossed hand grenades into the houses and bombarded them with gunfire.

Mordechai Ra'anan, leader of Etzel in Jerusalem (participant in the attack):
At 11 o'clock we blasted the first house; 15 minutes later, the second house; and so on, a house every 15 minutes. We regarded each house as an independent fortress.

Kalman Rosenblatt (of the Haganah men who came later to help the attackers)
We threw grenades into the houses before we entered them.

David Gottlieb (member of Lehi)

The Haganah accomplished in an hour what we had been unable to manage in several hours. They had good weapons, and they were seasoned fighters.

Hajj Mohammed Mahmoud Asaad

At Ain Rawas, under an olive tree, there happened to be a number of soldiers of the Arab rescue army that had retreated from al-Castal. The villagers fleeing for their lives asked them to come to the aid of the village. They could hear the sound of machine-gun fire. Their reply: "We have no orders to intervene."

Zaynab Mohammed Ismail Atiyya (Umm Salah)

My father and my uncle took up a position on the roof of the house... They noticed that the soldiers were approaching Abul Abed Salah. He was performing the ablution in the courtyard of his house, which was across from ours. They warned him, and he ran to his daughter's house next door. But the soldiers fell upon it and killed everyone inside—27 people: Abul Abed Salah's daughter, her husband, her mother- and father-in-law, her husband's brothers, and their families... My father and grandfather fired in the direction of the soldiers, killing the squadron leader and some of the soldiers. They blasted our house with mortar fire, and killed my father and grandfather on the roof. They stormed the gate of the house and pounded on the door. I was hiding with my children and my younger brother Mousa. They said, "Open the door," but I didn't open it. They threw a grenade, wounding my daughter Mariam's feet. They entered the house. My brother Mousa, who was 13 years old—they dragged him by the hair to the courtyard and began kicking him. I took out 250 pounds from my bodice and offered it to one of them, begging him not to shoot my brother. He took the money with one hand and fired his gun with the other. Then they shouted in our faces, "Get out of here, you sons-of-bitches!" My daughter Mariam—she was three—when she saw the soldiers kill her Uncle Mousa, ran to my father's wife on the second floor. She found her slaughtered, so she ran to the third floor. She found her Uncle Mahmoud bleeding. He asked her for water... My mother, may she rest in peace, told me that Mahmoud and my father clung to life for three days.

Naziha Ahmed Asaad

They came into the house. Two men and a woman, all armed. They killed my Uncle Radwan. They put my grandmother, my brother Omar, and me in the chicken house, and went in the direction of the village. Omar was two, and I was eight. Grandma carried Omar on her back and took us through the olive groves so we could go to Aunt Basma at Zahran's house. We encountered one of the Jews. He shot my grandmother, and she fell to the ground. My brother Omar fell from her back. I ran to Aunt Basma's house. The whole courtyard was littered with bodies, and the door to the house had been burned, the smoke still rising. Aunt Basma was sprawled in the doorway, all around her the bodies of her daughters and my cousin Fathi, who was three years old. Under my aunt's head was a pool of blood. Her head was bare, her headscarf lying beside it. I heard a whimper from inside the house, and weeping from the other direction. I called out, and a voice answered, saying, "I'm Fatima." I recognized her, for she was my age, and we used to play together. "Who are you?" she asked me.

"I'm Naziha," I told her.

"Come to me, come inside," she said.

"I can't," I told her. "Your house is burned. You come out."

"I can't," she said. "My head is injured. There's blood. I can't walk."

I went back to my aunt and put my hand on her brow and her head. I caressed her. Then I found my hands and hair had blood on them. I was frightened, and ran to my grandmother. I lay down beside her and Omar, and fell asleep.

Niʿma Zahran (Umm Mohammed)

They set up the mortar at 2:30. The first bomb, the second bomb, the third bomb... The fourth—may you never experience any such thing—like fire and smoke. We didn't see them, and they didn't see us. He said, "Open up, you swine." I didn't open up. The fifth one hit, our house became like a furnace, and we couldn't see each other anymore. "Open up, you swine," he said. I said, "If I open up you'll kill the children." He said, "I won't kill anyone." Who could have the guts to go near the door? It was enough to turn our hair white. But I raised my hand to open the door. "You only die once," I said. He was afraid to come in. He said, "You swine, with your Mohammed this and that, and your religion, blah blah blah..."

They took us to my Uncle Moustafa's house and put us in there. I found Ahmad Asaad Jabir's wife, and said to her, "Show me my father's house." She said, "What are you going to see? They killed them, 27 bodies in a pile."

In the road we saw Abou Jabr and his son Khalil Rashidah, there on the road to my father's house, the three of them face-down in a heap... I said, "Cousin, take me to my father's house." She said, "Go where? If you go, you'll die, 27 bodies in a pile. A little girl in her bed, they killed her."

They put us in my Uncle Moustafa's house at 3 o'clock in the afternoon. They brought the white flag, started shooting, and burned the village to the ground. They put up white flags, they occupied the village. They brought diesel trucks, the big ones, from the village.

Jamila Ali (Umm Mohammed)

Before we left the village, we were detained there for three days. After the three days, they opened the door and let us out... They took us to the bus. When we got to the bus there was a pile of villagers who had been killed, more than a hundred of them—maybe 104 or 105 people piled one on top of another. The Jewish woman took my brother-in-law, killed him, and threw him on the heap.

There were 500 armed men at Ain Karem, but not one of them came to our village to help us. We went in the trucks. They brought us oranges and said, "We feel sorry for you, pigs, even though you would have slaughtered us without mercy." The trucks took us away.

… They took us to Mehna Yehuda. They kept opening up the flaps and talking about the slaughterhouse they were taking us to, the furnaces they were taking us to, to burn us. Others said we were going to Abou Jebba. We're supposed to know who Abou Jebba is? They handed us over to the National Committee there, and that's where they left us. We stayed in Jerusalem for a month.

Abou Tawfiq al-Yasini

They took 14 people to the quarries and shot them. I saw that with my own eyes.

They threw them into the well, the Jouza well. They raised their flag over Mahmoud Salah's house on the western heights of the village—some of them thought it was the mayor's house. They searched the houses thoroughly, hoping to find money or gold jewelry. They transported provisions. They herded the wandering livestock—the chickens, goats, and sheep—into the alleyways of the village and brought them to the Jewish neighborhoods of Jerusalem. Only one thing remained: burial of the dead.

Moshe Barzili (of Lehi)

Sunday afternoon: We poured three barrels of oil over 30 corpses in the main street of the village. After half an hour, we realized that this was impossible.

Shimon Monita (of Haganah)

We thought that the bodies would burn. But it's not possible to burn bodies in the open air. It was for this reason that the Nazis built special crematoria in which fires would burn at an extraordinarily high temperature.

Yehoshua Arieli, leader of the Youth Brigade, the Gadnaa

Tuesday morning: We buried approximately 70 bodies in a mass grave. We blew up two groups of houses in each of which there were about 20 bodies.

They brought them gloves, protective coats, face-masks.

They buried 40 men, women, and children from the lineage of Aqal: the families of Radwan, Atiya, and Zahran.

They buried 31 men, women, and children from the lineage of Shahada: members of the families of Sammour, Zaydan, Hamdan, and Abdallah.

They buried 11 men, women, and children from the lineage of Jabir.

They buried 9 men, women, and children from the lineage of Hamida.

Eight from Eid's household.

Six from Hussein's household.

They buried Abed, the baker, and his son, of Hebron.

They buried the teacher, Hayat al-Belbeysi, who reached the Ain Karem road, then stopped and said, "By God, I'm ashamed of myself. It's my duty to go back and help the wounded, at least." She went back—she didn't go the rest of the way.

Sixteen

The evidence? There is no evidence, other than what can be surmised. But does the answer come as quickly and immediately as this? And who decides: functionaries in some organization, working from their offices thousands of miles away, or a person who has become so agitated that he made this decision on his own and carried it out or else delegated the task to someone else?

She interrupts the progress of her thoughts, and reverses direction. An accident, merely one of a thousand fleeting incidents that could happen to anyone anywhere, that happen to one person but could just as easily have happened to someone else. But how to explain that look, then? An altogether ordinary man, his features melting into the crowd of the station, the escalators, the train platforms. Did he follow her when she got on the train?

She had sat on the edge of her seat, poised to get up at any moment, shifting her eyes between the map posted above the door, to the left of it, to the window on her right. The train stops, and she reads the name of the station on the sign.

The train moves. She waits for the next station. Has he been glancing at her from time to time? Perhaps. Their eyes met suddenly. He was disconcerted. She noticed it, and found it odd, but didn't give it much thought. She went back to following the progress of the stations. One last station, and then the train set off. She got up and waited by the exit. The train stopped, and she got off.

Her participation in the conference seemed a strange thing. One of her colleagues said to her, "It's like sticking your head in a hornets' nest. A conference on Martin Buber on the occasion of the 25th anniversary of his death. The attendees will be Zionists who claim to be leftist and progressive. In short: a pointless ordeal. What *is* the point?"

"It won't cost me anything except an hour on the train to Cambridge Friday evening and an hour back on Sunday."

"And the effort you put into research?"

"I already have things to say on the subject. I sent them the title and a 200-word abstract, and they sent me the invitation."

"God help you!"

What was he so afraid of? An academic conference. Papers and discussion, and then everyone goes his or her own way.

Friday evening, on the green. A long rectangular table with a white cloth. Glasses, drinks, academics. Small groups calmly form and re-form. This one talks to that one, and then a third joins them. Minutes pass, and the first one turns toward someone, goes to him, and they walk together toward another group. One of its number slips away and heads toward the drinks table, stopping on the way to exchange a word with one of his colleagues with whom he became acquainted last time, or another whom he is just now getting to know. "From Egypt! I've always dreamed of visiting Egypt!"

Saturday. Three sessions. Three panels. Papers on Buber in Germany: his intellectual background, his role in confronting Nazism, his socialist thinking.

Sunday. Three panels. Buber: religion and politics. The ethical component of Buber's Zionism. Buber and the Arabs of Palestine.

Shagar read her paper. The critical comments followed just as she had foreseen: she had failed to understand the Jewish problem. She had failed to understand Buber, the great Zionist thinker, who had struggled in the cause of granting equal rights to the Arabs in Israel. Accusations of anti-Semitism, of a failure of objectivity, of a fanatical nationalist agenda. "Professor Abdel Ghaffar, you wrote a book on Deir Yassin. Did you know that Buber condemned the massacre? He condemned the massacre!"

"I do know that, sir. In that respect, he was generous to us!"

The chair of the panel intervened. "Please, let us not have interruptions. We'll give you a chance to comment, Professor Abdel Ghaffar!"

The chair gave her the floor. "Just five minutes," he said.

"Thank you—I don't need more than a minute. In Buber's work can be found every kind of colonialist discourse: the sacred mission of a chosen people spreading the light of civilization in a primitive desert; he deigns to allow the presence of its inhabitants to be taken into consideration. At all events, I am happy and honored to identify with Gandhi in this matter, albeit in a failed vision of the question of Palestine. Thank you."

What had possessed her to participate in the conference? Rancor is unacceptable grounds for an academic undertaking. Publication of her paper through the proceedings of the conference? Its publication in a specialized journal was a foregone conclusion already, without her having had to put herself to the trouble of attending this event. She could not come up with a persuasive answer. She turned off the television, made a cup of coffee, and sat down at her desk. She translated Gandhi's letter. The following day she picked up the work again, and translated Buber's response. A week later, she had completed the translation of both texts, and reviewed the draft of her paper in Arabic. She put the document in an envelope, sent it to Yusuf, in Cairo, authorizing him to publish it in a booklet. An answer to her question came to her only when she was returning from the post office. "Strange," Shagar murmured, "doing this or that you think you're being impulsive, and then you discover that your behavior is consistent, that there is a method to your actions, even though you weren't aware of it." The writing project on Buber and Gandhi, postponed for years, suddenly imposed itself. Because of the conference? The conference was only a prop. It was a response—both implicit and overt—to the chant that rose up around the culture of peace and the idea of a binational state as a solution to the problem of Palestine. Nothing new. Ideas set out by Buber 60 years ago. They didn't deceive that skinny, bare-chested, shaven-headed Indian, with his high-quality prescription glasses that enabled him to see from there, from distant India, what eluded some of the educated Arabs who stood just meters from the line of fire. In November 1938 Gandhi wrote:

> Palestine belongs to the Arabs in the same sense that England belongs to the English or France to the French... Surely it would be a crime against humanity to reduce the proud Arabs so that Palestine can be handed over to the Jews partly or wholly as their national home.

> The nobler course would be to insist on a just treatment of the Jews wherever they are born and bred. The Jews born in France are French in precisely the same sense that Christians born in France are French. If the Jews have no home but Palestine, will they relish the idea of being forced to leave the other parts of the world in which they are settled? Or do they want a double home where they can remain at will?

She jumped to Bayram:

Greetings to you and peace
From here to Judgment Day
For the miracles you performed
Long after the age of prophets had passed,
You who toy with your spinning wheel
And the stock market rises or crashes
Over London's head, as you spin
The fate of Lancashire of the spinners!
You, a sage whose utterances ever come true
Your philosophy's all in your loom
And in your disciples all around you
Hard at work with their shuttles.
The English live pleasurably

In the glory of their fleet,
And with a black nanny-goat, four years old
Their glory you defeat.

An Englishwoman passing by was staring at her in astonishment. Shagar realized that she had been reciting the poem aloud—had she been shouting, gesticulating with her hands? She laughed. She made her way to a restaurant she knew, ate, left the restaurant. The sky was clear, and so was her mood. She sang an old Abdel Wahhab song. She remembered Sitt Gulsun and her insistent objections every time she heard Shagar sing. May she rest in peace. She had been right. "I sang badly out of tune—and loudly, too." The thought didn't restrain her. She kept on singing.

She covered the distance from the restaurant to her house in an hour. It was late, and there were few passersby. Nothing happened.

Some days later, a visit to Wimbledon. She doesn't know the place. The train. The man. She tried to remember his features, but all she remembered was his discomfiture when their eyes met. No, not the discomfiture of a man whose gaze suddenly connects with that of a woman at whom he has been glancing furtively. Some other kind of unease that she doesn't understand. She got off the train, and then there was the station. On the main boulevard she turned right, as her friends had instructed her to do. She passed through an intersection, then another, and at the third one she found a small sign bearing the name of the street. She was almost there. She turned right into the street. A few more steps. It seemed as though a stone had fallen on her. She fell to the ground. Would more stones fall on her, or was someone going to beat her up? But why?

Shagar had not met Naji al-Ali. She didn't know, as she entered the street where her friends lived in Wimbledon, that Naji's house—now the home of Widad, his widow, and his four children, Khalid, Layal, Judi, and Usama—was in the same street, just a few paces from the place where she was headed. If Widad had been at that moment on her way to the train station or the supermarket on the main boulevard, she would have heard Shagar's cry. If Usama had been on his way home from school, he would have seen her laid out on the pavement, seen the ambulance pull up, and he would have run to his mother and burst in on her panting, "Mama, there's a woman up the road, they hit her, she's badly hurt, I saw her, Mama, collapsed on the ground, and the ambulance came and they took her to the hospital!"

Widad would murmur, "Oh, my God!"

Usama would not notice his mother's voice, strange, as if it came from down a deep, dark well. He wouldn't notice the sudden pallor of her face. He would rush upstairs, where he would stop all at once, lost, as if he didn't know whether his room was to the right or the left, or whether he wanted to go into the bathroom or into his room. He would head back downstairs at a run. "Mama, where's Khalid?"

"At the university."

He would enter the living room and sit down. Then he would get up, go back to his mother.

"Is Khalid going to be late?"

"Do you want to eat?"

"I'm not hungry."

None of this happened, but now, as I write about Shagar, I imagine it happening because I know Widad and Usama. I know the kitchen, the stairs, Usama's room, and the living room and Naji's sketches hung upon its walls. I know their house, the street, the Wimbledon train station. But why did I make this neighborhood the stage for the attack on Shagar?

Shagar is now sprawled upon the ground. She doesn't hear the intermittent wail of the ambulance's siren. It pulls up and stops. Two people get out of it, one of whom examines her. The other returns to the rear of the vehicle and comes back with a stretcher, upon which they lift her up. The swaying of the vehicle, the discontinuous siren, the light flashing on and off. The searing pain in her right leg. Did she drop a pot of boiling tea on her leg? Was she making herself a pot of tea? When? The pain in her head. She tries to remember. She loses consciousness.

On the plane that took her back to Cairo after the nine months she had spent living in England, Shagar said to herself, "The reckoning of wins and losses: the draft of a book on 1956 for which British documents were needed, a research project ('Gandhi versus Buber'), new friends, a damaged leg, and a crutch."

It wasn't an exact reckoning. She returned to find Karim not Karim. This, too, must be entered in the "losses" column.

Seventeen

When *Granada* was published, more than one critic inferred a connection between it and Palestine; there were some who thought I had drawn a parallel between the fall of Andalusia and the loss of Palestine. I was surprised by this analogy, which had never once occurred to me throughout the period in which I was composing the work. To a question put to me by a journalist I replied, "When I am able to write about Palestine I'll write about it, and I don't think I'll need to go back 500 years to do it. Moreover, I haven't conceded the loss of Palestine, and emotionally I cannot get to it by way of Granada." Then I surprised the journalist by telling him that *Granada* was a correlative of my fear throughout the Gulf War. And I meant it.

But, as I was researching Deir Yassin in order to write about Shagar and her book, *The Specters*, I realized that I was doing the same thing I had done when I wrote about Granada. In both cases, a map of the place was absolutely essential. An old map of Granada helped me locate the Rivers Darro and Shanil, Albayacin Hill and the opposite hill—where al-Hambra stands—as well as the Caesarea Market, Bibarambla Square... and so on. Studying this map, and later other maps, helped me to visualize the space which the characters of the novel inhabited, and within which they moved. I visited Granada twice after that, once at the end of the summer of 1993, after I had completed the first part of the trilogy, and then again at the beginning of the summer of 1994, two months after the publication of Part One, at which point I had completed only a few chapters of Part Two, *Maryama*.

I did not visit Deir Yassin—I have never had the chance to go to Palestine, but I referred to Walid al-Khalidi's two maps, which he had published in *Al-Hayat* along with his seven-article series, "Fifty Years after the Slaughter at Deir Yassin: A Village Confronts Zionist Organizations." The first map pinpoints the location of the village and the seven Jewish settlements surrounding it. Thick black arrows point to the four places from which the attack on the village was launched. The second map reconstructs the layout of the village homes, and identifies them with numbers that are cited in the article, such that the reader can refer to the map and know which were the homes of this family or that, and the positions and the movements of the defenders. In the course of repeated readings of the testimonials provided by al-Khalidi and others I obtained myself, I added to the existing map printed in black ink arrows in red and comments in blue, and these made it easier for me to follow, for example, the movement of Aziza Ismail Atiyya from her house on the western heights of the village to the communal oven: a red arrow and a comment in blue, "Aziza at 2 a.m."; or the movement of Hussein Atiyya at the first guard post (before dawn), after which he was barricaded with his comrades on the roof of Ahmed Asaad Radwan's house, from where he moved with his comrades, after they ran out of ammunition, to Mahmoud Radwan's house (also Aziza's house), and the one adjacent to it, that of Mahmoud's brother Hassan Radwan, where they continued the resistance.

I did all this without knowing exactly what I needed, or how to put this knowledge to work in my writing about Shagar and her book on Deir Yassin. But I was aware that I was doing something comparable to what I had done before when I was getting ready to write *Granada* (even though the characters in *Granada* were strictly from my imagination, while the characters from Deir Yassin were real, and some of them—those who delivered their own testimony—were still alive). I remembered what some commentators had written after the publication of *Granada*, the journalist's question, and my refutation. I felt unsettled, as now it seemed to me that matters were more complicated than I had thought. I wondered suddenly whether it is within the power of any of us to follow the threads that make up the fabric of his life. Take for example the woman weeping at the airport on that day in early February 1991.

Two weeks before that day—specifically, at 2 a.m. on January 17th, the telephone rings in her apartment in Budapest. Her husband's brother is calling from France to say, "The bombardment of Iraq has started—they're bombing Baghdad!" She wakes her husband and together they watch what every human being in possession of a television is watching: the CNN coverage; George Bush's speech, the newscasters' comments. Fair-haired Peter Arnett, and dark-haired Bernie Shaw. The woman and her husband hear Baghdad under fire compared to a huge Christmas tree. The newscaster—one or the other of them, she doesn't remember which one—says, "It's a magical, thrilling sight!"

This woman will not be able to return directly to Cairo, because most of the airlines have canceled their flights to the "Middle East region," as they call us. The plane bears her and her son northward to Switzerland, and then, after ten hours of waiting in the Zurich airport, south to Egypt. The woman doesn't cry in airports. Parting is heavy; she swallows it. It settles in her stomach like a ball of iron enclosed within the wall of her stomach and her clothes. She smiles, waves, says, "Goodbye!"

Her husband stands on one side of the divider, she stands with her son on the other. They call the passengers for boarding. Her husband holds out his hand to say goodbye, she clutches at his hand, beginning to weep. Weeping breaks into sobbing. Her husband entreats her to cancel her trip and go back home with him. "We can postpone the journey," he says. She shakes her head, dries her tears, and proceeds with her son onto the plane.

The woman is 44, but looks younger because of her face and small stature, despite the obvious gray in her hair. She usually appears self-possessed and strong, perhaps because of her profession, for she is a teacher, who stands in a great auditorium lecturing to hundreds of students at a time; or she might supervise a student preparing his doctoral degree, and stand up after the defense to announce to the audience that he has received his degree, and the student might be in his forties, with a wife and maybe some children who have come along to attend his defense. The job has aged her, or maybe tied her down, or educated her. It has trained her not to show a fragility that is her lot by heredity and natural disposition. The woman is afraid. As she bids her husband farewell, she does not realize she knows that, by the time she and her husband meet again, the war now raging will be over—with the United States victorious—and that, for decades to come, the fortunes of the region will be rearranged to its own disadvantage.

Am I oversimplifying? As I said before, who can separate the intertwined threads, who can separate fear of impending defeat from previous defeats? The woman weeps, quietly at first, but soon she is sobbing. She swallows her sobs, takes her son by the hand, they proceed together into the passageway leading to the plane. They sit, both fasten their seat belts, unfasten them. They rise, leave the plane, wait at the Zurich airport. They have lunch. They buy chocolate!

In Cairo, the woman goes to the university.

She returns home. She switches on the television and the radio at the same time. She tunes to one station after another searching for news. She hears the latest, and hears again what she has already heard.

She was sitting in front of the television. Was there a photo-documented broadcast being shown of the bombing of Baghdad, or were the images of Iraqi prisoners, or of interviews with American soldiers? Perhaps it was still shots of the Basra–Kuwait road: the destroyed vehicles, the corpses. She hadn't realized that these scenes would open up the doors of memory, letting out a flood of images unraveling all the way back to her roots: the bomber jets, the Egyptian soldiers in Sinai, Beirut Airport, the Palestinian camps, Beirut under siege, Sidon and Tyre and Nabatiya, and the region of al-Tuffah. An image floats up, of a naked woman walking dazed on a cold, cloudy morning, her bare feet wading through the mud in the street. Is it a presentiment of death? Her own?

She didn't realize that it was actually the harbinger of a new novel she was about to write. She continued with the academic year. The daily pressures of her work as chair of the department, which imposed upon her disagreeable administrative tasks she neither liked nor felt particularly skillful at, helped her to check her confusion and keep it under tight control. She seemed fine. In the summer, her father's illness grew worse, and then he died. In early fall, when negotiations between the Arabs and Israelis commenced in

Madrid, her composure dissolved utterly: she was unable to follow the first session, which was broadcast on television. She had not imagined that focusing her eyes and following some televised scene would require an effort, until that day, when she felt, after sitting in front of the television for five minutes, that she did not have the energy for it. She had hepatitis. Her mother looked after her for the three months during which she was confined to bed.

Writing *Granada*, followed by *Maryama* and *The Departure*, restored to the woman her balance, perhaps because the process of writing restored a will negated and paralyzed before the "desert storms," with their military equipment and their propaganda machines. She would write about people like her, who were living through a deadly moment in history, from which there was no escape. She would write the endings. But tackling history (familiarizing herself with it, and then knowing it) and the act of writing (beginning here and ending there, to create characters and time-frames and trajectories, to move quickly or slowly, establish a style and then substitute another one for it) gave her back her sense of mastery over her life, even if it was in a fictitious world.

She wrote about Granada, Valencia, and al-Pujarras. She didn't write about Cordova. Cordova was not part of the narrative. She visited it. Arab cities are so similar as to be nearly identical, sometimes: the great mosque set in its vast square, with the alleys and marketplaces around it. Al-Azhar in Cairo, the Umayyad Mosque in

Damascus, al-Zeitouna Mosque in Tunis, al-Fanaa Mosque in Marrakesh, and the mosque at Cordova. She wandered the old alleyways of the city, one passageway leading to another. Then suddenly: a great open space, ancient stone, a high wall, flocks of pigeons. The Grand Mosque. With the other visitors she passed through the Palm Gate into the exposed courtyard: the Court of Orange Trees. She stood in line, politely, calmly. Her turn came, and she bought a ticket for admission. The tourists around her had cameras slung from their shoulders. She went through a small side gate into the covered courtyard. She noticed the fragrance. She stared: a forest of columns, archways upon archways, muted light, and the fragrance. She observed that the passageways with open arches had long ago been filled in with stone, and thus converted to a wall dividing the inner courtyard of the mosque from the outer one—the open space planted with orange trees. The place had the architecture of mosques but the scent and dimness of churches. She went back to the columns, with their indeterminate color—pink? Not quite. A color that eludes names. Iron bars the height of the wall. She went closer. The treasures of the cathedral, constructed inside the mosque, were protected behind iron bars. The woman made for the nearest chair, and sat. She wept.

She left the mosque deciding to return to Madrid sooner than she had planned. In Madrid she waited for the departure time of her flight, oppressed by the burden of the hours. She wanted to go back to Cairo, to Egypt. How ironic! But a person cannot spend his whole life in direct confrontation with the harsh truth: hundreds of day-to-day minutiae at home, at work, among friends and family, cloud the picture, dim it, distract the eye, divert it from the naked reality, the deadly reality that appeared before her that day in Cordova. She went back to writing, but not about Cordova. Who would dare to write about Cordova?

I stop.

My writing is missing something, I say— Emile Habibi was brilliant, he knew how to make his reader laugh, and how to laugh himself, even in the process of conveying experiences that were mostly oppressive. Take for instance that extraordinary passage from his novel *The Secret Life of Saeed the Pessoptimist*, in which he conveys the experience of the Arabs dispossessed in 1948, who were forced to conceal their identities in order to survive on their own land, after the founding of the State of Israel. In the chapter "Saeed Changes into a Cat That Meows," Habibi writes that every time Saeed wants to tell his secret, the only thing that emerges from beneath his moustache is a mewling cat.

> Imagine your soul, after your death, entering a cat and this cat being resurrected and running around your house. Then imagine your son, whom you love so dearly, going out to play as all children do, and you calling him, meowing to him again and again, while he tells you again and again to shut up. Finally he throws a stone

at you. This makes you retreat, reciting to yourself the words of the great poet el-Mutanabbi in the gardens of Buwan in Persia: "In face, hand, and tongue a stranger.

That's how it's been for me for twenty years: meowing and whimpering so much that this idea of transmigration has become a reality in my mind. Whenever I see a cat, I feel uneasy, thinking that this might be my mother, may her soul rest in peace. So I smile at it, pet it, and even exchange meows with it.

Emile Habibi interweaves the comic with the tragic, wrapping tragedy in jests, his eye discerning various sorts of irony, no matter how harrowing the situation. I am not a satirical writer like him—what to do? But accuracy is one of the requirements of the act of writing, and to distill life down to an unmitigated tragedy is to risk dishonesty. For example, why did I not include the first part of Niᶜma Zahran's testimony? It has a curious air of superiority with respect to that man who came to hide in her house—he was afraid, and she wasn't. Her rage at this man sometimes even gets in the way of the story of the massacre. Fifteen minutes into the offensive, Niᶜma Zahran tells us, "I saw this shadow creeping up on me [she saw a man slinking toward her house]. He came up and said, 'The village is lost....' He shut the door and came in. The Jews came and started shooting at us... He said, 'Now they'll storm the house and start slaughtering us.' I was calm, not afraid, but he was so scared his hands were shaking. And when the Jew entered he asked, 'Who's that next to you—your husband?' I said, 'No!' 'One of your children?' I said, 'No! Look, mister, he's not my husband or a member of my household... he's not even a member of the *familia*!'"

Ni'ma Zahran wasn't laughing when she told this story, but Salwa laughed, and made us laugh, when she described her journey to the '48 territories after the '67 occupation and the opening of the borders between the occupied territories. The women of the village contracted with a driver who would convey them in his bus and take them on a tour of Palestine, now called Israel, to which they were forbidden entry. They boarded the bus and it started heading west. Imm Fakhri and Imm Atta sat next to each other. From time to time they treated each other to a pinch of snuff. Aziza drew a box from the pocket of her dress and offered it to her sister, who likewise reached for a box of her own and took it out.

"By God, sister Aziza, my snuff's better!"

"Just try these two pinches, sister Zarifa—there's none better than this!"

And each of them would put her thumb and forefinger into a box, take out a bit of the powder, and push it into her nose. Aziza would sneeze, and Zarifa would sneeze. Wisal would stand up abruptly, as if the sneezing had alerted her, and turn around to see her three children settled in the last seat of the bus. Seeing them there wasn't enough, though, so she would call out to them, "Bashir! Samir! Nabil! You boys all there?" She wouldn't wait for an answer to her question, but would face forward again and urge the driver, "Drive, man, drive!" It wasn't as if the driver had stopped, or the bus's only door (immediately to her right) had migrated to where her children were sitting. Who knew—this was the time of the Jews, and anything could happen!

The driver lost his way in the mountains, and found himself close to one of the settlements. He didn't dare get any closer. He stopped to ask directions. It was the cat, and not Wisal's children, that disappeared from the bus. The driver came back and made ready to set out again. But how could they set out without Abou Ammar? Everyone looked for him, under the seats, under the bus, in front of it and behind it. The cat's owner walked around calling him at the top of her lungs, "Abou Ammar... Abou Ammar!" The driver grew more anxious and said urgently, "Let the journey continue without incident, or the settlers will see us and fire on us!" At last the cat reappeared in much the same way he had vanished, so everyone settled down in their places. Imm Atta and Imm Fakhri went back to exchanging snuff, and Wisal went back to her sudden leaps from her seat and the inevitable query: "Bashir! Samir! Nabil! You boys all there?" She would see them with her very own eyes, turn to the driver, and say, "Drive, man, drive!"

A visit to Lake Tiberias wasn't on the itinerary, but the wishes of the older women prevailed. They said that the trip wouldn't be complete without a swim in Lake Tiberias.

Salwa chuckled as she told the tale of the old

woman's slip—a long one, of the type that fastened with a cord at the waist—which decided to swim off on its own. The woman tried to keep up, and when she couldn't manage it she had to content herself with watching its progress across the surface of the water. Maybe it was swimming to Syria!

Salwa didn't tell any more stories, because the '70s were not a time for telling stories; what, then, of the '80s—the latter part? Boys in the streets faced down the occupying army with stones and slingshots and old tires. And here was Wisal, running back and forth between her house and the prison and the military governor's post: one day because one of her sons is in jail and she's going to visit him; the next day because another has been arrested, and on the third day because a boy who threw a stone has come to her and she has given him a shirt different from the one the soldiers saw him wearing. "That's the one who threw a stone at us, the one wearing a red shirt."

"Mister, God knows without a doubt who is the boy wearing a red shirt who threw a stone at you. And here's a boy wearing a white shirt coming to visit his friend—what are you accusing *him* of?"

Then on a fourth occasion, because they raided her apartment and she got rid of her sons' documents by throwing them out the window: "The papers fell onto the soldier's head, it's true, and how was I to know they were standing under the window?" This time Wisal didn't run to the prison to visit one of her sons. But as she was herself on the way to jail, she still had it in her to tease the Israeli soldier. "I'm telling you, mister, you say a word to the warden and he'll bring me some of his biscuits. In the morning I like to dunk them in my tea with milk!" She recalled the look on his face and laughed.

Latifa, too, and Thurayya would laugh when they recalled stories of prison. Does a person laugh once the stress of the moment has passed, or does he laugh while in the midst of it, because laughter is such a strange, magical defense, which spills no blood but simultaneously protects and subverts the power relation between oppressor and oppressed?

I always wanted to write the story of Thurayya Habashi—Thurayya Shakir, whom we were accustomed to refer to as Thurayya Habashi, after her husband Fawzi Habashi. I listened to her one night in Hungary. She had come with her husband for a cure. I sat with her in her room at the hotel and listened to her story in all its detail. Years later Thurayya recorded part of the story in writing. She was arrested at dawn on March 28, 1959; they knocked on her door at 3 o'clock in the morning. They set about searching the house minutely, a process which took them two hours.

Then they told her, "Come with us, Mrs. Thurayya."

"Is this an arrest, or what?"

"No, we just need half an hour of your time, and you'll go home again."

"I went out and I didn't go back home until

exactly four years and four months later... I left three children: the eldest, Mamdouh, was eight; Hosam was six, while Nagwa was just a year old and still nursing."

Thurayya continues her story, "Our comrade Yvonne Habashi was imprisoned, and my children also have the name Habashi... I told this to the guard, so that she would help me, and she agreed. I was surprised at visiting time that the prison was entirely locked down. I escaped then to the lavatory and locked myself in, so that I'd be able to see the children when they came and entered Yvonne's room, because she was in the prison hospital... I looked and found that the whole place had been turned upside down in a matter of minutes. Officers came in and took over the room where Yvonne and the waiting visitors were... The children came, they had no idea... and there I was in the lavatory quaking with fear for them. The officer came to me in the lavatory and started pounding on the door, saying, come on out of there, Thurayya—I know you're in there, and I'm telling you, come on and see your children, missus, so I came out, but I was in a dreadful state, I was shouting, and saying that no one had any business touching them and that if anyone hurt them I'd drink his blood—and stuff like that, I don't know where it all came from... And then I hurled abuse at the guards. 'You can't do anything worse to me,' I told them. 'If they're not happy with you as the monkey you are, what are they supposed to do—make you into a gazelle?'

"I turned my attention to the children, hugging them fiercely. But what really bothered me was that the children were disturbed to see me in this abnormal state, shouting and cursing and hugging and kissing, all at once.

"About a week later I was surprised by a crew of military cops, in their red caps, who convened a court in the heart of the prison for 'the trial of Thurayya'... I was called, and I came from the cellblock, only to be startled by the arrangement of this trial. It's a scary thing—in fact the guard herself, as she was conducting me there, was shaking, saying to me, 'What did you do? They've turned everything upside down on your account.'

"I stood before them with my heart in my mouth—it was pounding so you could practically hear it across the room. I got hold of myself and asked for a chair to sit in, first of all. Then they started making their accusation against me and the long and the short of it was that I'd seen my children. Without knowing what I was doing I shouted in their faces, 'Aren't you ashamed of yourselves? All this uproar for what? To put on trial a mother who saw her children? Instead of prosecuting me, prosecute the unjust decisions that put a mother in prison without any cause, without at least permitting her to see her children and make sure they're all right. A mother who's committed adultery, a mother who's a murderer, or a drug dealer—any of them is permitted to see her children, but not me. And you come to put me on trial. Here I am, and I say I'll keep trying and trying and I won't shut up, and I'm telling you that right now.'

"I was beside myself, not knowing what I was saying or where all these words on my tongue came from, but every time someone addressed a word to me I answered him with twenty, until their boss shouted at me, Shut up!'

"I said to him, 'And why should I shut up? What are you going to do to me that's worse than prison? I don't think there's much you can do!"

Thurayya laughs as she recalls the story. Why? Because now that she's settled, between her children and her grandchildren, she's transcended all that happened? Does any of us have what it takes to transcend what happened? Does she laugh because she's a woman who laughs a lot? Because she has the gift of laughter and knows by temperament and experience just what its worth and value are?

Thurayya told about the day Intisar Khattab ate some documents and the notorious "day of dragging."

"Intisar was in charge of keeping documents—party papers, personal letters that had been smuggled in. Everything was written on Bafra papers—cigarette-rolling papers. Intisar put the papers in a tin can, a medicine canister. Then one time the warden and the superintendent entered unexpectedly and began a search. Intisar had hidden the medicine canister in her bosom, but before the search had been completed it fell out. Intisar snatched it and flew from the door of the cellblock to the prison yard. She ran, the guard at her heels. Intisar opened up the canister, swallowed what she could of the contents, and chewed up what she couldn't swallow. The commissioner was shouting, the warden was shouting, thinking Intisar was trying to commit suicide by swallowing pills.

"We laughed so hard we couldn't sleep."

And the day of dragging?

"It was only a few months after our arrest. We heard that Abdel Nasser had declared to a foreign journalist that there were no political prisoners in Egypt. I said, 'Then everything will be all right after all!' Fawzi was in prison in '48, when Moustafa al-Nahhas announced that there were no detention centers in Egypt; on the same day there was a general release of detainees, and Fawzi got out. I told my comrades what I thought, and we discussed the matter. We agreed that, after the morning lineup, we wouldn't head toward the door of the cellblock, but rather toward the prison administration—to the warden. We walked in on the warden, and Thurayya Adham said..." Here Thurayya Shakir smiled. "Because we had appointed her as official spokesperson, Thurayya Adham said that Gamal Abdel Nasser had announced that there were no political prisoners in Egypt, and she said we wouldn't return to the cellblock until a delegate from the presidency of the republic was brought in so that we could come to an understanding with him: either we were to be released, or they were to accede to our demands—we were demanding that prison conditions be improved, and that visitors be allowed, for these were entirely forbidden. The warden told us to calm down and go back to the cellblock, and he said he would inform the authorities of our demands. We refused. So the warden telephoned some official, and then we were surprised by the arrival of some armed soldiers who pointed their weapons at us, to intimidate us into returning to our cells. None of us moved. The prison door was locked down, and we heard the bugle sound. We found ourselves surrounded by the armed soldiers and another army of women prison guards, murderers, drug dealers.... For every one of us, three or four of them closed in, pulled us by the hair, and threw us down on the ground, beating and kicking the hell out of us, with their feet or with cudgels, leather straps, and canes. In the middle of this mayhem"—Thurayya laughs, she chortles—"I began to chant, 'Down with prison policies, down with the policies of lies and hypocrisy, down with the policies of oppression and terror!' I chanted, and we were dragged along the ground and flung one after another into the cellblock. But before the guard locked the door of the cellblock, Layla Shuᶜayb—who was petite, while the guard was tall and broad as a wall—pulled herself together, drew herself up, standing on tiptoe, raised her hand and, Wham! right on the guard's face. Later, when a delegation was sent to inspect the prison, including among its members Siza Nabrawi, they put us in rooms behind the prison. They locked us in and nailed up the windows. We shouted ourselves hoarse, but no one heard us."

Latifa al-Zayyat wasn't arrested in the campaign of 1959, for she had given up her partisan political work years before that. She was arrested in 1948, then again during Sadat's campaign in 1981. The times were changing, and we were making progress: internments didn't last four and a half years, but rather a few months, and women prisoners were not subjected to dragging and beating, or routine humiliation; also they were allowed to receive food from outside the prison, as well as some magazines and newspapers. In fairness, it must be said that the government strove for justice this time, for it didn't confine its arrests to Communists and Islamists alone, but distributed the arrests equally among all political groups, among Copts and Muslims, and men and women, and it gave everyone free publicity on the radio, on television, and in the front pages of the major national newspapers.

In my initial meetings with Latifa al-Zayyat, her laughter brought me up short. The woman was always surprising me with her continuous, sometimes abrupt, and loud laughter; and then she no longer surprised me—I got used to and grew to love both Latifa herself and her laughter. She was constantly laughing, but when she told me about her experience in prison, she laughed even more. In her autobiography, *Search Campaign: Personal Papers*, Latifa wrote about the dichotomy of incarceration and freedom, which for her was a lived experience, a part of her personal history. It was not merely an idea she was keen to explore because it concerned her; rather it was a thread—so she said—that gathered the vagaries of her own life and bound what had been to what was to come. To her this seemed a matter of life and death. She was so obsessed with it that she forgot laughter. She forgot it in the act of writing, but it was not absent from her oral narrative. Latifa al-Zayyat would laugh at herself and at her comrades in the cell as she told the story, so that the whole subject seemed like a comic play—no, not black comedy, despite the darkness of the experience, but rather a marvelous comedy that redeems the tale of stark realities by cleansing it of the blemish of fear, of bitterness, and of petty grudges. What remains is the lightness and transparency of the story, as well as the capacity of human beings to overcome adversity with humor.

Latifa, nearly 60, and full—not only in the figurative sense, but also in the literal sense of a body that has achieved its proper proportions— talked about prison. Her voice rose in a nonstop crescendo of staccato laughter. Her body shook and she got tears in her eyes, as she laughed and made us laugh, at herself, and at this one or that one of our women friends, who might have been sitting with us listening to her tales. She made fun of her own conduct, the sudden hysteria that overcame her because she couldn't find her dress, the one she had preserved with care, and safeguarded with every precaution, the dress that looked best on her... before the prosecution... for interrogation! "As if I had lost the jewel of my possessions!" I yelled and I argued, saying, 'Where did the dress go? Where's the dress? The dress has been stolen!' This hysteria infected the whole cell, and bedlam reigned, not because Egypt was lost, or Palestine, but because my dress had been stolen! It hadn't been stolen—I found it in its place. I had forgotten where I put it!

"Awatif joined us in the cell after they arrested her at the airport. She was wearing high-heeled shoes and a brown raincoat—she was perfectly elegant! She opened her bag and produced a tin of Swiss chocolate. She opened it: 'Please have some, doctor, have some, Amina...' It was as if we were paying her a visit to congratulate her on her son's marriage, and she was our hostess... in prison!

"When they called her for interrogation, she got all dressed up, went, and came back.

"'Is everything all right, Awatif?'

"'Oh, it's nothing—there's absolutely nothing to worry about.'

"'What sort of nothing?'

"Her face was relaxed and serene as could be. I said to her, 'All right, then—come sit down and tell us all about it, tell us everything from the beginning.'

"In the middle of all the talk, she said, 'The interrogator asked me whether I had attended an embassy party on such and such a day at such and such a time. I said, "I went—they invite me every year; there are university professors like me, journalists, diplomats, writers." You see, Dr. Latifa? Nothing at all.'

"'They didn't ask you anything else?'

"'No!'

"'Are you sure?'

"'They asked: "Were there military personnel?" I said, "There was a military attaché, and some others."'"

Latifa laughed and said, "I struck my own cheeks in despair!

"'What, doctor, what is it?'

"I said to her, 'How can there be nothing? They'll trump up charges against us that we're conspiring in favor of some other country!'

"Awatif was skeptical of this idea—maybe she thought I'd gone soft in the head. But of course what I said turned out to be right. They accused us of being collaborators. On the other hand, what would it matter if they called us 'The Case of the Apple'? Come on—an apple is an apple is an apple. If it were 'The Case of the Watermelon,' would it make any difference?"

Eighteen

And Karim? He didn't have the gift of laughter on that evening, or in the days that followed. He sat in the adjacent seat: his shirt buttoned all the way to the top, his skinny neck protruding from it, supporting the head held strenuously erect. His legs were pressed together, and likewise his arms, to the elbows, were held tightly against his trunk, then branched away from it like two sides of a triangle, ending at the hands with their interlaced fingers, planted upon his thighs. The way he sat, the boy appeared slender, with an elongated torso. He cut into space and made sure of it, carving out of it a domain for himself. Shagar gazed, trying to read his posture: had his shoulders shrunk, or did they seem smaller because they were drawn up so tightly? And the space between his eyes—how to read that? The lines of the face, unlike the lines in the palm of the hand, are a closed book. His eyes were open and like an abyss—how to read that?

Karim didn't laugh, didn't talk. Was it because the trial by fire he had just endured was still scorching his body? An affront, a thorn, too painful to retract? The successive beatings, the breaking of bones, the dogs, the torture by electric shock; one who has lost his mind, one who waits for release five years after the court's verdict that he is innocent. Karim didn't tell her anything about that. He was sitting, silent, and when he spoke, it was of other matters. Perhaps he wanted to protect her, and so he left her some latitude for a self-delusion that would permit her to say, "Karim was lucky—he wasn't subjected to what the others suffered!" He said he would tell her someday. Six months after he was released, he was arrested again.

"My God," Shagar murmured, "what kind of alternatives are these?" At the department meeting, she desperately defended Khalil. Was it for his intelligence and his exceptional talent that she liked him? Something else as well, something like attentiveness, an alertness of the spirit. He visited her in her office, borrowed some books from her; sometimes he would request permission to stay and discuss some subject or other with her. In the third year, Khalil replaced his usual attire with a short white *jilbab* and a skullcap. He let his beard grow, and the image was complete. She didn't comment—she minded her own business and left him to his. At the end of the year, and during the succeeding year as well, the boy achieved the highest marks—first in everything, across the board.

Before the department meeting, a colleague who veiled her head said, "Did you see Khalil? I talked to him about the *jilbab*, and I made it clear to him that it would be impossible for the university to give him an appointment if he let his beard grow and wore a *jilbab* and a skullcap. I talked to him at length, and—thank God—our Lord gave him guidance, and he listened to my advice." She was smiling now, proud of her accomplishment. "I saw him today at the college, and he was wearing a shirt and trousers. He kept the beard—that's it."

It was a stormy session. The professors were divided over nominating Khalil for appointment to a graduate fellowship and turning him down. The veiled colleague defended him, saying that he would settle down and come to his senses. We should send him on a foreign study assignment, to the United States or England, and he would outgrow all these childish things. Another colleague discussed the risk entailed in having Islamist types among the members of the teaching staff. The chair of the department said, "Naturally, Dr. Shagar is opposed to his appointment."

Was it the word "naturally" that provoked her, or had she already been annoyed by this whole discussion? It wasn't her habit to open a statement—any statement—with the word "naturally." She started with it. "Naturally, I am for his appointment. He is entitled to it. Academically he is the best of the graduates this year. From an intellectual point of view, he is a first-rate reader. He's also a gentle and decent young man."

The chair interrupted her. "And what about his tendencies?"

A colleague who was staring at her in astonishment said, "I took you for a person of secular inclinations, Dr. Shagar!"

She didn't answer him, but she offered up a defense of the boy's right to an appointment. He was appointed. He shaved his beard. He looked handsome and elegant, like a young film star.

Seven years. He didn't travel to study abroad, he didn't go to London or Paris or New York, whose pleasures might have damped his fires somewhat. Cairo schooled him as best it could.

Khalil got his Master's, then his doctorate. He became "the sharpest" of the instructors in the department, in the college, perhaps in the whole university. No one could get in his way. He was good at looking after his own interests. Shagar regarded him from a distance. She would have liked to know: was the germ implanted in him from the beginning, or did he pick it up from the streets of the city, with the result that he was thus blighted? What did you want, Shagar? Did you want him to keep his beard and skullcap and *jilbab*? To carry a gun and aim it at the right spot once, and the wrong one many times? To be persecuted or imprisoned, like Karim? Were there no other alternatives than these? While driving her car Shagar suddenly cried out, as if addressing someone in the passenger seat, "I want him to stay on the straight and narrow, not to be a hypocrite or a yes-man. Am I asking the impossible?"

"Khalil, I'd like a word with you." He sat down across from her, with the desk in between them. She said, "I'm angry with you."

He wasn't surprised. He gazed at her, and said, "I know."

"Do you know why?"

"I know."

"So what, then?"

"You've chosen to be beautiful, and to be defeated. I gave it a lot of thought, and then I decided that I didn't want to be defeated or persecuted."

"The easiest way out, and the most disgraceful!"

"You're oversimplifying, professor. A person chooses sometimes to work to change reality—this seems feasible to him. He bears the burdens of his choice, and there's no problem with that. I discovered that I don't have it in me to change the way things are, and I don't see that I have any power I might bring to bear for the sake of such change. In short, I found that the question was whether one was to be the wolf or the lamb. Better to eat than be eaten, I said."

"This is beside the point. I'm talking about personal integrity. You are not scrupulous in your conduct, Khalil—are you?"

He stared at her, smiling slightly. "What I said is not beside the point. You participated in the defense for both my Master's thesis and my doctoral dissertation, and in both cases you determined the value of my work."

"I'm not talking about your academic performance."

"I think about my academic performance at all times. It is what I will safeguard at any cost. I safeguard it and I rise, and I rise in order to safeguard it. I don't want to be like Gamal Hamdan, living alone and depressed, dying before his time. No, let me correct that: he died before he died. I will achieve academically, and guard that achievement by means of rank and power. Which is preferable, Dr. Shagar: for Gamal Hamdan to be the president of the university, or for his body to be discovered a few days after his death, the cause of which we don't know, whether it was suicide or a fatal isolation that overpowered him in the end?"

"You have to choose whether to be president of the university or Gamal Hamdan. Don't imagine that you can have it both ways."

He didn't reply. He said he was late for his lecture, and suggested that they continue the discussion at some other time.

She let him go. She went out and got into her car. "Why did I let him go?" she cried aloud. She got out of her car and went into the college. She went up to the department and looked at the schedule. She would knock on the door of his classroom and summon him from the lecture. She would seize him and teach him a lesson—with her cane, if need be. The old-fashioned style of upbringing? Why not? Necessity called for it. She knocked on the door and went in. "What is it, Dr. Shagar?" She looked at him, and looked at the youngsters seated before him. She mumbled something and left the room. It seemed to her as she headed once more for the college gate that she needed more than a cane to help her walk. She felt a profound fatigue, a desire to sit down and catch her breath.

Why had she not taken hold of the cane, brought it down on him, and beaten the living daylights out of him, until she succeeded in waking him up from his daydream? Why had she kept silent? Had he defeated her, or had she been defeated already, not having it in her but to watch the most beautiful of her children be stolen from her? Who was stealing them, and how? Were they babies, with no idea how to look after themselves? Yes, babies—infants! "Khalil is over thirty, you don't own him, no one owns anyone but himself. I'm his professor!" Shagar shouted, and then slammed her foot down on the brake. It was too late. Now she would have to get out of the car and deal with the problem. The traffic came to a halt, and the sound of car horns rose, before the driver accepted her apology and took the money to cover the cost of his broken taillight, which she had smashed when she ran into the back of his car.

The Faculty Council. Was there anything new? The senate was what it was: thirty professors around a table discussing their agenda, on the appointed day in the third week of every month. It was her habit to listen, to state her opinion calmly, to contain and restrain her outrage, so that all that would be apparent when she asked to speak was that she was expressing an opposing view, as is fitting at a respected council of distinguished professors. She would leave the meeting as if nothing had happened, get in her car, and leave. She would stop at the traffic light and see a driver in a car next to hers staring at her or laughing. She would realize that she was talking to herself. Once one of them made a comment: "Lunatics aren't allowed to drive—it's dangerous!"

"Go to hell," she replied.

She was fed up. She stood up, shouted at the top of her lungs. The dean said, "Calm down, Dr. Shagar." His words inflamed her further, and her voice rose still higher: "The issue is as plain as day, sir! The committee was formed for the defense of the dissertation. The two external examiners received the dissertation—both of them, not just one of them—and both of them told the supervisor that the dissertation wasn't good enough. They told him verbally, to save face and out of respect for collegiality. Instead of returning the dissertation to the student and asking him to make improvements to it, the supervisor went to the department meeting and said that the two professors had excused themselves because they were too busy, and he formed a new committee, which accepted the dissertation, discussed it, and passed it with First Honors. Does this make sense? What have we come to, doctor—what have we come to?"

The acting chair of the department intervened. "I do not accept what Dr. Shagar is saying with regard to our absent colleague. I do not accept this defamation of our department's academic credibility. You have no proof of what you are saying, Dr. Shagar!"

"This is what the two professors said. I heard about the matter, so I telephoned them. They assured me that after reading the dissertation they returned it, because it wasn't good enough."

"They did not write a report to this effect!"

Dr. Yusuf intervened. "Let's assume that they

erred in not writing a report documenting their rejection of the dissertation. Does this mean that the council should now authorize the granting of the doctoral degree with First Honors for a dissertation, when the two professors specializing in the topic have declined it?"

"It is a matter of viewpoint!"

"It is not a point of view," Dr. Yusuf shouted. "We are destroying the university with our own hands!" He rose to his feet, and roared, "You are destroying it!"

A clamor of voices broke out, some denying what Yusuf had said, the rest standing by him, even if they disapproved of the vehemence with which he stated his opinion. One colleague was saying, "Calm down, Yusuf, you'll have a stroke. You should see your face." He stood up, took Yusuf by the arm, and they went out.

The dean was rapping his pencil on the edge of the water glass that had been placed before him, calling on the council for silence. The acting chair continued what he had been saying. "I say it is a question of viewpoint. The dissertation didn't satisfy those two professors, God knows why. Two other professors, as well as the supervisor, evaluated it, with a different conclusion. Why are you creating problems out of nothing, Dr. Shagar?"

"A problem out of nothing? We're talking about the very core of the university's mission. The value of the research and the integrity of the professor! I repeat, to approve this result is a slap in the face of the college—it's a disaster!"

They voted. Seven out of thirty refused to approve the result. The council ratified the doctoral degree with First Honors. Shagar picked up her papers and left.

Shagar knew now that her fury on that day, and Yusuf's agitation, and the raised voices of everyone who contested the department's recommendation that the student be awarded a degree with distinction pertained not to this subject alone. This issue was merely the straw that—as the saying goes—broke the camel's back. It broke Yusuf's back literally, not figuratively. The whole college would follow in the pages of the newspaper something that was published concerning a university professor—he might not be from their college, but he was at the university. He plagiarized a book belonging to a departed colleague and published it in his own name. The victim's children didn't write to the newspapers—they went to court. The court's decision came down, confirming the theft. Before the council was convened, Shagar knew, and Yusuf knew, and everyone knew that the professor had not committed suicide, he hadn't emigrated to some remote island where no one knew his story or his book. And he wasn't standing in Tahrir Square castigating himself in penance for what he'd done. He came, smiling radiantly, as happy as could be, receiving congratulations, because the university had appointed him head of the department in which he taught. Yusuf gasped. Shagar gasped. The two of them sat down, dumbfounded. Neither of them uttered a word until they rose to attend the college council meeting.

At first glance, it seemed to her that the words "father of" or "mother of" must be missing from the announcement. All the same, she climbed the stairs as quickly as her leg and her cane would allow. She entered the dean's office and inquired. No words were missing. The paper hung on the notice board in the vestibule conveyed the news accurately: "Dr. Yusuf Ali Fahmi, a professor at the college, died yesterday evening. The funeral is set for noon today at the Mosque..." She didn't get into her car. She flagged a taxi, got in, and got out again in front of his building. The doorman told her the elevator was out of order. She ascended the five flights on foot. No sound came from the apartment. No one shouted or wailed. Were they at the hospital? What foolishness! She hadn't asked the name of the hospital. She knocked on the door. His daughter opened it and said, "Come in, Auntie Shagar." No one was crying. Not yet. Pale faces. Silence. His wife had not changed her clothes since the previous night.

"What happened? How?"

"He got home from the college at four in the afternoon. We had lunch, and then Samir asked him for help with his math homework, so he sat with him until seven o'clock. At 7:30 he said to me, 'Call me a doctor—I don't feel well.' He went to bed, and I called the doctor. I thought he had gone to sleep. The doctor came at ten. 'It's over,' he said. 'He's dead.'"

Two weeks later the dean summoned her. "I know how much the loss of Dr. Yusuf grieves you," he said, "but I don't understand why you keep repeating everywhere that the college council killed him. This sort of talk is not appropriate to an academic society, it is not appropriate for a professor."

"He wasn't ill. He had a heart attack because of what happened at the council."

"What is this, Dr. Shagar—an Arab film? 'Oh! My heart!' and then he dies? Fate and divine decree. His lifespan was written—or don't you believe in the judgment of God?"

She stood up. She got as far as the door, then turned and stared at him. "I don't like to think who will come after Yusuf. I see the coffin and the pallbearers, and I know it's the university that's in the coffin. It's a nightmare that comes to me every day—it comes to me when I'm awake, sir, not when I'm asleep!"

She slammed the door behind her. Rushing to get away, she tripped over her cane, and pitched forward on her face. The office boy helped her to her feet. "Are you all right, Dr. Shagar?"

She thought she had developed an inflammation of the liver. She went to the doctor, who ran the requisite tests. "Your liver is fine," said the doctor. "All functions are normal." How to explain this bitterness in her throat?

Her sense of loss at Yusuf's death was boundless. There were other colleagues whom she liked and respected, but Yusuf—there was no one like him.

He had come to London specially to visit her. It was only two days after she got out of the hospital. He rang the bell, and she opened the door. "Yusuf!"

He reproached her. "You have an accident, are admitted to the hospital, and I don't know about it? How can this be, how do you explain it?" As usual, he was right. She told him the details of what had happened. He smoked as he listened. Then he said, "Tomorrow ask the doctor whether there is any reason you shouldn't travel. She gazed at him quizzically. "You'll come back to Egypt," he said. "We don't need this country—come stay in your own house, your own university. There's no call for this outrage!" He was angry.

She smiled. "I'll stay until I finish my work in the archives."

"You are stubborn, Shagar, and no help for it. What if they get you next time, what if they kill you? What if..."

She interrupted him with a laugh. "I never said the incident was planned," she told him. "I said it was a possibility, only a possibility!"

No one killed her in that distant country. He was the one who went. He died of grief, at home, at his university. She would go to his mother in Upper Egypt and say to her, "Don't accept condolences for him. Your son was murdered. The university killed him." What nonsense is this, Shagar? No—it's not nonsense, it's the truth! Yusuf would have died every time the security forces stormed the university campus and pelted it with tear-gas bombs. He would have died the day the soldiers attacked the dormitories and killed Khaled Abdel Aziz al-Waqad. He said, "Shagar, the boy was seventeen. A freshman, Shagar. His family are poor—peasant farmers, barely able to rub two pennies together, and they sent him to the university to study. Five months, Shagar, and they told them, 'Come and get your son from the morgue.'" Yusuf swallowed death once, twice, three times. Then a final mouthful—less, perhaps—and he couldn't take it. It killed him.

Shagar traveled to Upper Egypt. She sat before the old woman. She kissed her head, but didn't say anything. She got on the train and went back to Cairo.

xₒ☙❧ₒx

It wasn't a funeral. The drums beat as military music imposed its rhythms on the campus. It impelled the students to assemble on either side of the procession to watch. "Rhythm?" The word brought Shagar up short. There was no rhythm, only a cacophony of shrieking sounds, intermingling.

"What's going on?"

"The annual."

"What does that mean, 'the annual'?"

"The annual festival. Is this your first visit to the university, ma'am?"

She had never seen it, never heard of it. It was something new, presumably. For the preliminaries, boys and girls carried various colored flags, just large colored flags not representing anything, and after these were the flags of the colleges, as well as signs: the name of the college would be written in a random script on ironed paper, which would be carried by a student who headed up a group of students from that college, boys and girls. Pharaonic costume, Turkish turbans, popular contemporary dress. Officers driving peasant farmers in chains, girls in evening dress, or in peasant dresses, others in traditional full-body wrap-dresses. A group of *mizmar*-players in folk costume. A masquerade party? wondered Shagar. How had the girl standing next to her heard her?

"They represent the history of Egypt."

"The history of Egypt? Where did they get those costumes?"

"From the closets."

What closets? Shagar didn't ask, although she found an explanation for the oldness and raggedness of the clothes. No one had thought of washing or ironing them. Perhaps the university had the funds to subsidize the requirements of amateur theater groups. Who was howling? A student. One of the students, in his rude and immature fashion, must be jeering at the parade. The voice got louder. It wasn't a student, male or female. There was a whole group howling! There was a sign, "School of Medicine." Another sign followed it, raised up on a wooden box wrapped in black. Written on the sign were the words, "One of the achievements of the School of Medicine." The students who were carrying the casket were the ones howling, laughing at the same time. Some of the onlookers joined in. The moaning mingled with laughter and mocking comments. My God—how was she going to give her lecture in the midst of this uproar? A student wearing a Napoleon outfit was afraid that the other students wouldn't recognize him. He held up a sign that said, "Napoleon and his wife, Queen Marie Antoinette!" No need for a wig— a veil serves the purpose. Another sign: "The School of Humanities," and behind it a horse-drawn carriage bearing three women students with their faces covered by veils in colors of red, yellow, and green—a different color for each girl—and behind them girls wearing hats and modern clothing. "The College of Fatima," shouted one of the male students, whereupon the whistles and remarks commenced. Shagar found herself leaning heavily on the student who was carrying the flag for the School of Humanities, and she snatched it from him. He pushed her hard. The tightly packed bodies of the students prevented her from falling to the ground. The boy retrieved his flag, and she left the scene. She headed for the office of the president of the university. She didn't find him. She left the administration building and made for the Humanities building. The dean's office.

"Is the dean in?"

"He's in a meeting."

She opened the door and went in.

"What is it, Dr. Shagar?"

She said nothing. She reached out and took him by the hand, pulled him out of his chair, and pulled him so he would follow her. He followed. She went down the stairs, with him by the hand. They went out the door of the college, and she pointed with her finger at the parade. "Look," she said.

He stared at her and smiled—laughed. "What's the trouble, Professor? It's the annual university festival!"

"A carnival?"

"No, not a carnival—"

She cut him off. "A saint's day, then?"

"A celebratory parade. Games and theater for the enactment of Egypt's history—are you not a professor of history, Dr. Shagar?" He smiled, and left her standing like a statue. No, she didn't stand like a statue. She shouted at the students, screamed at them. She doesn't remember what she said. She remembers that her voice was lost amid the beating of the drums, the blaring of the *mizmars*, and all the chatter. She turned and went toward the lecture hall. The microphone could not overcome the din created by the festival. She stopped.

She didn't return to the university for the rest of the week. When she did go, what the dean had said about her reached her ears: "Dr. Shagar has lost her mind. She barged in on me when I was in a meeting, grabbed my hand and dragged me away. I imagined that the college had caught fire, or some disaster was about to happen, but all I found was the parade put on by the colleges. She's lost her mind."

She didn't waste any time. She got a piece of blank paper and wrote:

To the Esteemed Dean of the College:

Greetings and salutations. I ask that you exempt me from all my responsibilities in the history department at the college, inasmuch as I burst into your room without cause, being about to set myself and the college on fire. You must have realized that all this sort of thing is a sign of madness. There is no doubt that the place for lunatics is not the university, but the insane asylum. Let me make myself clear, in case the meaning of my words has not come across: I am tendering my resignation.

—Dr. Shagar Mohammed Abdel Ghaffar

She left the college and went home. She made sure the doorman was informed: "I want no visitors. If anyone asks about me, tell them I've gone traveling." She went up to her apartment. She got a pair of scissors and severed the telephone cord.

Nineteen

Saïd's retinue set out from the big hill, in the direction of the canal region, and on 6 December 1861 they reached the entrance to the bridge north of Crocodile Lake. He visited the forced-labor trench designated as No. 5, one of the six fields into which that area was divided. Saïd spent there the following day, during which he visited the environs on that side of the canal; he saw as well the site that had been chosen as the point where the sea-canal would drain into Crocodile Lake. Saïd admired this site and requested that a private residence be constructed for him on the hill, which would have a prospect on the mouth of the sea-canal on the edge of the lake, that he might see and hear the rushing water of the Mediterranean Sea as it poured into Crocodile Lake.

Saïd left the bridge at nine o'clock on the morning of 8 December 1861, with De Lesseps and his entourage. They made a tour of the area that had been marked out as the site for Crocodile City (subsequently Is-mailiyya)... and from there he made another circuit around the Nafisha wells, then made his way to the farm at the well of "Abou Bal-lah," one of the company's original emplace-ments... At last he resumed his journey, arriving around noon at Toussoun Center, to the south of Crocodile Lake; the company had given the name "Toussoun" to this center after the son of Saïd Pasha...

At Toussoun a lavish reception had been pre-pared for the governor, and he entered the city mounted on horseback, De Lesseps be-side him, also riding his horse. They pro-ceeded between closely packed lines of Egyptian workers who cheered him, wishing him long life, while martial music played. Saïd Pasha's retinue, besides these two horses, con-sisted of six camels, saddled most handsomely and mounted by the most important mem-bers of the escort. Behind these was Saïd's pri-vate carriage, pulled by six mules, and then a division of the Egyptian army. Following this reception and its circumambulation of the es-tablishments that had been set up in Tous-soun, the visit was concluded and Saïd went back, returning to the capital of his province.

It wasn't the first time Shagar had read Abdel Aziz al-Shinnawi's book *Forced Labor in the Dig-ging of the Suez Canal*, but she absorbed herself in reading it as if it were the first time. On this visit, Saïd would reach an agreement with De Lesseps concerning a solution to the company's problem by implementing forced labor and transporting workers to the trenches against their will, or "biz-zour," as some of the peasant farmers put it when they were questioned by a British tourist, who recorded the expression verbatim, in the characters of the Roman alphabet. Every month 20,000 worked in the forced-labor trenches, with 20,000 on their way and 20,000 returning to their villages. They were distributed among the boats plying the River Nile; the trains bound from Cairo to Benha and Zagazig, or conversely; and the caravans across the great hill headed east on the outbound journey or westward on the return trip.

She placed a bookmark at page 130, where the expression "bizzour" occurred, and closed the book. She set it on the small bedside table and switched off the light. The most important meeting between Saïd and De Lesseps. In this meeting they would settle upon the provision of 20,000 conscripted workers to the regions where the excavation was taking place. Saïd would decide—or De Lesseps would decide and Saïd would concur—to reduce the size of the Egyptian army, dispatch the soldiers, and to direct them to the work in the excavation fields. Why does she keep going back to reading this book, which she has read several times, so that she now knows everything it has to offer? She shrugged her shoulders. There is a reason—there is always a reason.

x.꧁꧂.x

I wonder: this narrative, suspended between two lives—where is it taking me? I stare at the blank screen. Slowly my fingers move, tapping on the keyboard, conflating my story and hers. I stop, as if at a fork in the road. I ponder. I know that Shagar now, at this moment in which I sit at my writing, is walking alone in the streets. She has left the university and is no longer able to write: three files crouch upon her desk, each one containing the material for a book, each one waiting for her to open it, focus on it, and start to write it down. She sees the three files, reaches for them, opens them, and closes them again. She puts them back where they were. She leaves the house, gets in her car, heads toward the Abbas Bridge. She crosses over it to Manyal al-Roda Island. She crosses the Malek al-Saleh Bridge, and turns to the right. She parks the car and walks, the buildings set close together on her left, the river to her right—hidden, frogs croaking. A gap between two walls: water, and beyond that the palm trees; a fishing boat converted by some family into its permanent residence; a woman crouched upon the ground nursing the baby cradled in her right arm, while with her left hand she waves a fan at some ears of corn placed over glowing coals. On the other side, dilapidated buildings, and beyond them the ancient treasures of Egypt: the fortress, the churches, and the Mosque of Amr—nothing of these is evident to anyone passing by on the expressway.

She leaves the house, gets in her car, proceeds alongside the Nile toward the University Bridge, which she passes and heads for the Galaa Bridge. She crosses to the island. One side of the street: the Opera House. On the opposite side: the Mukhtar Museum; the statue of Saad Zaghloul in the middle; the bronze lions at either end of the

Kasr al-Nil Bridge; the three palms and then Tahrir Square. A little girl—about five years old, probably—darts among the cars, selling tissues. Children play soccer beneath the bridge. Security vehicles. Soldiers.

She leaves the house. The same route. The far end of the Kasr al-Nil Bridge. The three palm trees. The high-rise hotels. The British Embassy. The American Embassy, guarded by cement blocks that take up a section of the street. The statue of Simon Bolivar. Chairs lined up to receive mourners at the entrance to the Mosque of Omar Makram. A coffin, pallbearers, and a voice intoning verses from the holy book. She proceeds to Ramses Square. She parks the car in the railway station lot, and gets out. She crosses the street, circles the statue of the ancient Pharaoh. She goes back to her car. Tahrir once more. Kasr al-Aini Street. The hospital. The Prince's palace. The University Bridge. Then she turns to the left. She doesn't look at Mukhtar's peasant woman or the dome, between them the monument commemorating the martyrs of the university. She can't find it in her to look.

She goes back home, opens the door, closes it again. She tosses her cane aside and sits down. Has she gone mad, or are the walls closing in on her? Is she thinking? It appears that she is not thinking about anything in particular. Little bits of fluff and particulate matter catch the light and then disappear, like those nocturnal flying insects.

"Where have the stars gone?" Shagar cried suddenly as she stood on her balcony.

In the morning she got into her car and headed east. She passed the City of the Dead and the Citadel in the Muqattam Hills, then proceeded farther east toward the desert road: nothing but sand and gravel and bare hills. She continued until she saw the rugged mountain range stretching out on her right, a crescent-shaped mass. She murmured, "Ataqa: the western gate of the Isthmus." She didn't head toward the Isthmus. She bypassed it for the road connecting the three cities. She stopped and got out of the car. She crossed the strip of sand dividing the auto road and the channel. "The haunch of Egypt," "Nilotic Egypt's last line of defense," "a strong defense against a weak offensive . . . a weak defense against a strong offensive." What made her think of Gamal Hamdan at this moment?

She follows the line of brilliant blue. It looks innocent, not confessing its tale, mild on the surface, narrow, sharply defined, like the body of the Messiah. She notices three soldiers standing atop the mound of sand. Perhaps they are wondering why she has stopped in this place. They come down and move in her direction, approaching her. Boys carrying old-fashioned rifles. They look, then move on, distancing themselves from her. Do they know the story of the specters? Are they aware of them? Should she stop them, to tell it to them? And where to start?

The boy—he was standing there just like them, keeping watch, holding an old rifle. There upon the sandy gateway beyond the water. The boy fired suddenly. Was he afraid? The boy said, "Are we to leave the borders undefended?" He fired. They killed him. Did he know the story? Strange, strange—nothing is lost, nothing. She could, right now, take these boys, take the hand of one of them in her left hand, the hands of the other two in her right, as if she were taking them across the street to school. A few steps, it's just a few steps. They dig a little bit in the sand. She could call to them now, summon them to come stand with her at the edge of the water—here, too, it is possible for them to see everything. Before her, a freighter passes, borne along on the water, slow and deliberate. None of its captain or crew is anywhere to be seen—where is it coming from? From the distant countries of the north? From the south? They pay no attention—are they paying attention?

Shagar went her way, got into her car. She drove alongside the waterway. Al-Shallufa, Genifa, Kebrit, Fayid: the palaces of the wealthy. The summer retreats. Banana trees. Déversoir. The Ismailiyya heights: "the natural corridor between the Sinai and Palestine plains"—Gamal Hamdan again. Westward to the heart of the Delta. Eastward to the heart of Palestine. She entered the city and proceeded alongside a freshwater conduit. She turned right toward a site overlooking the lake. She sat down to have her lunch. The British forces embarked from here to Palestine. The Israeli forces came from Palestine and aimed their cannons here. The peasant farmers came from the north and south of Egypt. They returned home or died here.

Why has the voice stayed with her to this point? Why does the memory preserve some things and not others? The small radio with its wooden cabinet, plugged into the socket. Who is this girl, listening? The voice rises up clearly: "A decision on the part of the President of the Republic to nationalize the Universal Suez Canal Company of the Delta, an Egyptian shareholder company." "How comely you are, young Egyptian at the helm/ With the celebration underway on the canal/ A triumphal procession!/ Our president has told us nothing is impossible!/ The intruder has left/ He met his match in Egypt's son!" "Our forces have withdrawn to the second line of defense." "Where is the second line of defense located?" "I am stepping down, absolutely and finally." The broadcaster cries, "No!" Once again, gunfire on both sides of the waterway, for the entire distance connecting the three cities. A coffin—who is it that is being borne upon those shoulders? "With our spirit and our blood we will ransom you, Riyad!" "With our spirit and our blood we will ransom you, Gamal!" They cross over to the other bank. "Allahu Akbar," soldiers, flocks of pigeons. A coffin—who is it that is being borne upon those shoulders? Is it the coffin of the dean? The coffin of Umm Kulthoum, mistress of song? The coffin of the boy? "Day is done." "The lesson is over. Gather up the notebooks."

Shagar got back in her car and continued on her way. Al-Firdan. Al-Ballah. Al-Qantara. Al-

Kab. Al-Tina. Ras al-Ush. At last the free city: Port Said. Odd that monarchs give cities their names. They think of them as mules or horses. They immortalize themselves riding on their backs, in the form of iron statues. The cities have their cunning: they keep the name for themselves, but get rid of the rider and go with the grace of God, never looking back. She spent the night in Port Said.

The following day she retraced her steps. She stopped in Ras al-Ush. In al-Qantara. She stopped in al-Ballah and in al-Firdan. She stopped at Déversoir. Then she continued on her way to Suez. The sun was on her right, moving toward the hills. It vanished behind her.

She came to a stop and got out. She walked until she reached the bank of the canal. She sat down on the ground. The Cairo sky does not reveal the stars. She gazed at the sky. She saw the woman who, with her body, formed a roof over the horizon. Toward the Gulf, she touched the earth with the tips of her toes, and with her fingertips in the direction of the mountain of Ataqa. Between them, the pathway of the legs offers itself, ascending toward the belly spangled with stars, and then the arc descends, inclining toward the extended arms. A strange woman, who swallows her young in the morning, then each evening gives birth to them anew. Glittering stars festoon the river of her torso and its extremities. Nurslings encircle her many nipples with their mouths. A woman-cow. Shagar saw the cow. The arms and legs are lofty pillars, rising up. But who is this aged one riding upon the cow? His bones are silver, his hair is lapis lazuli, his crown turquoise. The vault of the sky is an udder—who is this little one bowed beneath her udder? The woman-cow disappears into the leaves of a sycamore, just her head peering out from behind the tree. Who is this, to whom she gives food and for whom she pours water? A woman-eye, at the portals of the horizon, opening her arms to receive those who come to the western hills. Where has the cow gone? Where did the lioness come from? She growls, demands blood. She runs toward the sunrise, toward the sunset. Whose blood is it that is flowing? Who has been born at this hour? The woman of the heavens swallows her young once more.

What's come over you, Shagar? The night's gotten deeper and deeper, as you sit there motionless, mesmerized by images that are nothing anymore except engravings on tombs. She shakes her head. Her eyes refuse to believe what they see. The woman is before her eyes, her body forming a roof over the earth, in space. On her head is a vessel, in her belly a vessel. Murderer-midwife. Shadows. Specters. The specters open their eyes, light their lanterns, traverse the underground waterway by night. Who is this they are telling their story to, filling him with determination, filling their noses with the breath of life? Who is this that laments morning and evening, will not be parted from his beloved and yet cannot reach her?

Whose voice is it echoing from on high? Where are his notebooks, where is the scale? Did you write everything down? What did you record, you with the face of a long-beaked bird? Did you scrutinize the reckoning and divide it all up in your notebooks? Have you preserved all your volumes in the catacomb? Are you loosening the bonds—when will you loosen the bonds? Will you open the mouth and release words from it? Open it and let them out, brighter than beams of light, swifter than hunting dogs, lighter than shadows.

She wasn't sleeping, her mind wasn't wandering in the past. Shagar was putting her house in order, setting her mind to rest.

She got into her car and set out, back to Cairo.

Author's Notes

✣ Mohamed Ezzat El-Bayoumi: the first of the student martyrs in the 1919 revolution; he died on March 11, 1919.

✣ Mohammed Abdel Maguid Mursi: a student at the School of Agriculture, martyred when struck by police gunfire in the student uprising of 1935.

✣ Abdel Hakam al-Garrahi: struck by police gunfire in the same uprising, and transported to the hospital; he died some days later, on November 19, 1935.

✣ Khaled Abdel Aziz El-Wakkad: martyred in the student demonstrations in protest of the bombardment of Iraq in February 1991.

The lines of poetry in the first chapter are from a poem by Cesar Vallejo of Peru. I translated them, substituting "all his loved ones" for "all the people of the earth," the phrase that appears in the original.

Sources for testimonials from the residents of Deir Yassin:

—Testimonials of Aziza Ismail Atiyya, Naziha Ahmed Asaad Radwan, Umm Eid, Hussein Atiyya, Ismail Mohammed Atiyya, Khalil Sammour, and Hassan Radwan are from the seven articles by Walid al-Khalidi, "Fifty Years after the Slaughter at Deir Yassin: A Village Confronts Zionist Organizations," *Al-Hayat* newspaper, 9–15 April 1998.

—Testimonials of Niᶜma Zahran and Jamila Ali were provided to me by Khairiya Abou Shousha of

Jerusalem University, and Adila al-Aidi, of the Khalil Sakakini Center in Ramallah.

—The testimonial of Zaynab Atiyya (Umm Salah) is from an interview conducted by Shafiqa Ayyad, reprinted from *Al-Bilad* newspaper, 6 May 1997, and an interview conducted by Reem Ubeidu, which appeared in an article entitled, "Fifty Years after the Nakba," in *Al-Nahar* newspaper, 16 May 1998.

—The testimonial of Umm Aziz is from an interview conducted by Shafiqa Ayyad, *Al-Bilad* newspaper, 5 June 1997.

—The testimonial of Mohammed Mahmoud Asaad was written in his own hand and sent to me by Khairiya Abou Shousha of Jerusalem University.

—The testimonials of Abou Tawfiq al-Yasini and Abou Mahmoud are from a BBC documentary film on the Arab-Israeli conflict.

—The testimonial of Abou Yassin is from a book by Sharif Kanaina and Nihad Zeitawi, *Deir Yassine: A Series of Obliterated Palestinian Villages*, The Center for Documents and Surveys, Bir Zeit University, 1987.

—The testimony of the Israeli officers is from *The Fifty Years War: Israel and the Arabs*, based on the BBC television series, ed. Aharon Bergman and Jihan El-Tahri (London: Penguin Books and BBC Books, 1998); a Zionist Organization of America study entitled, "Deir Yassin: History of a Lie," March 1998, www.zoa.org./archives; and the articles of Walid al-Khalidi mentioned above.

—The first part of the testimony of Sorayya Habashi is from "Testimonials and Visions," Committee for Documenting the History of the Egyptian Communist Movement, and the Center for Arab Research, Cairo 1998.

I would like to take the opportunity here to extend my most sincere thanks to Khairiya Abou Shousha of Jerusalem University, Adila al-Aidi of the Khalil Sakakini Center in Ramallah, Hosam al-Barghouti of Ramallah, and Islah Jad of Bir Zeit University, for their kindness in sending me whatever I requested of them by way of printed materials and testimonials.
                                                                —Radwa Ashour

Translator's Notes

This novel is rich in historical material both direct and allusive. Some of the references may be more familiar to an Arab readership than to a Western audience; not all of these call for annotation but I will expand briefly on four points in particular.

—The "Blood Libel" text quoted on pages 184–186 was first issued on September 19, 1982, as a statement by the government of Israel; on September 21 it was printed in the *Washington Post* and the *New York Times* as a full-page advertisement submitted by the Israeli Embassy in Washington, D.C.

—The phrase "the breaking of bones" on page 188 is a reference to an order issued by Yitzhak Rabin during the Palestinian uprising known as the First Intifada (1987–1993). In 1988 Rabin, known to many Arabs as "The Bone-Breaker," commanded soldiers in the Israeli Defense Force (IDF) to break the arms and legs of Palestinians in an attempt to put a stop to the Intifada.

—The words of the Mahatma Gandhi quoted on page 221 were written in Segaon, India, on November 20, 1938, and printed in *Harijan*, vol. 74, pp. 239–234, on November 26, 1938.

—The passage from Emile Habibi's *The Secret Life of Saeed: the Pessoptimist* on pages 234–235 is from the translation by Salma K. Jayyusi and Trevor LeGassick, published by Interlink Books, 1985.

I have now had the privilege of translating two of Radwa Ashour's novels, with her active support and participation, and for that honor I thank her, once again, *jazil al-shukr*: a profusion of thanks.

In 2007 this project received generous support from the National Endowment for the Arts, where I wish to thank most particularly Amy Stolls, who guided and encouraged me steadfastly throughout that year and even beyond. Thanks also to Paulette Beete and others, for featuring an excerpt from *Specters* in the NEA's 2007 Annual Report.

To Interlink Books I owe a debt of gratitude for taking on the publication of *Specters*. Pam Thompson, charged with the task of seeing the project through the stages from manuscript to book, has been much more than an editor: patient and good-humored, as well as skillful and dedicated. Hilary Plum has joined the effort in its finishing stages to lend her keen eye and insight to the painstaking elimination of loose threads and rough edges. I thank them both with all my heart.

Behind this and each of the translation projects I have undertaken stand a host of family members, friends, colleagues, and mentors who are too numerous to name individually, but whose inspiration has been, and continues to be, vital.

Last, but in some ways most of all: I take this opportunity to dedicate *Specters*, in its English translation, to Palestine.

—Barbara Romaine